HOW A REALIST HERO REBUILT THE KINGDOM

WRITTEN BY

DOJYOMARU

ILLUSTRATED BY

FUYUYUKI

HOW A REALIST HERO REBUILT THE KINGDOM:
VOLUME 1

© 2016 Dojyomaru
Illustrations by Fuyuyuki

First published in Japan in 2016 by
OVERLAP Inc., Ltd., Tokyo.
English translation rights arranged with
OVERLAP Inc., Ltd., Tokyo.

Seven Seas books may be purchased in bulk for promotional,
educational, or business use. Please contact your local
bookseller or the Macmillan Corporate and Premium Sales
Department at 1-800-221-7945, extension 5442, or by
e-mail at MacmillanSpecialMarkets@macmillan.com.

Follow Seven Seas Entertainment online at
sevenseasentertainment.com.
Experience J-Novel Club books online at j-novel.club.

TRANSLATION: Sean McCann
J-NOVEL EDITOR: Emily Sorensen
COVER DESIGN: KC Fabellon
INTERIOR LAYOUT & DESIGN: Clay Gardner
COPY EDITOR: Dayna Abel
PROOFREADER: Jade Gardner, Stephanie Cohen
LIGHT NOVEL EDITOR: Nibedita Sen
EDITOR-IN-CHIEF: Adam Arnold
PUBLISHER: Jason DeAngelis

ISBN: 978-1-626929-07-4
Printed in Canada
First Printing: September 2018
10 9 8 7 6 5 4 3 2 1

HOW A REALIST HERO REBUILT THE KINGDOM

Dojyomaru | Illustrations: Fuyuyuki

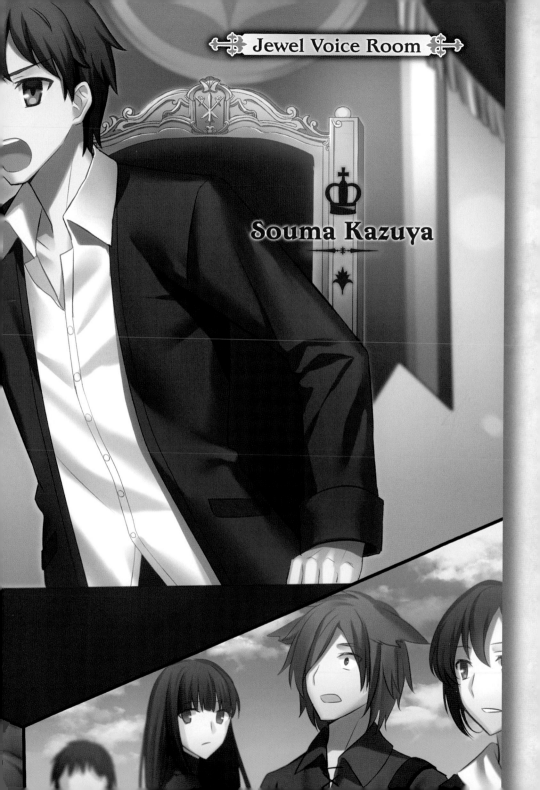

Souma Kazuya

The five diverse, talented people gathered by the Gift Proclamation—

Tomoe Inui

Poncho Panacotta

Jun

Contents

HOW A REALIST HERO
REBUILT
THE KINGDOM

I

Prologue

"**K**AZUYA...why do you think people build families?"

Grandpa asked me that question on a quiet autumn day. It was just after the Buddhist memorial service held to mark the seventh day following my grandmother's passing. I was alone in the garden with Grandpa, staring absently into the sky at the time.

I didn't understand the question, and as I struggled to find something to say in response, Grandpa answered. He looked like he'd had an epiphany.

"So that they don't have to die alone. It occurred to me again and again as I was caring for your grandmother. Though we lost our son and your mother so soon, you were still here for us. Because of that, we had a sense of fulfillment in our lives. The bonds we've formed will last even after we ourselves are no more. For any living being, there can be no greater source of pride."

"Grandpa..."

"That is why I want to tell you this. Kazuya, build a family. And, once you have, protect them, come what may. You've always been a sensible boy...no, I suppose I should say you always tended to think about things rationally."

I was silent.

"But listen, you mustn't do that when it comes to family. Once you've taken their hands, never let go. Put your life on the line and protect them to the bitter end, no matter what. If you do that, I'm sure you'll be able to think 'I lived a good life' when your time comes. Just like your grandmother...and just like me."

"You're making this sound like it's your last will," I teased, but Grandpa nodded in complete seriousness.

"I'm getting on in years. These may be the last words I'll leave to my grandson, who will one day be alone."

At the time, I could say nothing in response.

Now, as if he had only been holding on so he could see me get accepted into university, Grandpa had left to be with Grandma.

"I know," I whispered to myself in that house where I was now alone. "I haven't forgotten your last will, Grandpa."

To build a family, and protect them, no matter what.

Holding that promise close to heart, I would begin my new life. That was how it was supposed to be.

◇ ◇ ◇

"O Hero! It is good that you have heeded my summons," said a middle-aged man who had just appeared before me. He was of average build and was attempting to sound majestic. I'd have put his age at around forty to fifty years old. He wore a red cape thick enough to serve as a coat, and atop his head sat a gleaming golden crown. I could tell at a glance that this guy was a king.

Was the gentle-looking young woman standing at his side the queen, then? She was a beautiful woman with platinum blonde hair, wearing a beautiful dress. She looked like she was only around thirty.

Let's take stock of the situation, I thought. *A needlessly high ceiling, rows of marble pillars, and a red carpet beneath me. Soldiers standing at attention on either side and mixed in with them a person who looks like your stereotypical prime minister.*

It was a place that looked like it came out of the opening of an RPG. There was a king, a palace, and that "O Hero" line I'd just heard.

Okay, calm down, I told myself. *Panicking will not improve your situation. The first order of business is... right, I'll start by gathering information.*

"Wh-why do you look at me like that? Are you upset that I have called you here?" the King said nervously as I stared at him.

"That's not it. I just don't have a good grasp of the situation. Could I ask you to explain?"

"Y-you certainly are calm. It is most enviable..."

"Your Majesty..." I began.

"I-it is nothing!"

The prime minister cleared his throat, and the king jumped a little. Seeing that little interaction, the queen giggled, and the soldiers looked on with wry smiles. From that exchange, I could see the King truly was the good-natured man that he seemed.

I sensed that he lacked the aura of command required of a nation's ruler but also that he was the type who was loved by the people. Still, that was neither here nor there.

I posed my question with deliberate calmness so as not to intimidate him. "So, if I'm the hero, does that mean there's a demon lord invading or something?"

"You certainly do catch on quickly. It is precisely as you say."

I was speechless. *Seriously...? This isn't a dream, right? No, I just wanted to try saying that. I can distinguish between dreams and reality. This doesn't have that hazy dream-like sensation. All four of my senses, excluding taste, were reporting to me that this was the real world.*

This is...reality...let me say it again. Seriously...?

"I-is something the matter, Hero? Why do you suddenly clutch your head?"

"No, don't worry about it. I just felt a little dizzy." My head had started to hurt, but for the moment, I'd have to put up with it. "I'm fine now. Please, explain the situation."

"A-are you certain? Very well, I shall explain."

The king then launched into a lengthy explanation of the world's history, like you might see in an old RPG. It was long-winded enough that, if this were a game, I'd have been hunting for the Skip Text button, so I'll summarize for you readers a bit.

First, he spoke about this world.

The world was made up of the supercontinent Landia and several islands of varying sizes. On Landia, there were many countries, large and small. In addition to humans, these were populated by beastmen, elves, dwarves, and dragonewts, among other races. There were countries where these races coexisted, countries where one race had preferential treatment, countries which forbade entrance to all but one race, and more. These countries took many forms, and they struggled against one another for supremacy at times. However, ever since the Demon Lord's Domain appeared, it seemed that all these countries had, on the surface, taken a position of mutual cooperation.

Next, the king spoke about the Demon Lord's Domain and the Demon Lord.

Around ten years ago, in the northernmost reaches of the supercontinent, Landia, a dimension called the "Demon World" had appeared, and monsters of many sizes and shapes had poured out, throwing the Northern Countries into chaos. The countries had formed an alliance and organized a punitive force to send into this Demon World.

However, that punitive force had been annihilated. In the Demon World, there were "monsters" which had minimal (or, some would theorize, no) intelligence, as well as "demons" who were intelligent and powerful fighters. The demons were the ones who had annihilated the punitive force. Furthermore, though it had not yet been verified, people whispered about the existence of a being who ruled over the demons, a "Demon King."

After that battle, the countries had lost their main fighting forces, and none of them had the power to defend themselves against the monsters that appeared from the Demon World. The demonic forces, which had until then held only the equivalent of a small country, laid waste to the Northern Countries and came to rule a third of the continent. This territory was now called "the Demon Lord's Domain." While their advance had stopped for the moment, it was said that this was because the expansion of the front lines had spread the demons and monsters thinner, making it possible for the individual countries to hold the line against them. That didn't mean mankind had any decisive way to turn things around. In the frontline countries, things had bogged down to a stalemate.

Following that exposition, the king talked about this country.

This was the Kingdom of Elfrieden, a medium-sized nation in the southeast of the continent. It was ruled under a monarchy. It was a country originally founded by many races working together, and though the king was a human, those of other races were accepted here without discrimination. Regardless of race, everyone held citizenship, and aside from "king," they could take any job they desired. Even the prime minister who had been complaining to the king earlier was a half-elf, with both human and elven parentage.

Because they did not border the Demon Lord's Domain, there were few monster attacks. However, the country had been weak to begin with, and the national treasury was not exactly in good shape. Food shortages had been especially bad in recent years, and that had only exacerbated the problem of refugees dispossessed by the expansion of the Demon Lord's Domain drifting here.

There were dark storm clouds on both the domestic and international fronts.

Apparently, relations were tense with the Gran Chaos Empire, the largest country on the continent, excluding the Demon Lord's Domain. The Empire was the country which shared the longest border with the Demon Lord's Domain and was also the country that had directed the first invasion of it. After their loss against the Demon Lord's Domain, the Empire was apparently requesting war subsidies from other countries. To put it simply, they were requesting that countries who were far away from the Demon Lord's Domain provide financial support to those that were close to it. Though these were "requests," when they came from the most powerful country in all the world, they were closer to ultimatums. One of those requests had come to this kingdom, but under current circumstances, it would be difficult to pay.

Finally, the king talked about the "hero summoning," which had brought me to this world.

Apparently, in the request for war subsidies that came from the Empire, there had been verbiage which had said, "If you are unable to pay, carry out the ritual of hero summoning which is passed down in your country and turn that summoned hero over to the Empire." It was abundantly clear that this country had no means to pay, and perhaps that had been the Empire's intention all along. Perhaps they wanted to use a hero for his fighting potential, perhaps they wanted to dissect one and study him, or perhaps they had no interest in one to begin with, and they merely wanted to use the Kingdom's failure to respond to their request as a *casus belli* to invade. With no way to know what the Empire wanted, speculation had led only to more speculation, and the kingdom became suspicious of everything.

In response to their situation, the kingdom had decided to perform the hero summoning ritual. They had not yet decided upon whether to turn the hero over or not, but if they succeeded, it would at least give them a card to negotiate with. For that, they needed to respond to the request and show they intended to perform the ritual.

Now that you've heard this much, I'll bet you've probably already guessed that the king never thought he might actually manage to summon a hero.

"Hey!" I shouted at him without intending to, and the king jumped back in fright.

"Eek! I am most sorry!"

"Oh, sorry," I said. "I lost my composure for a second there."

Even though he acts like this, he's still a king. I'll have to refrain from any further rudeness.

Still...had I really been summoned by coincidence, with no one really expecting anything from me?

"So, what do you plan to do?" I asked the king after taking a moment to calm myself.

"A-about what?"

"The whole 'turning me over to the Empire' thing."

"That is...what should I do? It is a real pickle." The king really did seem troubled.

That surprised me a little. I had expected him to plead, "The Empire is scary! Please, go and serve them for our kingdom!" as he cried and begged me to do it. He looked pretty fainthearted, after all.

"What is there for you to agonize over?" I asked. "You're afraid of the Empire, aren't you?"

"I am afraid! That is exactly why I am agonizing over this!"

"If I may interject, allow me to explain," the half-elf prime minister said, stepping forward. "At present, there is a clear difference in power between our country and the Empire. We simply are not in a position to say no when the Empire asks for something. While we are stuck in that situation, you are the sole lucky card that has fallen into our hands. Once we play that card, however, we have nothing left to use when negotiating with the Empire. Even if we can survive this time by doing as they say, what will we do the next time something comes up? Next time, we might only have succeeded in giving up our only card."

I was silent. It wasn't hard to see what he was saying.

What had happened to northern Fujiwara after they had given up their only card—Minamoto no Yoshitsune—was a good example. Those who cave in to intimidation and let go of the only card in their hand will have only a dark end awaiting them.

"What is a hero, anyway?" I asked.

"It is said that a hero is 'one who leads the change of an era,'" the prime minister replied.

Hmm...so it's not just someone who slays that Demon King?

"Isn't that a wee bit vague?" I asked.

"We don't have much in the way of documentation, you see."

"Please don't hold a ritual if that's the case."

"I cannot apologize enough for this state of affairs," the prime minister said formally.

Giving me the routine bureaucratic apology isn't going to help... still, this is a problem. There's not enough information to act on. Which means what we need most right now is time.

"Sire, I have a proposal."

"What is it? You may speak freely."

"Can we talk about what's going to happen from here on out? Not standing here, somewhere where we can sit down and discuss it at length. Just me, you, and the prime minister."

"Hm. What do you think, Marx?"

"That would be fine." The prime minister, whose name was apparently Marx, nodded in assent.

Since I had their agreement, I made another request. "Please gather all the materials you can on this country, as well. Focus on the balance of payment reports as well as materials on agriculture, forestry and fisheries, economy, trade and industry. Also, gather documents on land, infrastructure, and transport. We might be able to scrounge up the money the Empire is demanding. I'd like the materials you have on heroes as well...but, well, that can wait."

"Very well. I will have them gathered at once," said the king.

We took a break at this point, and I was called to the king's governmental affairs office later.

Sitting on a comfy sofa across from the king and Prime Minister Marx, we held meeting after meeting. We talked about basically everything there was to talk about: this country's industry, economy, tax system, agricultural policy, military preparations, foreign affairs. We discussed it all.

The meetings went on for a full two days. This was partly because I asked questions about every minute detail of the materials I'd had them gather and partly because they latched onto the policies I was proposing to a bizarre degree. From partway through the meeting, the king paid rapt attention to me, as if he had become an entirely different person.

It was now two days later. The soldiers guarding the door would later tell everyone that, when the king left that room, his expression was uncharacteristically bright and cheerful, and that his was the face of a man who had come to a decision.

The day after our three-person meetings had come to an end, the king gathered the VIPs of the castle in the audience chamber and proclaimed loudly, "My people, I ask you to heed my words closely."

"I, the thirteenth king of Elfrieden, Albert Elfrieden, hereby abdicate my throne to the summoned hero, Souma Kazuya! Furthermore, I hereby announce the engagement of my daughter, Liscia Elfrieden, to Sir Souma."

The room fell silent. Everyone had been struck mute. The only one present who remained calm was the queen.

This bombshell announcement completely blindsided me.

HOW A REALIST HERO REBUILT THE KINGDOM

CHAPTER 1

Fundraising

O N THE THIRTY-SECOND DAY of the fourth month in the 1,546th year of the Continental Calendar, the throne was ceded to Souma Kazuya.

It happened in the capital of the Elfrieden Kingdom, Parnam.

This city was where the residence of the Elfrieden Kingdom's king, Parnam Castle, was. A town had risen around Parnam Castle, and the circular walls surrounding it were reminiscent of a city-state in Europe in the Middle Ages. The roofs in the nobles' quarter and the peasants' quarter were uniformly orange, and this suited the classic image of the town well.

Parnam Castle was in the center, connected to large roads at the north, south, east, and west gates. The roads were always busy with carriages and large mounted beasts. Aside from the main roads, there were also countless smaller cobblestone roads radiating out from the castle, and these small roads were connected by even smaller roads. Seen from the air, it would have resembled a spider's web, or perhaps a snowflake. These roads were lined on both sides with merchants and tradespeople, and they were always bustling.

Since today was a holiday, as well as the first day off since the new king, Souma (though, with the crowning ceremony not yet having taken place, he was technically only acting king), had been given the throne, the marketplace was even busier than usual. The sudden change of monarchs had caused tension in the castle town for a little while, but once they heard that the throne had been ceded to the summoned hero—and that the former king, Albert, had announced his abdication of his own will, and that Souma was betrothed to Princess Liscia, the former king's daughter—the confusion naturally died down.

Because the former king had ruled through "being loved," the rumors settled down to:

"Well, if the king is fine, I guess it's okay."

"Yeah, the pressure really seemed to be getting to him. I'm glad he has that weight off his shoulders now."

"He'll be able to take it easy now. It's best for everyone this way."

The people's interpretations of what had happened were largely favorable. It seemed the king's lackadaisical manner was in tune with the national character. Having had the throne foisted on him, Souma had worried that a resistance movement might rise against the sudden change, but he was a little let down when it never happened. Regardless, it was another peaceful day in Parnam as people of many races went about their business.

As if cutting through that peaceful afternoon, a white horse galloped down the cobblestones.

The horse was spurred on by a beautiful young girl in a red

military uniform that looked like it could have come out of *The Rose of Versailles*. She was sixteen or seventeen years old with fair skin and platinum blonde hair that streamed behind her in the wind. Her tight-fitting uniform accentuated the well-balanced lines of her body.

A beautiful girl riding a white horse made for a picturesque scene in its own right. The people she passed on her way let out gasps of admiration, which turned to cheers when they realized she was their country's princess.

"Congratulations on your betrothal, Princess!"

"We wish you happiness!"

The people sent her their warmest regards, with no idea how she herself felt about the matter. Of course, it was unlikely she could hear them now, anyway.

"Father, Mother...please, be safe!" Liscia Elfrieden whispered to herself with a pained look on her face.

"Father! What is the meaning of this?" Liscia demanded, raising her voice at the sight before her.

The king's bedroom was a room large enough that the king-sized bed did not dominate it, and each and every piece of furniture was exquisitely designed. Originally, this bedroom had been meant to be the private quarters of the royal couple, so it should have been turned over to Souma when he ascended the throne. Souma, however, didn't want to go through the trouble of moving in, so he had given permission for the former royal couple to stay, and they were still using it. Souma, incidentally, had brought a simple bed into the governmental affairs office and slept there.

When Liscia ran into that room, out of breath, she was greeted by the sight of her parents not only elegantly enjoying tea on the attached balcony, but dipping scones in cream, raising them up to each other's mouths, and saying:

"Say 'ah,' darling."

"Ah."

Liscia fell to the ground, but quickly stood back up, and marched up to the former king, Albert, with anger in her eyes.

"Father, when I heard your throne had been usurped, I hastened back from my patrol outside the capital! So, why is it that I now find you two feeding each other without a care in the world?!"

Liscia, in addition to her title as a princess (though, following the abdication, she was now the new king's betrothed), had also graduated from officers' school and held an officer's rank in the army. She was not especially high in the ranks, but due to her noble birth, she was often tasked with attending Royal Army funerals, or with other missions of a special nature. This time, she had been on a regional patrol, so she had rushed to the capital upon hearing of her father's abdication.

"There was no usurpation, really. I abdicated of my own will," her father said calmly.

"Why would you suddenly do that?!"

"I had become certain that this man would make a better king for this nation than I. This is a decision I came to as the one entrusted with this country, and I take full responsibility for it. I will tolerate no objections."

In that one moment, Liscia saw the dignified authority of the man who had, until just recently, carried a nation on his shoulders, and found herself unable to object any further. "Urkh...but how could you decide my engagement without even consulting me?"

"You may discuss that between yourselves. The betrothal was something I forced on him to begin with. If you do not want it, I doubt Sir Souma will force the matter."

"Motheeeer!" Liscia shouted. She turned to her mother for help, but Elisha just smiled.

"Meet Sir Souma for yourself first. This is your life, so you must decide what you will do with it yourself. Whatever your decision is, we will respect it."

With not even a straw to grasp at, Liscia's shoulders slumped.

She departed the room of the former royal couple and walked quickly across the palace.

It had been some weeks since she had left this palace for her regional patrols. Something about the palace she had been away from for a few weeks caught her attention. Many of the servants were running around—the guards, the maids, the bureaucrats, even the ministers—anyone and everyone was running. The sight of pudgy ministers running about and gasping with sweat beading on their foreheads was so surreal that she could only stare, dumbfounded.

It hadn't been like this before. The castle she remembered had been a place so relaxed that it felt as if time just flowed slower there. The maids, the ministers...everyone walked slowly, and it was so quiet you could hear the palace guards training in the courtyard from anywhere in the palace. Hadn't Liscia joined the

Officers' Academy because she had been sick and tired of that atmosphere?

But what now? No matter where she went in the castle, the sound of footsteps echoed.

Liscia called out to one of the maids who was rushing past. "Can I have a moment?"

"Why, Princess! How may I be of service?" the maid asked, slowing.

"Um...everyone in the castle seems to be in an awful hurry. Is there something happening?"

"No, nothing in particular."

"Are you sure? It felt like everyone was rushing to do something..."

"*I* am. Ah, but perhaps it is our new king's influence. When we see how that man works, it makes us feel bad if we don't work, too. I couldn't stand to be slow myself, either...ah, I'm in the middle of something right now, so I will take my leave!"

"I-I see... do your best."

As she watched the maid speed off, Liscia was speechless.

For him to make even the maids feel this way, just how hard does the new king work?! Just what kind of guy have I gotten betrothed to?!

Liscia found herself wanting to bury her head in her hands even more.

At last, she came to the king's governmental affairs office. When she opened the door, the first thing that she saw was a mountain of paperwork. On a desk large enough that two fully-grown adults could have slept atop it, the papers were piled high and looked ready to spill over, but that wasn't all. When she looked around, she saw a number of bureaucrats sitting at another long table, fighting a losing battle with yet more bundles of paperwork.

As Liscia stood there, dumbfounded, a young man spoke to her from the other side of the mountain of paper.

"You, whoever just came in."

"Huh?! What?!" Snapped back to her senses, Liscia had let out a strange cry, but the speaker didn't seem to care at all.

"Can you read? Can you do math?"

"D-don't mock me! I've certainly been taught that much!"

"Well, perfect. Get over here and help me with the work."

"Just who do you think you are, asking me to help...?"

"Just do it. That's a royal order."

Saying this, the person behind the paper mountain stood up.

For the first time, the two came face to face. This was the first meeting between the new king, Souma, and his betrothed, Liscia.

Liscia would later describe her first impression of him as "a young man with tired eyes."

In stories where a hero is summoned to another world, the hero sometimes gains powers as a result of being summoned. It seemed the people in this world all had some ability to use magic, so where was the harm in hoping I might have gained the ability to use magic, too? Technically, I *had* been summoned here as a hero.

So, right after the throne was ceded to me, some priestly-looking guys carried out an inspection of my abilities.

Apparently, there were various types of magic that people could use, and they had devices that could test it. This one looked kind of like a stone slate. When a person touched the slate, that person's magic type and abilities were displayed in that person's head. Not even the people of this world understood the principles behind how it worked, but it seemed there were a fair number of these sorts of out-of-place artifacts in this world.

So, I got my diagnosis, and here was the power I'd gained: [The Power to Transfer Consciousness into an Object and Manipulate It]

It was an ability that let me transfer my consciousness into objects I touched, and I could manipulate up to three of them simultaneously.

It sounded more like a psychic power than magic, but the lighter the object, the more freely I could control it. I could get an overhead view of whatever I was controlling, as well. What was more, in addition to my own consciousness, I could have that object move under an independent consciousness, as well. Using an object as a medium like this, I could think about multiple things at the same time.

While there was the limitation that I could only move around things close to me, being able to make things move around at will was neat. Like I was triggering a poltergeist effect.

So, that was why I named my ability "Living Poltergeists." Sounds like I have a case of junior high syndrome, maybe?

Having gained my Living Poltergeists, one thing immediately came to mind:

"This is going to be *so* useful for doing paperwork!"

Copying my consciousness into three pens, I could review multiple documents simultaneously with parallel thinking, and by manipulating those three pens, I could sign off on them. *Man, ever since I learned I had this ability, I've gotten so much more work done.* Actually, without that ability, the giant mountain of paperwork that had piled up in the confusion since I had been given the throne would probably have buried me in an avalanche by now.

Yeah, I know what you want to say. I get an ability, and it turns out to be mostly good for handling deskwork more smoothly?

While I was getting good use out of it, whenever I thought about it as a hero's power, I could only think, "How did things turn out like this?" I mean, even if I hadn't gotten super powerful magic that would let me take on hordes of enemies at the same time, I'd have liked some defensive magic that would at least let me protect myself.

Well, wishing for things I couldn't have wasn't going to get me anywhere. As a matter of fact, it was a useful power to me.

Today, as usual, I was fighting the mountain of paperwork with my Living Poltergeists. While I was doing so, someone entered the room with a thunderous noise that sounded like they'd tried to kick down a perfectly good door. When I peeked through a gap in the paper mountain, I saw it was a young woman in a military uniform.

With her regular features, skin so pale as to be translucent, and silky platinum blonde hair, she was so gorgeous that at any other time I would have been captivated by her beauty. However, having pulled three consecutive all-nighters, I saw not a beautiful girl but just a new source of labor.

After calling her over and practically forcing her to sit next to me, I pushed two stacks of paper in her direction. "Please compare these two sets of documents and look for places where the values, or the number of items, don't agree and mark them."

"Huh? What? What kind of work is this?"

"What kind, you ask? Digging for buried treasure. That's what." I explained to the perplexed girl in uniform. "For 'unaccounted-for expenditures,' to be precise. One pile is requests for budgetary appropriations, the other is income and expenditures reports. Even if the amount requested and the amount spent match, if the number of items differs, that can be indicative of either wasteful investment undertaken to fully use up their budget, or embezzlement disguised as investment. We'll check those, and if any laws have been broken, we'll make each of the responsible parties pay to make up the loss. If we uncover personal embezzlement, we will mandate repayment, and in the event they cannot pay, we will arrest the offender and seize their assets."

"U-understood."

Perhaps she had been intimidated by the threatening air of a man who had gone without sleep, because the girl nodded along as I talked.

Good.

Around two hours passed with her working quietly next to me.

At last, the girl in military uniform spoke to me, her hands never ceasing their work of checking documents as she did. "Hey."

"What? If you're tired, you can take a break whenever."

"No, that's not it... I haven't introduced myself yet. I am Liscia Elfrieden. The daughter of the former king, Albert Elfrieden."

I stopped moving my pen. "You're the princess, huh?"

"I don't look like one?"

"You were in uniform, so I didn't notice. But...yeah, maybe you do look princess-y."

At this point, I finally took note of how attractive she was.

"I'm...Souma Kazuya. Technically, I'm the new king."

Liscia turned to face me. She was pretty close, and we looked into one another's eyes. Unlike me, who was just taken aback, her golden eyes seemed like they were trying to evaluate me. After we looked into one another's eyes for some time, Liscia slowly opened her mouth.

"I'm not a princess anymore. Because you usurped the throne, my current position is a little unclear."

"Usurped...? Your father pushed the throne and all his duties on me, I'll have you know. Honestly, why do I have to go through all this pain and hassle?"

"Seriously, what happened? I know you're the summoned hero, but how did that suddenly turn into you taking the throne?"

"You tell me. I just did what I felt I needed to in order to protect myself..."

I explained what had happened around the time of the summoning ceremony to Liscia.

When I had been summoned to this world, I'd been on the verge of being handed over to the Empire. The king hadn't seemed enthusiastic about the idea, but seeing as he had no other plan, if the Empire had put pressure on him to do it, he probably wouldn't have had any other choice. There had been no telling what might happen to me if I were turned over to the Empire, so I asked the king to choose the "do not hand over the hero" option.

My proposal to the king and prime minister was that they pay the war subsidies to buy time, and with that time, push forward with policies that would build a strong and prosperous country. If the Empire was saying "hand over the hero in place of war subsidies," all we had to do was pay the subsidies. If we did that, they would lose any justification for interfering in our affairs. It was not an actual threat, no matter what it seemed like. To keep up appearances, the Empire would not insist on it any further. That was my reasoning. We would use the time bought this way to pursue country-strengthening policies which would let us stand on equal terms with the Empire.

The two of them had objections, of course. They had said this country had no means to pay the war subsidies. But, after inspecting the materials they brought me, I was able to show that if we sold off some state-owned facilities, enacted caps on government spending, and the king turned over some of his "personal assets," it would be possible to pay.

I had gotten into my university's School of Socioeconomic

Studies (with the subject I had selected for the "socio-" part of the entrance exam being World History, by the way), and my dream for the future had been to become a local government employee. This was all within my field of expertise.

Hearing this plan, the king had taken on a ponderous expression, but the prime minister, Marx, was enthusiastic. He must have ultimately decided that, rather than turn over the hero to preserve the status quo, enacting economic reforms was more likely to leave the country with a future. The king became more enthusiastic as we went on.

As the guy who suggested it, I knew I'd probably be expected to put in a lot of the work on those reforms, but only as a single bureaucrat in the finance ministry...or so I had thought.

"And then he pushed the throne off on me."

"Um, well...sorry."

"It's nothing you need to apologize for. If anything, you're a victim in all this, suddenly finding yourself engaged to me."

"Well, yeah... wait, huh? Which of us is higher-ranked now? Do I need to be super polite and formal?" She looked unsure of whether she should speak to me as a commoner would to a king or as a princess who was candidate to be queen.

"We can keep it casual, I guess?" I said.

"Sure."

"Also, don't worry about the betrothal thing. I'm just holding on to the throne for now. I'll probably quit this whole king gig in a few years, anyway."

"Huh? Why?!"

"Because I only ever planned to work hard enough to earn the subsidies for the Empire so that I wouldn't be turned over. Now that I've been handed the throne, I'll do enough to get this country on the right track, but after that, I'll leave it to the people of this country to handle the rest. Of course, we can tear up the engagement then."

I gave Liscia a reassuring smile.

◇ ◇ ◇

"I'll probably quit this whole king gig in a few years anyway." My eyes went wide when I heard Souma say that.

He makes it sound so simple. Does he even realize how difficult that would be?

Even someone like myself, who had focused so much on military matters that my political knowledge was a bit weak, could see the situation our country was in. I believe the word was "checkmate." Food shortages, economic malaise, the influx of refugees caused by the invasion of demons, plus pressure from the Gran Chaos Empire. We had nothing but uncertainty bearing down on us.

For that reason, I could somewhat understand my father's decision to immediately abdicate the throne to someone he sensed was more capable. Still, considering all that, was it even possible to get this country back on track? Even supposing he somehow could, would the people allow a king who had accomplished such a great feat to retire so easily?

"So, do you think you can secure the funds for the war subsidies?"

"Hm? Yeah. I've already secured the funds to send to the Empire."

"Huh?"

"Right now, I'm trying to squeeze out the funds for my reforms. They'll cost even more than the war subsidies, after all."

Wait...wait, wait, wait, wait! He's already secured the funds? The amount the Empire requested was so massive that it was equivalent to the national budget, from what I heard!

"Where did we have that kind of money...?"

"I sold off, like, a third of the treasure vault."

"The treasure vault...our national treasures?! Don't tell me you sold off our national treasures! You didn't, did you?!" I closed in on Souma, who looked very blasé about the whole thing. "The national treasures belong to the whole country! Just arbitrarily selling them off is a betrayal of our people!"

"Now, now, just calm down. If you say they're the property of the people, I'd say selling them for the benefit of the people is all good."

"Even so, there must have been objects with historical and cultural value..."

"Oh, if that's your concern, I had those set aside. All I sold were jewels and ornamental objects that had material value."

Souma looked through the paperwork for the treasure vault inventory. "Treasures were divided into three categories: Category A (items with historical or cultural value), Category

B (items without historical or cultural value but with monetary value), and Category C (everything else). We only sold items from Category B. Rather than sell the stuff in Category A, if we put it on rotating display in a museum, it's likely to serve as a more permanent source of income."

"Well, maybe... what about Category C?"

"Magic tools, grimoires, and the like. Honestly, I'm not sure how best to handle them. You could say they're like weapons, in a way. We can't sell them off or put them on display without the proper precautions. That full set of Hero Equipment looked like it might fetch a nice price, though...mind if I sell that?"

"Please, don't..."

Technically, you're supposed to be the hero...ah, wait, you're the king now, aren't you?

"But, if we have all this money, shouldn't it go to the military? In officers' school I learned 'spend always on defense, never on tribute.'"

"Let me answer that pithy saying with another one. 'Time is money.' Which is to say, by offering the war subsidies as a sacrifice, we can gain the one resource our country most needs right now: time."

"Why do you have to talk in such a roundabout way?"

"Don't worry about it. Anyway, even if we were able to strengthen our forces, it would all be for naught if we can't also get domestic issues under control. Until the food and refugee issues are resolved, we're only going to continue losing the support of the people. Once that happens, we'll be left with a fragile state that's easily thrown into riots with a little agitation by foreign actors."

"No...the people love this country, too. They wouldn't riot..."

"You're being idealistic there. 'Only once one is clothed and fed does one learn manners.' In the end, you can't have morals or patriotism on an empty stomach. If you're too busy looking after yourself, you can't afford to look after others."

Souma's eyes were cold as he said this. It was a harsh and realistic view. That alone made me feel he was on the mark. From the look of him, you would expect him to be a weak man, yet somehow... he looked so reliable.

◇　◇　◇

After spending another day working, I was finally able to secure a certain amount of funds. While I wasn't exactly flush with cash, I would have the money I needed for my reforms for the time being. I managed to extract all this money from just my direct holdings, without having to touch the Three Dukedoms, so I'd have liked some praise for that, at least.

Looking around the room...it was a disaster. Bureaucrats were passed out on their desks, others were leaning back asleep in their chairs, their faces looking skywards. On the sofa, Liscia had lain down and was snoring softly.

I moved over to her quietly, sat on the sofa's armrest, and watched Liscia sleep. In the end, this girl had stayed up until close to dawn helping me with my work. Even though she must have wanted to say a thing or two to say about being forced into an engagement with me...

I patted her sleeping head. Her silky hair slid smoothly between my fingers. The excitement from being set free after such a long job must have been affecting me. Normally, I'd have been too embarrassed to do this sober, but just sitting here like this made me happy.

"Mrm..."

Liscia groaned, so I pulled my hand out of her hair. The next moment, Liscia opened her eyes and sprung up. Maybe she was still a little groggy, since she was looking around all over.

"Good morning, Liscia," I said with a wry grin.

"M-morning...huh? Did I fall asleep...?"

"We've hit a good stopping point now. Do you want to go back to sleep?"

"Oh, no. I'm fine. What about you, Souma? You haven't slept, have you?"

It looked like she was fully awake. I was happy to see her showing concern for me, too.

Lifting myself from the armrest, I stretched my arms wide.

"I plan to have a good long rest after this, but...could you come with me for a bit first?"

"Hm? Where to?"

"For a before-bedtime walk," I said.

In the light of near-dawn, Liscia and I bounced along on horseback.

While breathing in the morning mist, Liscia's horse sped along with a *clip-clop, clip-clop*, not bothered in the least by the weight of two people. Liscia sat in the front holding the reins, while I was behind her with my arms around her slim waist, holding on for dear life.

"Hey, don't squeeze my belly so hard," she objected.

"No way. This is pretty scary."

"Pitiful. Normally shouldn't you, as the man, be the one holding the reins?"

"Well, it's not like I had a choice. I've never ridden on a horse before."

In modern Japan, there was rarely any chance to ride horses. At best, I'd ridden on a pony at the petting zoo as a child while someone else led it on a leash.

"In this country, pretty much everyone from peasant farmers to the nobility can ride, you know?" she told me.

"In my world, there were many more convenient vehicles."

"Your world...tell me about it, Souma."

"Hm?"

"Did you...leave behind any family, a lover maybe, in the other world?" Liscia asked me hesitantly. Was she trying to be considerate of my feelings?

"No, nobody. My last relative, my grandpa, just passed away the other day..."

"I'm sorry."

"It's nothing to apologize about. Grandpa had lived a full life. That's why, well...nobody's waiting for my return, so I guess I don't feel the need to go back in any hurry."

"Oh...you don't." Liscia seemed somewhat relieved.

As we talked, the horse kept clip-clopping along. It was around six in the morning, maybe. The time when people finally started to stir. As we passed through the shopping street, no shops were open yet and there was almost no one out. Passing through the castle town, we reached the wall that went around the capital. We came up to a massive gate, the likes of which I had only seen in foreign fantasy films, and after speaking to the guards there, we went outside through a small door beside it.

Liscia did all the talking here. If the newly-ascended king had told them he wanted to go outside the city without any body-guards, I doubt they'd have allowed it. So Liscia, who held an officer's rank, told them, "I have been dispatched outside by order of the king," and played it off as part of her duties.

Once we safely passed through the gate, Liscia added, "Since I said it was a royal order, there's going to be a record of it. Who knows what Marx is going to say to us later."

I ignored her complaints.

After a short trip through the city streets, we finally reached our destination. "Stop here," I said.

As she stopped the horse, Liscia looked at me questioningly. "This is where you wanted to come? All I see are farmers' fields."

Indeed, there was nothing but verdant fields of green leaves here. Green fields, wet with the morning dew, as far as the eye could see. This was the place... no doubt about that.

"This is the place I wanted to show you, Liscia."

"These fields? I suppose they're pretty when they're wet with the morning dew like this..."

"Pretty...huh. Even though it's because of *this* that people are *starving to death*."

"Wha?" Liscia's eyes widened in surprise.

I sighed. "Take a close look. These 'inedible fields' are the root of this country's food crisis."

◇   ◇   ◇

*Inedible fields...*that was what Souma had called the fields spread out before me, looking at them bitterly. Souma had said he'd wanted to show me these fields, but I still didn't understand why.

"What do you mean?"

"Exactly what I said. All of the fields you see here are cotton fields."

"Cotton fields...ah! That's what you meant by inedible!"

Cotton flowers were grown to produce cotton thread. Sure enough, these fields didn't grow anything you could eat.

Souma sat down there, resting his elbows on his thighs. "Jumping straight to my conclusion, it's the excessive increase in the number of these cotton fields that has caused this country's food shortages."

"Come again?"

Did he just sort of off-handedly say something incredible now? The cause of our food shortages?

"While I was sorting through the paperwork, I noticed it. With the expansion of the Demon Lord's Domain, the demand for clothing and other daily necessities has skyrocketed. Of course, the demand for the raw materials has shot up, too. With the selling price of cotton flowers rising and being able to sell as much as you can produce, the farmers have entirely stopped growing the food crops they had produced up until that point. Crops grown to sell to others instead of to eat are called cash crops. Which is to say our farmers have turned to growing only cash crops, which has led to a lowering of this country's food self-sufficiency rate."

I was speechless. The cause of this country's food shortages...

I had always assumed it was bad weather, or that our country just had poor soil to begin with. Here was a concrete reason, and yet I, who had lived in this country for more than ten years, hadn't seen it. Meanwhile Souma, who had been summoned here only a few days prior, had managed to.

"If I were to go a bit further, I could say it's the cause of this country's poor economy, as well. When the food self-sufficiency rate drops, you must import from other countries to avoid starving. However, imported food involves transportation costs as well, so the price of food rises. That puts pressure on household budgets, but you can only cut food costs so far. If you don't eat, you'll starve, after all. Of course, if you're going to trim the fat somewhere, it's going to be in nonessential and luxury goods. This change in spending practices is causing a downward spiral in the economy."

What had I been looking at? Had I just been a private citizen, it would have been fine to laugh scornfully at my lack of insight. However, I was a princess.

The ignorance of those at the top kills those at the bottom.

"I'm...a failure as a royal." I lost all strength, falling to my knees there. In all my life, I had never so keenly felt a sense of powerlessness as I did now.

Seeing me like that, Souma let out an "uh," and an "um," scratching his head, before resting his hand on my head.

"Don't let it get you so down. We've secured the funding we'll need. It's not too late for agricultural reforms."

"What are you planning to do?"

"Place limits on the growth of cash crops, bring back the growing of food crops, and improve our self-sufficiency rate. The country will pay subsidies to help support that transition. First, we'll replant the fields with beans, which have a wide range of uses, and potatoes, which are resistant against famine, and over time I'd like to increase the number of paddy fields. After that…"

Souma spoke eloquently of his plans for agricultural reform. He used a lot of words like "paddy fields" that were unfamiliar to me, but as I looked at his face in profile, he seemed so radiant.

I felt I could understand why my father had abdicated the throne to him. He was what this country needed most right now. We had to do whatever it took to keep him tied down here. Our betrothal had probably been meant as another chain with which to bind him.

I guess I can't afford to be upset about the engagement being decided without my input.

Souma had said that once he got the country on track, he would return the throne, but we couldn't let him do that. It would be a loss to the country to have a man of such rare talent leave. It needed to be prevented at all costs.

He says he has no family in his old world. If I were to become his family here, could I keep him in this country? I wondered. *As his fiancée, if I can just make the marriage a fait accompli...wait, the best way to make it a fait accompli...would basically be...doing that with him...*

The thoughts that came to my mind left my face flushed red.

"So, in the mountains we'll...hey, Liscia, you listening?"

"Eek! Wh-why, yes, I'm listening."

"Hm? Your face is all red, you know."

"It's just the sunrise! Think nothing of it!"

My cheeks were on fire. I was ready to just die of embarrassment.

From there on, I don't think I heard a single word of Souma's explanations.

CHAPTER 2
Start from X

THE TECHNOLOGY in this world was kind of all over the place. On Earth, technology had moved from manpower, to the water wheel and windmill, to the steam engine, and then on to the combustion engine. It was a series of incremental advances.

If you wanted to fly freely through the sky, before you could build an airplane, you would first need to discover the concept of lift, and a propulsion system (the internal combustion engine) would need to be created. In order to create that propulsion system, you would need to understand the system behind how things burn. In the history of Earth, new technologies had always been built atop other technologies that had laid the groundwork for them.

However, in this world, there were mysterious creatures and magic. If you wanted to fly freely through the sky, you could just ride a wyvern. These people had skipped past the concept of lift and propulsion systems and just gone flying.

In a world where you can create fire, ice, and more with magic any time you want to, the difference between what is possible and what is not becomes extreme.

In this world, they had large tamed beasts that could haul as much as a four-ton truck.

There were steel battleships, only they were drawn by massive sea dragons.

There was no electricity, yet the nights were bright in this country. The street lamps had lightmoss in them, which stored light energy during the day and was phosphorescent at night, keeping the town lit.

They didn't have gas, so they used firewood, ovens, and fire magic (or magic items) to cook.

There were no aqueducts. However, all around town, there were wells with water elemental spells cast on them which drew water from deep below the earth. Those are enough examples to make my point.

In this country, even without science, many things could be done with magic. Turning that around, if you were to take away their magic and mysterious creatures, this country's civilization would not be that advanced. Comparing it to a point in our own world's history, they were probably in the late Middle Ages or early modern period, at best. The feudal system was still intact, and the industrial revolution a long way away.

That was the kind of country I was now king of.

◇ ◇ ◇

"Liscia, agricultural reforms don't happen overnight," Souma told me at breakfast. "So, for the time being, I suppose we'll have to increase our imports from other countries to compensate."

I sat across from Souma, nibbling on my toast as he talked. On the narrow table, there was a basket of bread as well as plates with scrambled eggs, sausage, and salad for two on them.

"But didn't you say imports are expensive, and that causes a decline in consumer spending?"

"I did. That's why we'll probably end up having the country buy up goods, then resell them at domestic prices for a time. We'll take a loss on the tariffs, but we need to bear it for now. I'd like to make up the shortfall with exports, but first we'll need to find a replacement for our current primary export, cotton."

"Sounds hard... anyway, let's set that aside for a moment." I asked the question that had been bothering me for a while now. "You're the king, so why in the world are you eating in here?!"

This was the castle cafeteria. What's more, it was the general cafeteria which the soldiers and maids used. What we were eating right now was the A-Set lunch for this morning. The king of a country was sitting amongst the guards, eating the same food they did. There were limits to how little dignity a king could be allowed to have.

"The constant curious glances from the guards and maids are starting to hurt, you know!" I protested.

"Don't let it bother you. The whole castle is being frugal right now, so I can't allow wasteful spending on my meals."

"Didn't you say austerity measures were a bad influence on the economy?!"

"If you just accumulate the money you're saving, yes," he said.

"But if the extra money is used properly, it makes the economy go 'round."

"Still, that doesn't mean we have to eat here."

"Well, do you want to eat this stuff at the big royal table? It'll feel even more unsatisfying that way."

"You may be right, but still..."

It felt wrong eating with all these people watching us. Even if I was used to it from my days at the officers' academy, I was technically Souma's fiancée, a person under the scrutiny of the masses, and to their eyes, here we were having a rendezvous. How could I stay calm like that?

I sighed. "If we're cutting back on food costs, should I speak to my parents? They're always eating cakes and such at teatime."

"Oh, that's fine. Those are all 'offerings' anyway."

"Gifts, you mean?" I asked in surprise. Could our people afford to do that?

"Well, they're from large stores and stores owned by the nobility, you see. Even with a guy like me as king, being a purveyor to the royal family is prestigious, apparently. We still get sent a lot of stuff, even with the food shortages."

"Please, don't speak ill of yourself like that," I said. "You're a king now."

"A lot of the foods are sweet, but they don't have a long shelf life. Since I don't have much of a sweet tooth myself, I give them to the former royal couple or the maids and have them write reviews. Then, for the ones that are rated highly, I give them a royal warrant of appointment. It's gone surprisingly well."

"So that's why..." I murmured.

Lately, I'd been hearing "all's not quiet on the weight-loss front" from the maids. There had even been reports that some of the maids were joining the guards for training.

I'd better be careful, myself, I decided.

In contrast to me as I made promises to myself, Souma was looking off into the distance.

"I-is something the matter?" I asked.

"No, it's just...if the food budget were tighter, we might be subsisting on a diet of cake three times daily...hahaha...I nearly put 'if they have no bread, let them eat cake' into practice myself."

"If people didn't know the circumstances, there could be a revolution over those words," I said.

"You two seem to be enjoying yourselves."

When I turned in the direction of the sudden voice, I saw a young man in the fluted armor (minus helmet) of the Royal Guard. He was tall, with a sufficiently sturdy frame, and from behind his long, straight blond hair peeked a beautiful face that probably made him popular with the ladies.

"Why, Sir Ludwin," I said.

"It has been too long, my princess. No...perhaps I should call you my queen now."

"Um, well...I'm not either of those at the moment, actually."

Seeing our exchange, Souma had a "who is this guy?" look on his face.

"Souma, this gentleman is Sir Ludwin Arcs of the Royal Guard," I said, introducing him.

Despite his youthful age—just under thirty—Sir Ludwin was a genius who had been made head of the Royal Guard. In times of peace, the head of the Royal Guard was responsible for security in the capital as well as Parnam Castle, but in times of crisis he was also given command of the king's personal forces, the Forbidden Army. Though, that said, practical military control of the country lay in the hands of the Three Dukedoms.

"The Three Dukedoms" referred to the two dukes and one duchess who held control of the land, sea, and air forces. The current holders of the Three Dukedoms were as follows:

General of the Elfrieden Kingdom Army, Duke Georg Carmine. A beastman with a lion's mane. He commanded his troops with the intensity of a raging fire, striking fear into the hearts of our enemies.

Admiral of the Elfrieden Kingdom Navy, Duchess Excel Walter. A sea serpent descended from pirates. She was an incredible woman, adept not only at fleet battles but also in politics.

General of the Elfrieden Kingdom Air Force, Duke Castor Vargas. A dragonewt. He was king of the skies and leader of the stars of the Royal Army, the Wyvern Knights.

In exchange for swearing fealty to the kingdom, their families were allowed to hold territory within the kingdom, where they were given self-rule.

At the time of the kingdom's founding, this kingdom having been created by the coming together of many races, this system had been put in place to protect their races from friction with the others. However, even now, with all the races living in harmony, the system still remained in place. In exchange for territory, their families put their lives on the line to defend the country they loved. That was the pride of the Three Dukedoms.

However, at present, the Three Dukedoms had taken their forces and were secluding themselves in their own territories. It seemed these three, with their great love and respect for the former king, had not yet recognized Souma, who had ascended the throne in a manner that looked like he was usurping it as their liege. That was the source of Souma's current worries.

If you combined the three duchies, they made up a third of the country. Without their cooperation, Souma's reforms would be difficult to accomplish.

I myself had written to Duke Carmine, who loved me like a daughter, several times, asking him to meet with Souma directly. His reply was always "As yet, I see no cause to trust him."

He was a man who was resolute in his convictions, but I had never known him to be so blindly stubborn. So why was he being so stubborn this time? For my part, I hoped he would accept Souma as soon as possible.

Without any idea how I was feeling, Souma was shaking hands with Sir Ludwin. "I'm Souma Kazuya. Technically, I'm the king of this country now."

"I'm Ludwin Arcs. I've heard rumors of your hard work from the civil servants."

"Well, you tell those civil servants, 'if you have time to gossip, work harder' for me."

"Hahaha, I'll do that. Would you mind if I joined you for breakfast?"

"It's fine with me."

"Thank you."

Sir Ludwin brought over a breakfast tray and sat down next to me. "So, how are things going? With these reforms of yours, I mean, Your Majesty."

"Not so well," Souma complained between bites of toast. "We're especially suffering from a lack of qualified people. At present, I've inherited the previous king's advisors...in other words, the people who left the country alone until it got this bad. Setting aside Prime Minister Marx, the rest are all useless."

This country was an autocratic state. The will of the king was strongly reflected in its politics.

There was a Congress of the People which all citizens had the right to vote for representatives in, but it was merely a place where laws and policies to "suggest" to the king were drafted, and these laws and policies would later be "suggested" to the king by the prime minister. In short, it was a glorified suggestion box, and whether these suggestions would be implemented or not was entirely up to the king.

Though, that said, if the king were to just do whatever he pleased, he would lose the hearts of the people, and would likely see himself deposed by the Three Dukedoms.

Furthermore, when the king wished to consider different policies, he could summon advisors other than the prime minister. The king would confer with his advisors, deciding if his policies would be effective or not. The selection of advisors was left to the king's sole discretion. He could hire whomever and however many he wanted.

In truth, even before taking the throne (in this kingdom, from the time one was a prince), a prospective king would begin to gather people who might become his advisors. But with Souma having ascended the throne so suddenly, he had none.

"People who can tell me the things I want to know and who will work hard at the tasks I set them to," he said. "Those are the sort of personal retainers I want."

"I understand. All those who stand above others long to have capable underlings," Sir Ludwin said.

"Is it the same for you in the Forbidden Army?"

"Yes. Most of the graduates from the Officers' Academy request to be assigned to the armies of the Three Dukedoms. While they call us the Forbidden Army, we're basically just the capital's defense force. It's not a popular posting, is it, Princess?"

"Well...I guess not. Most of my classmates went to the armies of the Three Dukedoms."

I was in the land forces, but that was because there was no point in me joining the Forbidden Army, since it existed to protect the royal family.

"Well, there you have it. These days, the Forbidden Army has a lot of misfits and eccentrics in it. We even have a mad scientist who drifted over to us from the Weapons Development Branch."

"Oh, now that sounds like someone I'd want to meet!" Souma said.

Seeing Souma's enthusiasm, Sir Ludwin replied, "I'll introduce you sometime." He laughed wryly.

After that, we made small talk for a while and then parted with Sir Ludwin.

When I get back to my room, I'll send another letter encouraging Duke Carmine to meet with Souma, I thought to myself.

◇ ◇ ◇

"We really do suffer from a lack of capable people!" I complained.

"I-I suppose..." Liscia said.

I tried to persuade Liscia, but she looked a little bewildered.

Because I had been working my ability so hard, it might have leveled up. Lately, I could move up to four things at the same time (effectively, I could do the work of five people), but even with that, it was only the equivalent of having one extra person. A person who lacked any knowledge or skills that I myself lacked. What I needed were people with knowledge I didn't have. People with skills I didn't have. I desperately wanted to have people like that.

So, I decided to gather them.

"That being that, I think I'll use a Jewel Voice Broadcast."

"A Jewel Voice Broadcast?"

The Jewel Voice Broadcast was a system for delivering the voice of the king to all regions of the country. In the Jewel Voice Room in the palace, there was a floating jewel that must have had a diameter of around two meters. The jewel was said to be imbued with the magic of the spirits of air, sylphs, and the spirits of water, undines. It would deliver the king's voice to all around the country, and in towns with the appropriate setup, it could even project his image. Past kings had apparently used the Jewel Voice Broadcast to unveil a new constitution or to declare war on another nation, that sort of thing.

"I'll bet you'll be the first to use it to gather capable people," Liscia said, seemingly impressed.

Was it really such a wild idea? "How do you normally gather them?" I asked.

"Through personal connections or holding written exams and hiring those who pass."

"Aren't those methods pretty biased? What's the literacy rate in this country?"

"Half the people can read, and three-tenths can write."

"That's no good at all. Only three-tenths of the population can take the exams."

"Just so you know, that's average in this world," she said.

Hmm...guess that's what happens when you don't have compulsory education.

"Anyone can be taught to read and write," I said. "Surely, the quality of a candidate shouldn't be decided by his or her ability to afford lessons. It's seven-tenths of the population. Just how many diamonds are you planning to leave in the rough?"

"There's nothing I can say against that," Liscia said, sounding ashamed.

Though, I suppose she's not the one I need to be telling this to, huh? Really, this country needs to be fixed from the ground up.

"So, what conditions are you going to use in your call?" she asked.

"I'm considering the wording. Though, really, I intend to borrow the words of a great man I admire."

"A great man?"

"Yeah. A 'crafty hero in a troubled land.'"

◇ ◇ ◇

"If you have a gift, I will put it to use!"

Through capital, city, town, and village alike, Souma's voice echoed. His image was projected into the capital, the cities, and even the larger towns as well. The receivers in the larger areas released a mist into the air, then used the refraction of light to recreate the scene taking place inside the Jewel Voice Room.

To put it in modern terms, they were receiving a video feed from the filming location and projecting it live onto a mid-air screen. The quality was grainy, but people were excited to have their first glimpse of the new king.

Some were bewildered by his youth, others by his plain appearance. The fault for this lay with Souma, who had felt it too bothersome to put on formal attire or even his crown.

Just seeing Princess Liscia standing at his side without looking particularly tense reassured the people. Though they had heard he hadn't forced the king to abdicate and usurped the throne, until they saw him for themselves, they had still harbored some uncertainty. Especially in the case of Princess Liscia, whose dignified beauty had made her something of an idol to the people. Some had voiced concern for her well-being.

As they went about their business, Souma's speech continued.

"My people, our country is faced with a crisis of heretofore unseen proportions! The grave matter of the food crisis, the economic downturn which stems from it, the influx of refugees from lands seized by the Demon Lord...any one of these things alone would be a serious malaise which threatened this country. Yet, there is still more! The Empire has expanded its influence, and some of our neighbors watch us with eager eyes, ready to pounce! The former king, recognizing that this situation was beyond his power to solve, has entrusted this country to my humble self.

"To recognize what one cannot do, and to make way for one who can...even when one knows it to be the right thing to do, it is never an easy choice. In times of peace, the former king would have had the capacity to be a great ruler."

For a moment, Princess Liscia thought, *that's giving him way too much credit* with a bitter smile, but no one noticed.

"However, these are troubled times! In times of turbulence, we seek in our rulers not a person of saintly virtue, but someone willing to get their hands dirty, willing to stubbornly do what it takes to survive. Not a ruler who is above average in all things, but a ruler who will not give up on survival, and on that one point excels beyond all others. Because, ultimately, that is what will protect your families and livelihoods! That is why the former king entrusted this country to me! I am tenacious, and on this one point I am superior to the former king.

"At present, I am in the process of launching many reforms. However, we face an overwhelming lack of capable people to aid in their implementation. Therefore, I am putting out a call to the gifted amongst you. I say to you again: if you have a gift, I will make use of it!

"In these confused times, what we need is not those who are, on average, better than others. It is those who, in one aspect, stand head and shoulders above all the rest. The form that gift takes matters not. It matters not if you have any qualifications beyond that gift. If there is one thing about which you have the pride to say, 'I am better than anyone else at this,' come to stand before me!

"Schooling, age, class, origin, race, gender...none of these matter to me. Whether or not you can read, do arithmetic, have money, are of sound mind and body, are beautiful or ugly, or have a scratch on your shin, it does not matter! If you can think, 'at this one thing, I am better than others. At this one thing, I will not lose out to any other person in the country,' then show yourself before me! If I decide your gift is something the country needs, you will be welcomed as one of my personal retainers!"

The new king's passionate speech put a shine in the people's eyes.

As they listened, they must all have been racking their brains for something they were more gifted at than other people. At the same time, though, even if they found something, they were probably all thinking they wouldn't be hired if it wasn't useful in some way. As that feeling of resignation set in, it became a dam blocking the flood of enthusiasm that was building from the impassioned speech.

The king was seeking capable people who could solve this country's problems. Everyone found it hard to imagine that their own gifts would be of any use to the country.

"I am sure that, among you, there are some who are hesitant to believe their gifts can be of use," Souma said, as if aware of the people's hesitation.

"However, that is not something for you to decide on your own! I, the king, will decide whether the country needs your gift! I care not if others deride your gift as worthless! I will be the judge of that! So, have no hesitation! Come and unveil your gift before me!"

Souma paused for a breath to calm himself.

"If you are still hesitant, then here is what we shall do. If your gift is proven to be without compare in this country, in the name of the Kingdom of Elfrieden, I will issue you a Certificate of Peerlessness, and you will receive a cash prize. How's that for a little motivation, people?!" The image of Souma pumped his fist into the air.

At that moment, a great cheer rose up in every city worth calling a city across the country. The dam inside the people's hearts had broken. It was the same in the capital.

"Oh...! I can hear the cheering in the castle town from here. Glad you're all fired up," Souma said, breaking into more casual speech.

Standing by his side, Liscia wanted to hold her head in her hands, but no one seemed to mind.

"You can nominate yourself or someone else," Souma said. "If the nomination is for someone else, three-tenths of the award goes to the nominator. If there are people locking themselves away and playing hermit when this country is in crisis, I want all of you to go and drag them out. Also, for gifts like 'I'm stronger than others' or 'I'm good at singing' where there is room for competition, we will have the candidates compete amongst themselves in advance to choose a single representative for that gift, so be ready for that. All right...I think I've said everything I need to."

Finally, Souma closed out his Jewel Voice Broadcast with the following words: "Now then, O gifted ones, come shake my hand in the capital, Parnam."

Liscia glared reproachfully at him after the broadcast ended. "What was with that last line?" she demanded.

"Just going with the flow," Souma said with a laugh.

Now, how will the people react? Will the people he wants come to the castle? she wondered. *Here's hoping lots of people come...*

◇ ◇ ◇

In history, there are some scenes which are easily dramatized by later generations. There are some conditions for this:

First, it must be the turning point of an era.

Second, it must have a certain flair when dramatized.

In the Sengoku Period, it would be the scene where Oda

Nobunaga performs part of the Noh play *Atsumori* before the Battle of Okehazama.

In *Romance of the Three Kingdoms,* it would be the scene where Liu Bei recruits Zhuge Liang after paying three personal visits to him.

In Roman history, it would be the scene where Caesar says, "the die is cast," as he crosses the Rubicon.

Then, if one were to ask which scene from the era in which the throne was abdicated to Souma was most often dramatized in later years, the answer would likely be this gathering of capable people.

Before Souma, five gifted young people were summoned. Of them, the king would welcome just one with wholehearted joy.

Seen from Souma's perspective, this was one of his greatest accomplishments. From one other person's perspective, it was the turning point in the Cinderella story of their life. From the perspective of "one who watched that scene through eyes unlike those of others," it was to become "the turning point of an era."

In this scene, there were *three* main characters.

I had worried about how many people would come, but the response was far greater than I had anticipated. Not placing any limits on the type of gift and offering a cash prize had probably helped.

Now the capital was packed so full of people, we'd had to place restrictions on the number of people allowed access to the palace. The situation was so overwhelming that the officials, including Marx, had been running around like mad since morning.

It felt to me like way too many people had turned up, but apparently, since I had put out such a wide call, the masses had rushed to the capital to see what kind of people would catch the king's attention.

When people move, things move, too.

Merchants who sensed a business opportunity had gathered to set up shop, so the castle town looked like there was a festival going on. It was an unexpected shot in the arm for our economy, but at the same time, it also meant more work for the officials.

Now, as for the all-important recruitment drive, the response to that was massive, as well.

A multitude of diverse gifts, some immediately useful, some of no apparent use at all upon first glance, were on display at the judging station. There, five officials judged whether the participants' gifts were unique. If they were acknowledged to be, prize money was awarded, no matter what that gift was. Liscia and I were in a separate room, reading the reports from the judges and picking out the people we liked.

There really were a lot of applicants, but that also meant a considerable amount of overlap in their gifts. The competition was particularly fierce for the "Gift of Martial Ability," "Gift of Talent," and "Gift of Beauty," so they were deciding on a number one for each category at another site.

At each of these sites, spectators enjoyed watching the proceedings, named "Best in the Kingdom Martial Arts Tournament," "Kingdom of Talent," and "Elfrieden Pretty Girl Grand Prix."

By the way, after this, by request of the merchant's guild, these tournaments became a yearly event in Parnam and attracted many tourists.

Also, the Elfrieden Pretty Girl Grand Prix invited rumors that it was actually being held by the king to choose his mistresses. As a result, all the nobles who wanted to tie their own lines to the royal family sent their relatives to participate. When Liscia heard the rumors, I did get some cold looks for it later.

The judging process had originally been planned to last for one day, but instead it lasted for three. Those with gifts that made me think "this is what I'm looking for" were brought before me on the fourth day.

I was seated on the throne, with Liscia standing at my side. (Technically, while we were betrothed, the marriage hadn't been held yet, so she wasn't allowed to touch the queen's throne.) One step down from us, Prime Minister Marx stood to our right, and Captain of the Royal Guard Ludwin to our left.

We had hauled the jewel from the Jewel Voice Room into the throne room, so this scene was being broadcast around the kingdom.

Five young people were brought before us.

One had silver hair and elven ears, a girl who looked like a warrior with some muscle showing through her brown skin.

One wore a black robe which covered his whole body, a thin young man with a somewhat listless look on his face.

One looked distinguished, but in a different way from Liscia, a beautiful blue-haired girl with a gentle air about her.

One had little fox ears sprouting from her head, a rustic-looking girl of around ten.

Finally, one was a fat middle-aged man drenched in sweat.

"Your Majesty. The many gifted people of this country who came in response to your summons have been recorded in a ledger. These people here are those possessed of especially rare gifts."

When Marx said this, the fat man prostrated himself before me, jumping to do so with the speed of a grasshopper. The blue-haired pretty girl did the same, her every move filled with grace, and the fox-eared little girl awkwardly followed suit. The black-robed young man watched them all sleepily, bowing before me last.

The elf-eared girl remained standing. Everyone present was shocked.

"You are before the king. Will you not prostrate yourself?" Ludwin cautioned her in a quiet but forceful voice.

The elf-eared girl seemed not to care. More than that, she looked me in the eye and said, "I ask your forbearance, as this is the custom of my tribe. The warriors of my tribe do not lower their head before any but their master. And, for our women, to not lower your head before any but your husband is proof of your chastity."

"Still..." Ludwin argued.

"I don't mind." I held up a hand to stop Ludwin from arguing with her. "We're the ones asking them to help the country. There's no need to be so uptight."

"As you wish, Your Majesty," Ludwin said, backing down easily.

He did that knowing what would happen, I'll bet. He acted in a way that keeps people from taking us lightly, while still showing how tolerant the king is. He's an impressive actor. In that case, I'll have to live up to expectations and play the tolerant king.

I rose from the throne and turned to face them.

"Please, do not prostrate yourselves before me. It is I who am in the position of asking you for a favor. Do not stand on ceremony. Go ahead and be at ease."

The four of them rose quietly. I looked to Marx, indicating that he should continue.

Marx nodded, beginning to read from some sort of scroll. "We will now announce the gifts held by these individuals and carry out the awarding of prizes! Madam Aisha Udgard, dark elf from the God-Protected Forest, step forward!"

"Yes, sir!" This time, the elf-eared girl meekly obeyed.

She looked less than twenty years old, but I had heard dark elves remained youthful for a long time, so their appearance and age didn't match. She had brown skin and an attractive silver ponytail. Wearing chest armor and gauntlets, she was dressed like a warrior. Her slender legs peeked out through the slit in her waist cloth. They were moderately muscular and looked quite healthy.

Dark elves, I thought. *One of the minority races of Elfrieden, they are a race with a high level of combat ability. Instead of cities, they reside in the God-Protected Forest and are granted autonomy as protectors of the forest. They have a strong sense of racial unity and reject outsiders...huh.*

While acting like nothing was out of the ordinary, I manipulated the gloves I had left imbued with my consciousness in the other room to flip through the *Elfrieden Children's Encyclopedia* (since it was aimed at children, the entries were short, which made it useful when looking up information quickly) to read the article on dark elves.

The dark elves in this country weren't fallen elves that had lost the blessing of the gods, like you might see in a lot of fantasy settings. It seemed it was just that the pale-skinned blonde elves were called "light elves," and the brown-skinned, silver-haired elves were called "dark elves" to distinguish between the two.

"This one has shown herself to be remarkably gifted with martial ability. She was the winner of the Best in the Kingdom Martial Arts Tournament. That achievement shows she truly is fit to be called the greatest in this kingdom, and for this, we praise her!" Marx declared.

Huh, so she's the winner of that martial arts tournament. She must be tough, then. There was just one thing that concerned me. "I put out a call for capable people who will help the kingdom, but will you help me when the time comes? I've read that dark elves are loyal only to their own kind."

"It is no longer an era where we can survive just by protecting our forests. If this country falls, the forest will be threatened. Some feel that we dark elves need to change. I am one of them," Aisha said clearly.

"Well...that's a rather liberal statement for one from such a conservative race," I said.

"True. I am seen as a heretic. However, if we don't do something...King Souma?"

"Yes?"

"I do not need the prize money. Instead, I ask you to allow me to address you directly."

The hall was abuzz. Aisha was trying to make a direct appeal to the king. Even in Japan, there was a time when that would have been a capital crime. It seemed this country was no different.

Liscia and Ludwin's hands went to their swords, but I motioned for them to stop.

"I will allow it. Say what you will."

"Souma?! That's not—!"

"She was ready to risk a lot to say this to me. As king, I should hear her out."

"Thank you. I will speak, then." Aisha puffed out her chest with pride and spoke. "Recently, there have been many incursions into the God-Protected Forest by other races. They harvest mushrooms and other edible wild plants, hunting down the forest beasts. I understand that you have a food crisis; however, if you steal these things from us, we will be the ones who starve! We have had no choice but to take up arms against the intruders. Even now, there are clashes taking place throughout the forest. King Souma, please, crack down on the offenders!"

"I see..."

Basically, she wants me to forbid the people who are going without food from hunting or harvesting wild plants in the forest. When there's a food crisis, if you go to an area where distribution is limited, the crisis is even deeper there. If there just so happens to be a forest with plentiful resources nearby, I guess they might enter it even in the face of dark elf attacks.

"Sure, you've got it. Regarding the God-Protected Forest, there are already laws restricting entrance, so I can't issue a new ban, but I'll see to it that food aid reaches the people in the vicinity at once. If, even after that, there are still those trying to enter the God-Protected Forest, we will recognize them as poachers and prosecute them."

"Thank you. You have my gratitude."

With those words, in place of bowing, Aisha brought her hand to her chest and closed her eyes. I wasn't sure if that was a gesture of gratitude or just a pose showing relief at accomplishing her task.

"Still, Aisha, poaching is an unspeakable crime, but if we think about the future, would it not be wise to consider trade with those outside the forest? Aren't there things in the outside world that draw your interest?" I asked.

"Well, yes, but...we have no likely trade goods."

"Hmm...what about lumber? Don't you have some from periodic thinning?"

Living in a forest, they must have had more wood than they knew what to do with. In the outside world, on the other hand, demand for it was high. That ought to make a decent trade good, but...

"Periodic thinning...what might that be?" Aisha asked with a serious look on her face, and I couldn't help but be dumbstruck for a moment.

Huh? Don't tell me they don't do periodic forest thinning in this world?

"I'm referring to the periodic felling of a set number of trees to maintain the forest..."

As I said this, I glanced to Liscia, Marx and Ludwin, but all of them shook their heads. Apparently, this was the first they'd ever heard of it. It was the same with Aisha.

"To protect the forest...you cut down trees?"

"Of course. If you leave trees alone, they just keep getting bigger, and their leaves and branches spread out. If they block out the sunlight, young trees can't grow. Besides, if they're growing too densely, it impacts their lifespan, so you end up with nothing but old trees that are thin and weak, like bean sprouts. That sort of bean-sprout forest is easily destroyed by snow and wind. On top of that, if the sun doesn't reach the undergrowth, it all dries up. That causes the land to lose its ability to hold water, which can be a cause of landslides. This is all common knowledge...right?"

Looking around me, it was like seeing a collection of bobble-heads that could only shake their heads left and right.

Aisha suddenly prostrated herself before me. "King Souma... no, Your Majesty!"

"Wh-what?!"

"I humbly beg your forgiveness for my earlier rudeness!"

"Uh, I didn't even care, but...wait, is it okay for you to lower your head like that?"

"I do not mind! Because, from this very moment, I pledge to serve you loyally for the rest of my life!"

Whoa, whoa, hold on. What's going on here...?

"Use my life however you will! My body, my heart, my chastity, I offer to you! If you tell me to fight, I will fight! If you tell me to love you, I will love you! If you tell me to become your concubine or slave, I will do it! If you tell me to die, I will die!"

"Where did this crazy loyalty come from?! What happened in the last few minutes?!"

"However, before you order me to die, I ask you heed my final request!"

"Huh? You're ignoring me?! You're totally ignoring me?!"

"Please, as soon as possible, come to the God-Protected Forest!" Then she slammed her head firmly against the floor once more.

At this point, even Liscia was thoroughly taken aback.

That self-harming kowtow is practically a threat.

"Okay, let's hear your story," I said. "Basically, you want to bring me to the God-Protected Forest, right?"

"That is precisely it! And, at the God-Protected Forest, please teach us this 'periodic thinning!' In recent years, the God-Protected Forest has been facing exactly the issues you just spoke of, Sire! Where the trees are dense, they become thin and weak, young trees don't grow, the water is muddy, and when wind or heavy storms come through, they strip the land bare. With your words, I have at last learned the cause!"

"The God-Protected Forest has a history stretching back thousands of years, doesn't it? Nobody noticed this before?" I asked, only for Liscia and Aisha to nod ashamedly.

"The trees in the God-Protected Forest are long-lived to begin with," Aisha said. "That is why, up until now when they're reaching the end of their life cycle, nobody noticed."

"That's right," Liscia said. "This isn't just their problem. We don't do periodic thinning in Elfrieden's mountains either, so the situation may be the same everywhere."

"Well, anywhere they don't rely too heavily on the forest should be fine. When the old trees fall, new ones grow in anyway. Even if a natural disaster wipes out a bean-sprout forest, it will recover in ten years or so. Nature works in cycles like that, after all."

"Wouldn't that be devastating to the dark elves of the God-Protected Forest?" Liscia asked.

I'll bet it probably would. They live in the forest itself, after all. If the forest disappears, we'll have ourselves an instant set of refugees. I don't need any more refugees, so I'd better act quickly.

"I understand. Let's head to the God-Protected Forest at some point in the near future."

"Ohhhh! Thank you, Sire!" Aisha cried.

"However, when I come, you'll have to permit the entry of a certain number of people. It looks like forestry management is going to be a task for the entire country. I'll take this opportunity to hold some classes on how to establish the forest industry."

"As you wish, Sire," she said.

"Good. Ludwin."

"Sir."

"It sounds like she wants to serve me, so I'd like you to see what Aisha is capable of. We know her martial prowess as an individual, but whether she can become a general and lead troops remains an open question. If she has the potential, I will make her the general of an army. If not, I will hire her as my personal bodyguard."

"Yes, sir. I understand."

Much later, after testing her, Ludwin would tell me, "She does have potential as a general. However, her ability as an individual fighter is greater, and it would be a waste to use her as a general." She was the convenient Lu Bu type, apparently, the kind of fighter who could act as a general but could also be sent in alone to wreak havoc. From then on, I would keep Aisha at my side as a bodyguard.

That was the end of Aisha's turn, but things had gotten pretty intense with the very first person. I'd just been planning to hand out awards quickly then call out to anyone who looked useful.

Please tell me the other four don't all come with so much baggage.

"Next, Sir Hakuya Kwonmin, step forward," Marx said.

"Yes, sir." With his name having been called, the black-robed young man leisurely strolled forward.

He was a young man of around twenty wearing a distinctive outfit that looked like he had combined a pastor's cassock and a kannushi's traditional kimono and then dyed the resulting outfit black. His shoulder-length black hair looked unkempt. He was pale and slender, looking like more of an indoors-y type. He acted listless, but his sleepy eyes were fixed on me.

"This man, though his recommendation came from another, has demonstrated the gift of wisdom!" Marx announced. "He has memorized the laws of this country, and his knowledge and memory are believed to be without peer in this nation!"

That's like being able to recite the entirety of the Six Codes from memory, I guess. That would be amazing, yeah. If he's here by some-one else's recommendation, he's one of the ones signed up by a relative, huh. I wonder what it is. Something is tugging at the back of my mind here.

"Your gift is splendid," I said. "If you wish it, I will recom-mend you for a bureaucratic position in the Ministry of Law. How about it?"

"No, just the prize will be enough," Hakuya said immediately, shooting down my proposed recommendation. "I only came here because my uncle who looks after me said, 'At your age, you need to stop sitting around doing nothing but reading books and go do something useful for society,' and sent in the application without asking me, so I don't need excessive rewards."

"These books you mention, are they all law related?" I asked.

"No. I don't focus on any specific genre. Law, literature, tech-nical manuals, I'll read anything."

"I see."

I wonder why. There's something bothering me here.

"Hmm...in that case, how about you become the librarian for the archives in the palace?" I asked. "There are probably books in there that you won't find on the open market, and with your authority as librarian, you'll be able to read them."

"Oh, that does sound nice. If that's the case, please, let me do it." Finally, something I could recognize as a happy expression crossed Hakuya's face. He seemed satisfied.

Seize every opportunity, as they say. It was probably better for me to keep an interesting card like him in my hand than to let him go.

"Next, Madam Juna Doma, step forward."

"Yes, sir."

Trading places with Hakuya, the blue-haired pretty girl stepped up.

She looked like she was around the same age as me, nineteen, but the air she had about her made this woman feel more mature than her age. With her fluffy hair trailing behind her, she was the picture of beauty as she gracefully bowed her head. While her clothes weren't very revealing, the top half resembled a dirndl from Austria, while the bottom was transparent and showed her legs, like you might see in an Indian dancer's sari. Around her hips was wrapped a frilly piece of clothing.

Were it not for the piercing look I received from Liscia, I might have admired her beauty for a full hour.

"Yeah. I haven't forgotten my job, so stop glaring," I murmured.

"I don't know about that..." Liscia responded, looking away angrily.

Marx coughed and cleared his throat, saying, "Sire, this one has shown she is gifted with a rare beauty and singing ability. With those gifts, she took the crown at both the Elfrieden Pretty Girl Grand Prix with her beauty, and at Kingdom of Talent with her singing. Truly, she is the most beautiful songstress of this generation."

A double crown?! Now, that's impressive. "Sometimes the heavens *do* bestow two gifts, it seems," I said.

"You are too kind," Juna responded calmly and elegantly to my somewhat awestruck praise. "I have heard that the Doma family are descended from loreleis. Singing is in my blood."

Loreleis...they're sea monsters who use their beauty and their songs to lead sailors to their doom, right? Certainly, her beauty and those flowing blue tresses did make me think of loreleis. "I'd very much like to hear you sing."

"If you wish, I can."

"Sure. This scene is being broadcast around Elfrieden right now through this jewel. Could you sing a little song to cheer up our countrymen?"

"A song to cheer them up, is it?" Juna seemed troubled. "Most of the lorelei songs passed down in my family are sad love songs, you see..."

"Ohh, if there's some code or something holding you back from singing one, that's fine."

"No, I just don't know any. If I could hear one, I could learn it right away, though."

"Hmm...ah, how about this, then?"

I pulled out my smartphone. It was one of the few things I had on me when I'd been summoned to this world. I opened my music folder, picked a song that jumped out at me, then walked up to Juna and put the earbuds in for her.

"What might this be?"

"Something like a machine that plays music, I guess? Anyway, I'm playing it now."

Juna's eyes widened.

The moment I pressed the button, Juna's body shuddered. She seemed bewildered at first, but she was getting used to it, as her body gradually got into the rhythm. Then, five minutes later, she pulled out the earbuds.

"I have it memorized."

"Already? You really can memorize it the first time you hear it?"

"Yes. Now, let me sing it for you."

I returned to my seat and she began to sing.

The song was Masashi Sada's "Ganbaranba." This cheerful song, which had even had a *Minna no Uta* short made for it, was distinctive for using rap in Nagasaki dialect mixed with the Kyushu children's song "Denderaryuba." Grandpa was a fan, so I had listened to it with him together a lot.

Still, I was impressed with this lorelei. She was even managing to sing the rap parts in Nagasaki dialect. These were completely incomprehensible to people from the Kanto region, but she sung them flawlessly.

By the way, Liscia told me later that she couldn't understand the lyrics. I could understand the language people in this country speak, and they could understand my Japanese, but it seemed that was part of my power as a hero. I could even write in the world's language. What I tried to write in my head got translated into the language here, so even though I couldn't read it afterward, I could write it.

So, the Japanese (in Nagasaki dialect) that came out of Juna's mouth was in an unknown language for the people of this country. Still, even without knowing the words, if a song is good, you can still get into it. Everyone listened to that catchy tune and enjoyed it.

A few minutes later, amidst roaring applause, Juna finished her song and bowed.

"That was a fun song. Thank you."

"No, I should thank you," I said. "Your singing was wonderful."

"If possible, I hope you will teach me more of the songs of your country, Your Majesty."

"I'd very much like to have you sing them. Oh, I know! Hopefully we can increase the number of jewels, but even if that's not possible, we could eventually convert the Jewel Voice Room into a recording studio so that the people can hear your songs all the time."

"My! That would be like a dream come true, Sire." Juna wore a smile of heartfelt bliss. It was a marvelous smile.

"I'll be counting on you when the time comes," I said. "You did a great job today."

Juna stepped back, and now it was the fox-eared little girl's turn.

"Next, Madam Tomoe Inui of the mystic wolf race, step forward."

"Y-yesh!"

Her voice breaking, the young girl with animal ears who looked to be around ten stepped forward with her right arm moving at the same time as her right leg.

The mystic wolf race... I thought. *I guess those aren't fox ears. They're wolf ears.*

She was adorable with her suntanned skin and cute little round eyes. The clothes she wore were just a little shabby, though. They were torn in places and, perhaps because she was tense, the fluffy tail that stuck out from her rump was standing up straight.

Yup, I want to stroke it.

"Young though she may be, this one has the exceptionally rare gift of being able to talk to birds and beasts. When we brought her to the stables, she was able to correctly tell us everything from the horses' current state of health to their history. According to her, the horses told her these things. Truly, it is a godly ability."

The gift of talking to animals, huh? Looks like we have an astonishing little beastwoman on our hands here.

As I thought about it, next to me Liscia quietly whispered, "The country of the mystic wolves is far to the north. There shouldn't be any in this country."

"A refugee, huh?" I murmured. *Ah, that would explain the beat-up clothes then, wouldn't it?*

With the expansion of the Demon Lord's Domain, several countries and villages had been destroyed. Those who had lost their lands had fled south, becoming refugees in other nations, and they were starting to put pressure on the economy. Different nations dealt with them in different ways. Some proactively took them in, while others moved to expel them. That said, even when it came to the countries taking them in, most either forced them into hard labor such as mining or sent them out as additional manpower to fight against the demons, so both types of countries were hell for the refugees.

Even in my kingdom, refugee camps had sprung up outside the capital Parnam. At the moment, the decision on what to do with them was still "on hold." If we helped the refugees when we didn't even have enough food to feed our own people, riots might well break out. If we expelled them or forced them into hard labor, we would have to deal with the refugees' resentment. If they went into hiding and turned terrorist on us, that would be terrible. As things stood, they were causing a decline in public safety, but we had no choice but to maintain the status quo.

To offer a helping hand to others, we need to be in a good place to help ourselves first, I thought.

"I said if they had a gift, I would put it to use, and I don't intend to twist those words," I said out loud. "If she has a gift, it doesn't matter if she's a foreigner or a refugee. We're in no position to be particular about such things, after all."

"You're right."

When I said that, the mystic wolf girl who had just been introduced hesitantly opened her mouth to speak. "Uh...um...King Souma..."

"Hm? What is it?"

"Um...well...uh, I also...have something I'd like to say..."

Because she was extremely tense, she spoke as if forcing the words out. It was hard to make out what she was saying.

"Did you have something you wanted to say? I don't mind. Please go ahead."

"Yesh...um...actually..."

"Hm? What? You need to speak up or I won't be able to hear you..."

"Um...I..." Tomoe had tears in her eyes. She was still young enough to be called a little girl, so it was painful to see her with a face like that.

"I understand. I'll come over to you, so don't cry anymore," I said.

"Awoo..."

I walked over to the girl's side and crouched down next to her, putting my ear next to her mouth. As the one in charge of guarding me, Ludwin had a disapproving look on his face, but I ignored him.

"Now I should be able to hear you," I said. "Say whatever you like."

"Yep. The truth is..."

What she whispered to me next made me doubt my ears. I stood up and stared at Tomoe's face.

"You're certain of this?"

"Y-yep."

"Have you told this to anyone else?"

"N-No...nobody but my mom..."

"I see." I sighed. It was half relief and half worry when I thought about what was to come. This was more than just some rare gift. This girl had the potential to be a "bombshell" to this world.

Calm down. Breathe. Don't let anyone here notice how agitated you are.

"Whew...I'm a little exhausted. I'd like to take a little break here."

"Souma?"

When I said that, Liscia looked at me dubiously. The others had about the same reaction, but I ignored them, boldly raising my voice.

"I would now like to take a thirty-minute break. The presentation of awards to the remaining two, this girl included, will take place after that. Madam Juna."

"What is it, Sire?" When I called her name, the lorelei songstress stepped forward.

"Right now, our countrymen are watching us over the Jewel Voice Broadcast. It would pain me to make the people just wait during our break. So, could I ask you to keep them entertained with your singing for half an hour or so?"

"Of course, Sire. Our songs are the pride of my family. I will sing my heart out for them." With those words, Juna gave an elegant bow.

Our eyes met for just a moment. It felt as if she were checking with me: *There's a reason for this, isn't there?* Even so, she chose not to ask, doing as I had requested.

Even without her beauty and singing, I would want a considerate person like her among my subordinates.

While Juna was buying time for me, I gathered those I could trust in the governmental affairs office. This included myself, Liscia, Marx, Ludwin, and Tomoe. That was all. As for Aisha, who didn't want to be separated from me now that she had sworn her loyalty, I had her stand outside the door to ensure no one was listening in.

"Is all of this caution really necessary?" Liscia asked in bewilderment, to which I responded with a nod.

"We are in a very bad situation. Did anyone hear what Tomoe said earlier?" I checked with the other three, but all of them shook their heads.

"I didn't hear. Her voice was so quiet."

"Neither did I."

"Me either."

"Is there any risk people heard her over the Jewel Voice Broadcast?"

"That should probably be fine," Liscia said. "It's not that sensitive."

As soon as I heard that, I felt as if a great weight had been lifted from my shoulders.

"Is it that bad?" she asked.

"Yes. It was literally a bombshell statement."

Everyone's focus narrowed on Tomoe, causing her to shrink into herself even more. It seemed like it would be hard to get her to talk, so I answered on her behalf.

"She can converse with animals. You all heard that, right?"

"Yes. It's an incredible gift, isn't it?"

"She used that power to talk to a demon, apparently."

The moment I said that, the room went cold. Everyone was speechless, just mouthing voicelessly like a bunch of goldfish. Before I go into detail about it, there are some things you need to know first.

What people in this world thought of when they talked

about demons and monsters was slightly different from what people in my world thought. In the world I came from, monsters were not "people" or "plants and animals." They were seen as aberrations.

However, in this world, the words "person" and "animal" were defined very broadly.

To be more specific, humans, elves, beastmen, and dragonewts were all "people" and fell under the category of "mankind."

In the categories of "plants and animals," even at four meters tall, a red grizzly was still a mammal. Even if it looked like a dinosaur, a monitor lizard was still a reptile. Even if it was as big as a person, a giant ant was still an insect. Even if it ate people, a man-eater was a plant. Furthermore, gelins—the slime creatures that did things like merge together, split apart, melt, and more—also fell under the "plants and animals" category, for some reason.

By the way, dragons and the like were called "god-beasts," and they were categorized separately.

The reason none of these creatures were called monsters was because they were native to this world. Since they were part of the ecology of this world all along, each of them had their own habitats away from where humans lived. As a matter of fact, the eight-legged horses in this country would all be Sleipnir by the standards of the world I came from, and the livestock such as cows and chickens all looked like they had been designed to look more monstrous.

However, if you asked what monsters were, the term referred to things like chimeras, which were a mishmash of different animals fused together, zombies, skeletons and other undead types, as well as goblins, orcs, and ogres, which looked almost like people, but no one would mistake them for sentient beings.

Ever since the Demon World had appeared, there had been a large outbreak of these monsters in the north, but even before the Demon World's appearance, they inhabited areas known as dungeons that were all around the continent.

Dungeons were underground spaces with a mysterious ecology. I was used to seeing them in games, but they actually existed in this world. Incidentally, I heard that in this world there were people called "adventurers" who made their living by exploring these sorts of dungeons, protecting merchants, eliminating dangerous beasts that tore up the fields, and slaying monsters that came out of the dungeons.

Before the Demon World appeared, monsters had been thought to lack intelligence. As a matter of fact, the monsters in dungeons, even the almost humanoid ones like goblins, only possessed intelligence on the level of animals.

However, among the monsters in the Demon Lord's Domain, there were those that behaved as if they were intelligent.

These monsters acted in groups, used weapons and magic, and could put together strategies. They acted almost like "people" did. When mankind had failed in its invasion of the Demon Lord's Domain, their lack of fuller knowledge about the existence of these monsters was the biggest factor in their defeat. Mankind had chosen to call these intelligent monsters "demons" to distinguish them from more animalistic monsters.

Now, let's get back to the story. Basically, Tomoe said she had spoken with one of these demons.

Apparently, up until now, no one had ever succeeded in talking to a demon. With the sudden appearance of an army that spoke a foreign language, and with hostilities ongoing no less, understanding one another just wasn't going to happen.

Liscia drew in closer to Tomoe.

"Just what did you talk to, and what did you talk about?!"

"W-with Mr. Kobold. They're different from us...they're short, and their whole faces, not just their ears, are doglike...on the day before our village was attacked, he said, 'I can't bear to see those with the same scent as me attacked. Hurry and flee.' It was a miracle I could understand what Mr. Kobold said, but...thanks to him, we were able to avoid trouble..."

"So, to sum it up...demons have a clear will of their own, is that it?" Ludwin said, as if groaning.

The people of this world only thought of demons as slightly smarter monsters. Like locusts swarming over the land, or barbarians who delighted in slaughter. From what I had heard, that wasn't a mistaken impression when it came to monsters. However...for demons, perhaps another viewpoint was going to be necessary.

If demons had their own will, like Tomoe was suggesting, mankind might have been fighting a war against the demon race without realizing it. A war with no channels of diplomacy, at that. With their families being killed, their houses razed, and their countries stolen, mankind held great resentment towards

the monsters and demons. If this was a war, it was possible the demons resented mankind in the same way.

"If this knowledge spread to all of the other countries..." I began.

"...there would be chaos," Liscia finished.

Liscia and I both slumped our shoulders.

I didn't think dialogue would be possible with each and every demon or monster from the Demon Lord's Domain. Those we could talk to, like the kobold who had let the mystic wolves escape, might only be a small portion of them. However, if people were to find out that even some of the demons are like that, the demon race would stop being the common enemy of all mankind.

Right now, even if it was only on the surface, all the other countries were united against the Demon Lord's Domain. If this information were to spread, what would happen to that? If it meant they tried to sue for peace with the demons, that would be great, but it would be completely unsurprising if some of them put their own country's interests first, siding with the demons to invade other countries. If that were to happen, mankind would fall to pieces.

"Do you think the Empire knows?" I asked.

"I'm not sure," Liscia said. "It was only with Tomoe's unique gift that someone was finally able to communicate with them. Even if they do realize it, they'd have no way to verify it."

"So, basically, our country has a monopoly on this information for the time being. Good grief..." This was one hell of a thing to have fall in my lap.

She's like a bomb. I can use her as a trump card, but if I mishandle her, it could all blow up in my face.

"I-I'm sorry..." Tomoe was wincing, so Liscia poked me.

"Oh, no, we aren't blaming you," I said quickly. "Actually, I'm glad you came to this country. It chills me when I think what might have happened if you had gone to another country instead."

"Still, are you going to conceal this information?" Ludwin asked. "If people find out we hid such vital information, isn't it possible we would be condemned as an enemy of all mankind?"

"You have a point." I wanted to clutch my head when Ludwin pointed that out. "Doing a bad job of hiding it and then having people think we're harboring ambitions as a result isn't a great plan. Besides, if this is a war, the current situation where both sides are fighting a war of extermination is not good. To make sure the war doesn't continue until one side is wiped out, we need to leak the information out little by little."

I need to resolve myself. I continued to speak, looking at those around me. "We'll leak something that sounds like nothing more than a hypothesis to the other countries. Something like 'Maybe there are those among the demons we could talk with.' If we do that, they should be a little more cautious. At the very least, they should try to discover if there's any truth to the rumors."

"As part of that process, isn't it possible they will find out the same information we have? Wouldn't that eliminate the value of concealing it?"

"You're wrong, Marx. Our trump card is Tomoe herself."

"M-me?!" she squeaked.

I nodded firmly to Tomoe, whose eyes darted about in bewilderment. "Even if the demons do have wills of their own, there needs to be some means of communication to negotiate with them. For instance, while the other countries are still searching for a way to negotiate with the demons, we can talk to them using Tomoe as a mediator. That is a huge advantage."

I didn't know how much our kingdom would be able to negotiate on its own. However, by having our own independent line of communication, we could prevent a situation where another country monopolized the right to negotiate and refused us any opportunity for dialogue. In exchange, we would be taking a burden on ourselves, but that was far preferable to leaving our kingdom's fate in the hands of another country.

"So, Tomoe, our country needs to do everything it can to protect you," I said.

"P-protect me...?!"

"Yes. It's no exaggeration to say that, right now, you're far more important than some guy like me. Honestly, if this information leaks out, the moment you get abducted, this country is ruined."

"No way...you're making that up...right?" Tomoe looked around restlessly, but no one denied it.

It was no exaggeration to say Tomoe held this country's fate in her hands. While I would never do it myself, another country might have pretended they had never heard any of this and "disposed" of her. That was just how important Tomoe's existence was.

"So, to keep you under the highest level of guard we can, I

want you to live here in the palace. If it comes down to it, we might not be able to protect you in the refugee camp."

"Awoo..." Tomoe moaned.

"Hold on a moment," Marx raised his hand. "If we have someone not of royal blood living at the palace, might that not draw unwanted scrutiny?"

"Hmm. Well, tell me how we can welcome her as royalty, then."

"You say that like it's so easy... there are a number of ways a common person can become royalty. One would be for you to adopt her, Sire. However, as the wedding has not been held yet, this is not possible. Your wedding ceremony will take more than a year to prepare, after all."

"You heard him, Liscia," I said.

"Hey, don't throw this over to me." Liscia quickly looked away.

Living with Liscia as my wife and Tomoe, who's already around ten, as my daughter, huh... yeah, I just can't imagine it.

"Anything else?" I asked.

"You could take her as a secondary wife, Sire."

"That's...all kinds of messed up."

She's young enough to be in elementary school, pal. It brings to mind that image of Blackbeard saying, "You damn lolicon."

Marx cleared his throat. "She is just barely within the acceptable age range for a political marriage, I believe."

"Souma...ten years old is a little young..."

"Why are you blaming *me*, here?!"

Now Liscia's looking at me coldly. I'm not into that stuff, okay?!

"Hey, wait, the former royal couple can just adopt her."

"Hmm. I believe that would be acceptable." Marx snickered.

That bastard. He said all that stuff when he already knew that was possible!

"That sounds good! I've always wanted a little sister!" Liscia said.

"Whu-whuh!" Tomoe cried in confusion.

Liscia hugged Tomoe tight, causing her to sputter and panic. As for Liscia herself, she had a more relaxed look than I had ever seen on her face.

Come to think of it, since Liscia's my fiancée, Tomoe's going to be my sister-in-law. A wolf-eared loli sister-in-law...that's too many character attributes.

"But, but...I have a family. My mom and little brother are waiting for me in the camp," Tomoe said, breaking free from her prospective big sister's excessively touchy-feely embrace.

"Ohh, the adoption is only for appearances' sake, so you don't have to worry about that. If you become my sister-in-law, your mother and brother will be family, too, so I don't mind if they live at the palace as well. We'll provide some funds for them to live on, and if they want to work, we'll give them something to do in the palace."

"Well...in that case...okay," Tomoe accepted somewhat timidly.

Good. That doesn't quite wrap everything up nicely, but I think I've done what I can for the moment. I've somehow gained a sister-in-law in the process, but, hey, she's cute, so it's all good.

"Now then, let's get back to the hall," I said. "We're keeping Madam Juna waiting."

It's been almost thirty minutes, after all. She probably can't draw things out much longer.

"For now, we'll only give Tomoe the prize money as her reward. If the former royal couple were to suddenly announce they were adopting her, that would be like telling everyone that something's up. We'll let some time pass and then announce it another day. I'd like you all to act with that in mind, got it?"

"Yes, sir!" everyone replied.

◇ ◇ ◇

Thirty minutes after King Souma called for a break, the award ceremony resumed. Right now, the mystic wolf girl was being praised. As that scene unfolded, I, Hakuya Kwonmin, stood watching with the other prize winners.

"Your gift is remarkable," he told the wolf girl. "I hope you will put it to use for our country."

"Y-yesh! I undershtand!"

She's stuttering all over the place, I thought. *How adorable.*

What could that adorable little girl have said to alarm the king so badly that he had called for a break? What's more, that little girl was the only one who had been called aside during the break. It was clear that it had been something important, but there was no way for me to know what it was now.

From the time I came here, I had been observing the king in question. He looked ordinary. I had heard he'd been summoned as a hero, but he looked exactly like any of the common townsfolk. He didn't wear a crown, carried no scepter, wore no cape, and though their design was unusual, when he stood there in those casual clothes, he didn't look like a king even while standing in front of the throne.

If I looked for it, occasionally his eyes took on a statesman-like appearance. He was a very hard man to pin down. From the way he had acted so far, you might say he was a passable king, I suppose.

With the dark elf warrior's direct appeal, he had shown magnanimity and, even without intending to, he'd found a solution to her problem. From what had happened with the mystic wolf girl, it seemed he could ad-lib where necessary, too. It had been a little awkward, but, well, I'd give it a passing grade.

However, his real trial would start here.

The fat man beside me was sweating profusely, though I couldn't tell if it was cold sweat or greasy sweat. I turned to look at him. It was his turn to receive his award next.

On the way here, he had told me himself what his gift was. And, as far as I was concerned, his was "the gift this country needs most right now."

When he sees him, what will that young king's judgment be?

Will he look down on the man's appearance (a big round belly and a pudgy face), which no one would call attractive, even as empty flattery?

Will he make a laughingstock of him in front of the entire country? Even if he doesn't go that far, will he miss the importance of the man's gift?

If he does any of those things, I...

"Next, Poncho Panacotta of Potte Village, step forward!"

"Y-yes, I'll do that, yes!"

When Prime Minister Marx called his name, the fat man named Poncho walked forward with heavy steps, his round belly wobbling. The comical way he walked drew laughs from all around. Even Princess Liscia struggled to suppress a smile.

When I looked to see the king's reaction, his face was serious. Not smiling, not displeased, just looking at Sir Poncho with a serious expression.

"This one's gift, as you may have guessed from the look of him, is for eating," Marx said. "During the application process, a number of people claimed to have the 'gift of being a big eater,' but none could defeat him. Furthermore, his stance towards his pursuit of food is unusual. He has traveled the world, eating the famous and bizarre dishes of each region. In his own words, 'If it was edible, I ate it.' However, it seems he has spent his entire fortune on traveling and eating, so he is not as well off as he might appear...ahem. Regardless, it can be said that he has a gift that is unique in our country, so..."

"I've been waiting for you!" The king was moving before Marx could even finish reading the explanation. When he reached Poncho, he took his hand with both hands, not hiding his elation in the slightest. "I'm so glad you responded to my call! You're the sort of person I've been waiting for!"

"Huh...uh...what?" Sir Poncho's eyes darted around. His brain couldn't keep up with the situation.

Eventually, his mind caught up, and his face stiffened.

"M-me, Your Majesty?"

"Exactly! You're the one this country has been waiting for! More than any of these other gifted people, I'm glad that you came! I always thought that if someone like you was among the civil officials, it would be worth recommending they apply!"

"D-do you feel that strongly about me?"

"Yeah. Your knowledge from wandering around eating famous and bizarre foods will be the key to saving this country!"

When the king said that, Sir Poncho cried a flood of tears. "I-I...everyone's always called me a fatty...an idiot wasting his money on food...as for me, I only went around eating because I wanted to eat, so I thought they were right...can my gluttony be of service to this country?"

The king patted the crying Sir Poncho on the shoulder. "Let them say what they want about you. No matter how trivial something is, if you master it, it's a gift. Be proud! The appetite you didn't hesitate to spend your fortune on will save this country! Please, share your wisdom with me!"

Hearing his king's earnest request, Poncho wiped away his tears with his sleeve. "Y-yes! If my knowledge can be of help, please use it, yes!" he responded cheerfully.

When I looked around, most of the audience were standing there, mouths agape, unable to digest the situation. During that, King Souma returned to the throne, then turned to Marx and said, "In this country, there is a tradition of the king rewarding meritorious servants, or those for whom he has high hopes, with a new name, isn't there?"

"...Ah, yes. That is correct, Sire."

"In that case, Poncho, I bestow upon you the name Ishizuka. In my homeland, this was the name of an 'insatiable seeker and evangelist of food.' Work hard, so as not to bring shame upon that name."

"Y-yes, sir! Thank you, yes!"

This was the explosive moment in which Poncho Ishizuka Panacotta was born. The first person King Souma had personally welcomed as one of his retainers was the rotund man with the vigorous appetite, Sir Poncho.

I wanted to cry out for joy. Splendid! This was a king who had his priorities straight!

Whether he would hire Poncho or not had been a touchstone for this king. I had thought that if he failed to recognize the man's value but hired him on the potential he might someday be of use, that would be a pass. If he had chosen not to hire him solely based on his appearance, that would be a failure. I never dared to imagine he would welcome him so enthusiastically. This was a happy miscalculation for me.

This man may well save this country.

I felt something welling up from within me.

It looks like I won't be able to just watch any longer.

"King Souma, a word with you, if I may," I said.

◇　◇　◇

"King Souma, a word with you, if I may."

With the awards all handed out, just as I was about to declare an end to the ceremony, the young man in black robes—Hakuya Kwonmin—stepped forward and took a knee. Now his sleepy eyes were wide open. Just by doing that, he mysteriously had an entirely different air about him now.

Feeling something like a slight premonition, I turned to Hakuya and asked, "Do you have something to say?"

"Indeed. Though I stand here on the recommendation of another, it is now my wish to recommend myself."

A self-recommendation. Does he want to sell me on his merits himself, then?

"Hmm...I've already promised you the position of librarian to the palace archives. If you want to make a self-recommendation, does that mean you're dissatisfied with the post? What is it you seek?"

"Should it be at all possible, I wish to place myself in your service, Your Majesty."

"But not as a librarian?"

"Correct. With my wisdom, I seek to support your supremacy."

"M-my supremacy?"

Supremacy is a bold thing to claim, I thought. *If he means to support that with his wisdom, what does he plan to become? A general handling military and foreign affairs, or a prime minister handling internal affairs...?*

I looked straight at Hakuya. "Amusing, but do you have a gift great enough to accomplish that?"

"I humbly submit that I do."

"You can do more than recite the law from memory, then?"

"With all due respect, I believe I have told you as much. 'Law, literature, technical manuals, I'll read anything,' I said. I have information on every field of study stored inside my head."

"I see..." Now I knew what had been bothering me before. Though he could recite the law from memory, he had said he read all sorts of books. That meant his knowledge wasn't limited to just law. For him, the laws he'd memorized were just one small fragment of the diverse knowledge he possessed. "Why didn't you say so earlier?"

"I sought to judge whether you were a ruler worthy of my service."

"Then does this mean I'm worthy?"

"You receive a passing mark, I suppose."

What insolence, I thought. *Still...he's amusing. Is he boasting, or does he have the skill to back it up...? Either way, there's no way to know just yet, I guess.*

"I'll leave you to Marx!" I said. "Judge this one's gift and give him a position suited to it."

"Very well, Sire."

"Thank you very much."

Marx and Hakuya both bowed.

A few days later, Marx would rush into the governmental affairs office, crying, "Sire, would you ask me to teach a wyvern to fly?!" It was an idiomatic expression from this world for trying to teach someone who knows more than you.

At this time, I had no way of knowing that this had been my

first meeting with the man who would come to be known as the Black-robed Prime Minister.

◇　◇　◇

In history, there are some scenes which are easily dramatized by later generations. There are two conditions for this:

First, it must be the turning point of an era.

Second, it must have a certain flair when dramatized.

In Elfrieden history, the scene most dramatized in later years was "King Souma's Gathering of Personnel." It is said that there are three main characters in this scene.

Seen from Souma's perspective, this was one of his great accomplishments. From the perspective of the man who would come to be called the Black-robed Prime Minister, Hakuya Kwonmin, it was to become the turning point of an era. From the perspective of a certain other person, it was the turning point in the Cinderella story of their life.

However, there are different theories on who that third person was.

Some say it was the Warrior of the Eastern Wind, Aisha Udgard, who, despite being a dark elf who lived in the forest, swore her loyalty to the king, and from that point on was always at his side serving him.

Some say it was the Prima Lorelei, Juna Doma, who was recognized by the king, learned the songs of his country, gave birth to the concept of a lorelei, which was the word that came to mean an idol singer in Elfrieden, and was loved by king and people alike.

Some say it was the Wise Wolf Princess, Tomoe Inui, who, despite being a refugee, was instantly adored by King Souma and Queen Liscia, and taken in as the queen's adopted sister.

However, the one most featured in dramatizations was Poncho Ishizuka Panacotta.

Mocked by all around him for his weight, this unspectacular glutton of a man was, through "The King's Gathering of Personnel," able to turn his life around. For the people exhausted with their daily lives, this true story moved them and gave them energy, and so it came to be dramatized many times.

It seems odd to call the tale of a rotund man a Cinderella story. Yet, despite being a little scatterbrained, he was hard not to like. He was loved by all, and so they said it suited him perfectly.

In addition, because the King's emotional welcoming of Poncho was broadcast throughout the kingdom, it had the unexpected side effect of many gifted people gathering in Elfrieden, thinking, "If even a guy like that can become important, so can I..." From this event, in later years, a new proverb meaning "start with small things" was created.

"Start from Ishizuka."

HOW A REALIST HERO REBUILT THE KINGDOM

CHAPTER 3
Let's Create a Broadcast Program

AROUND THE TIME the commotion from Souma's personnel gathering had settled, a certain ghost story began to spread in the castle town of the capital Parnam.

According to the tales, there was a mannequin that roamed the streets at night. It was the type of doll you saw in clothing shops—faceless, with arm and leg joints. Carrying swords in both hands, it stalked the streets night by night, hunting animals and monsters.

One adventurer said this:

"A while back, I took a quest from the guild to escort a peddler and was walking around the streets at night, y'see, when we had the bad luck to get surrounded by some subspecies of gelin (those gel things). They're weak individually, but this time there were a lot of them, and the battle was going badly. Then a mannequin carrying swords in both hands tottered along from the direction of the palace and attacked the gelins. It was such a creepy sight that we bolted right away, but...I wonder what was up with that thing."

Another adventurer said this:

"It was a week ago. I took a mission from the guild that said, 'A group of hobgoblins has crossed the border to the north and is traveling southwards. We want you to intercept them.' We were waiting in a valley along their route to intercept them, but wait as we might, they never appeared. Something seemed strange, so we went scouting for them, and what we found was a mannequin standing in the middle of a pile of brutally killed hobgoblin bodies. Thinking it was some new type of monster, me and my warrior buddy attacked it, but it parried us with two swords it carried. When our mage tried hitting it with fire, it ran off at an incredible speed. That thing...it's probably a new autonomous weapon created by the demon king, don't you think?"

There were many sightings, and though many said it was a ghost story, it was almost certain that it existed. However, when the adventurers' guild recognized its existence and quests to capture or destroy it were issued, all sightings stopped.

After that, some wondered if it hadn't been a prank by someone.

◇ ◇ ◇

"...So, well, there are rumors like that going around in the castle town, you know?" Liscia told me.

"Oh, yeah, are there now?" I asked.

As I lay back on the sofa, my hand with the needle not stopping as I responded to her, Liscia, who was sitting on the bed, took on a slightly upset tone.

"What? Don't stories like this interest you?"

"No, it's not like that, but..."

"Souma, you're the king, so shouldn't stories that are causing unrest in the castle town be important to you?" she said.

"You don't need to worry about it. That mannequin won't be showing up again."

"Do you know something about it?"

"Yeah, sorta..."

I packed the cotton while I gave vague answers. Now, I just had to sew the back closed and it would be done.

"And, hold on, what are you doing there, Souma?"

"What? Exactly what it looks like. Sewing."

"No, I'm asking why you're coming to my room to sew!"

"Well, where else would I go? My room's still the governmental affairs office, after all."

Recently, the amount of work to be done had settled down a bit, so while my Living Poltergeist pens were working, my main body could rest like this. Though, that said, the governmental affairs office where my bed was always had a lot of officials coming in and out of it, so it was a bit hard to take it easy there.

"Besides, you know how Aisha's been lately..." I added.

"I can guess," she said.

Recently, Aisha had become so clingy that she would never leave my side.

When a dark elf pledges their loyalty to someone, they pride themselves on staying by that person's side and protecting them until the day they themselves die, apparently. That was why Aisha had appointed herself as my bodyguard, and whether it was work time, meal time, or sleep time, she tried to follow me everywhere I went, even into the bath and toilet. I thought it was problematic to have someone who hadn't even officially been hired yet so close to the king, but she was beautiful, highly loyal, and her skills were well known, so Ludwin and the royal guards turned a blind eye to her.

As for Hakuya, who had taken over the post of prime minister from Marx, he'd said, "Is it not lovely to be surrounded by such beauties? The princess, Madam Aisha, Madam Juna...it matters not to me which you choose, but please hurry up and give us a child. It will bring stability to the royal house."

That's a hell of a thing to say so easily. Good grief.

While I was thinking about that, Liscia came over and poked me in the back.

"I bet you don't actually mind the attention, do you?"

"Give me a break. Just when I was finally able to get some rest... wait, huh? Come to think of it, where's Tomoe?"

"Tomoe is over in Mother and Father's room. Mother's taken a liking to her."

Just a few days ago, Tomoe had come to the castle to live as Liscia's adopted sister. Of course, as we had promised, her family had come with her, too.

Incidentally, Tomoe's mother worked at the palace day-care facility, which we had set up as an experiment to help encourage the advancement of women in society. She stayed with the wet nurses, caring for other people's children at the same time as her own. This day-care facility was a hit with the young maids, who said, "Now I can get married without worrying."

With maternity leave being nonexistent at present, women were often dismissed the moment they got pregnant. That was why, unless they became a king's mistress, most of the maids spent their entire lives single.

But I digress. Basically, it meant Tomoe had two mothers in the palace. She had seemed a little bewildered at first, but now both of them adored her.

Liscia stood up and, resting her hands on the back of the sofa, she peeked over my shoulder. "Still, when you have time off, you sew...? Is that a doll?"

"Oh, this? It's Little Musashibo."

I finished sewing up the doll's back, presenting it to Liscia.

"Little Musashibo?"

"Yeah. He's from my world...something like a rare and exotic beast, I guess?"

Little Musashibo was a cute super-deformed mascot based on Musashibo Benkei from the city I lived in. He had a white silk face, a Buddhist priest's stole and prayer beads, and big bushy eyebrows that looked imposing but with adorable acorn eyes underneath. People liked that gap, so he was well received.

By the way, the city where I had lived had absolutely no connection to Musashibo Benkei. So why Benkei then, you might wonder? Well, because long ago Saitama Prefecture was known as Musashi Province. That was the only reason.

Now, you might ask, "Then, wouldn't Musashi Miyamoto

or Musashimaru have worked just as well?" or, "If it's because of Musashi Province, doesn't that cover all of Saitama?" but to do so would be boorish.

You don't think, you feel. That's just how mascot characters are.

"Urkh...it makes me mad how surprisingly cute it is," Liscia said, looking at the Little Musashibo doll. "Still, why would you make something like this?"

"Well, actually...turns out my Living Poltergeists works really well with dolls."

With those words, I focused, and Little Musashibo began to move before our eyes. He used his short little arms and legs to break dance. That he was good at it only made it more surreal.

Liscia stared, dumbstruck. "What is this...?"

"When I use it on a pen, all I can do is make it float around, but with a doll, I can move it around almost as if I were inside it. What's more, with dolls, the limits on distance go away."

Up until now, I had only been able to manipulate objects up to 100 meters away, but with dolls, I was able to send them not just into the castle town but beyond the walls.

"That's certainly impressive, but...what are you going to do, become a street performer?" Liscia looked exasperatedly at Little Musashibo.

"Ha ha, now there's an idea. Maybe I'll quit being king and make a living on the road."

"Don't be silly. I won't let you abandon the job halfway."

"I know that. Anyway, here's the important bit."

I gave Little Musashibo two short swords. When I did, despite being made of felt and stuffed with cotton, Little Musashibo managed to hold two swords that would have felt heavy in the hands of a grown man. Little Musashibo posed like Musashi Miyamoto with his two swords.

Liscia's eyes went wide. "No way...it's a doll, right?"

"It seems that when a doll holds something, it's counted as an optional item for the doll. What's more, it can freely use any items I equip it with. As a test, I gave another doll some weapons and tried sending it to fight monsters. It managed to fight just fine."

"A doll fighting monsters. Wait...the mannequin from the rumors!"

"Yeah. I used a doll I happened to find around the palace to experiment."

I had never imagined there would be rumors about it, though. I had tried to do my tests at night when there wouldn't be people around to see, but maybe that had just made it feel even more like something out of a ghost story.

"Thanks to that, I found out they can hold their own against monsters. On top of that, the more experience they gain, the better the dolls get at moving."

As I said that, Little Musashibo spread the arms he was still holding the short swords with wide, spinning in circles fast enough that you almost expected a "whoosh" sound effect to pop up. He looked like a big spinning top, but he was actually like a revolving saw turned sideways, so he was more dangerous than he looked.

"Is the training undergone by the dolls reflected on your main body?" Liscia asked.

"If it were, that would make it one ridiculous ability. Sadly, no; even if the doll learns to use a technique, I can't reproduce it myself. Maybe it's because I don't have the muscle strength for it? My body's still weak."

"Hmm...why not work out?"

"I think it's a more effective use of my time to improve my ability to control the dolls than to try to get stronger myself. No matter how much I work out, I'm not going to get tough enough that it's better than keeping three strong dolls around me."

"That's not how a hero fights." Liscia said, exasperated.

Sadly, I had to agree with that assessment.

In fantasy works from my old world, my job class would have been Doll Master or Puppeteer, probably. Those sorts of jobs tended to be mid-range support types. That's a long way away from the mid- to close-range attacker type impression most people have of a hero.

"When I watch you, I can feel my image of what a hero is falling to pieces..." Liscia said.

"Ha ha ha..." I chuckled. "Don't worry. I feel the same."

In roughly a month since I was summoned, all I had done was domestic politics. Since all I planned to do for the next few months was domestic politics as well, could I really call myself a hero? No, I could not. (Rhetorical question.)

Suddenly, a knock came at the door.

"Excuse me," someone said, entering with a bow.

It was the palace's head maid and Liscia's personal attendant, Serina. An intellectual beauty who was five years older than Liscia, she was as talented as she appeared, a woman who knew how to get her job done.

When Serina saw my face, she lowered her head reverently.

"Your Majesty, Sir Hakuya sends word that Sir Poncho and the others have all gathered."

"They're here, huh? I've been waiting!" I rose from my seat eagerly, taking Liscia by the hand. "Let's go, Liscia."

"Huh? What?!"

When I suddenly grabbed her hand, Liscia blushed.

"Oh, my word, Princess," Serina said. "To think you would blush just from holding hands...with such innocence, how will you ever attend to your nightly duties with His Majesty?"

"Serina?! What are you saying?!"

"Please, let me hold your child soon. You do know how babies are made, yes?"

"Augh! You're always teasing me!"

Serina was a capable maid, but she had a bad habit of being downright sadistic to cute girls. Her mistress, Liscia, was no exception. Well, I guess that meant their bond of trust was strong enough to allow it. So long as she didn't turn that sadism towards me, she was a very capable worker.

"Well, we're heading off," I said.

"Hey, wait, Souma," Liscia objected.

"Take care!" Serina called. As we left the room, she saw us off with a bow.

We picked up Aisha along the way, and by the time we arrived at the meeting room, all those who had been summoned were gathered.

At the round table in the center of the room sat Hakuya the prime minister, Tomoe my sister-in-law, Juna the lorelei, and Poncho Ishizuka Panacotta. If we excluded Ludwin, who was occupied with another matter, and Marx, who had relinquished the title of prime minister to Hakuya and now managed the palace, everyone who had been present for the gathering of personnel was here.

"Your Majesty," they all said, rising.

"Please, remain seated," I told them, holding out my hand. "I'm the one who called all of you here."

Liscia and I took our seats, as well. Aisha was the only one who remained standing, hovering behind me so she could act at once in case anything should happen. Honestly, it was bothering me having her stand there, so I asked her to sit, but she stubbornly refused.

Weren't you supposed to follow your master's orders? I thought, annoyed. *Well, we'll set that aside for now.*

"Everyone, thank you for coming," I said. "I give you my heartfelt thanks."

"N-n-n-not at all! I-i-i-it was nothing!" Poncho stammered.

"Sire, do not bow your head so easily," Hakuya said. Beside the flustered Poncho, Hakuya had a disapproving look on his face. "If the one at the top abases himself so, there may be those who come to look down on him."

"Any dignity I can only maintain by acting self-important is dignity I don't need. Besides, I think of all the people in this room not as retainers or citizens, but as comrades."

"You're too kind, Your Majesty." Juna gave a slight bow. Those little gestures of hers always made for such a pretty picture.

Tomoe, on the other hand, was so nervous she was stiff. Her clothes last time had been falling apart, but now she wore what looked like a miko outfit with a miniskirt, which was apparently a traditional outfit for mystic wolves. "A-am I your comrade as well, my king?"

"No, no, Tomoe, you're my sister-in-law, remember?"

"Oh, right."

"Yep. So, don't call me your king, call me 'Big Brother Souma.'"

"Ah, no fair! Call me 'Big Sister,' too, then!" Liscia cried.

"Um...Big Brother Souma. Big Sister Liscia," Tomoe said with upturned eyes.

"Nice!" Liscia and I both gave Tomoe's cute reaction enthusiastic thumbs-up.

Thwack! Thwack!

We got whacked upside the head with a paper fan. It was Hakuya who did it.

"You two, it's taking us forever to get on with things, so please cut that out."

"We're sorry..." we both earnestly apologized.

By the way, that paper fan was something I had given to Hakuya when he had taken the position of prime minister, saying, "If I act too far out of line, don't hesitate to slap me upside the head with this." It had been a joke to try to get the too-serious Hakuya to lighten up, but as you would expect from a man who was the greatest genius in the history of Elfrieden (or so Marx claimed), he was putting the paper fan to brilliant use.

"So how does a retainer slapping his king with a paper fan factor into the royal dignity?" I asked.

"It pains me to do it, Sire, but this is a royal order, you see," Hakuya said with a cool look on his face. "That aside, Sire, you'll have to explain to everyone why they've been called here."

"Oh, yeah, that's right...Poncho."

"Y-yessss!"

With the conversation suddenly turning to him, paunchy Poncho stood up so vigorously he almost knocked his chair over. He was as rotund as ever, but he was more suntanned than he had been during the royal audience the other day.

"Have you prepared what I asked you for?" I asked.

"Y-yes! With your cooperation, Sire, I was able to visit all the places it took me eight years to go around to before in a matter of two weeks."

"Cooperation...what did you do for him?" Liscia looked at me dubiously.

"Oh, he means that I cleared things with the countries involved and let him use one of the royal family's royal visit wyverns to get around."

Royal visit wyverns were used by the king when he traveled abroad. The Forbidden Army had only a handful of them. Poncho's task had required speedy transportation, so I had loaned him one. Most wyverns belonged to the air force, but with their general, Castor, being uncooperative, asking him to loan us one of theirs probably wouldn't have worked. It was such a headache.

"Well then, Poncho, show us what you've gathered," I said.

"Y-yes! In here, Sire, I have the 'ingredients there is no custom of eating in this country' that you requested, yes!" With those words, Poncho pulled out a big sack.

When Liscia saw it, her eyes went wide. "Hey, that's the Hero's Sack!"

"Yeah. It fits a lot more than it looks like it should, and, on top of that, food put inside it doesn't rot as easily. I thought it'd be perfect for gathering ingredients, so I lent it to him."

"Even so, you shouldn't...oh, whatever." Liscia slumped her shoulders in resignation. "So, what was it? Ingredients there's no custom of eating in this country?"

"More precisely, it was 'ingredients eaten in foreign countries and select regions of our own country, but for which there is no general custom of eating in this country,'" I said.

Different places have different foods, and different people have different tastes. You often hear of things that are thrown away as inedible in one place being appreciated as a delicacy in another. Even in Japan, in some regions you could find things that would make you say, "Huh? You eat that?" to the point that there have been programs like the *Ken**n Show,* which have focused on the subject.

"Right now, our country grows things like cotton, tea, and tobacco, so we're replacing them with food crops," I explained.

"However, we won't see the effects of that until autumn, at least. So, to keep the people from starving until then, a plan with immediate effects is needed."

In order to resolve the food crisis, serious reforms over a long period of time would be necessary. However, during that time there would be people starving, and there was the worry some might starve to death at this rate. What was more, the first to die would be babies of nursing age, with their weak constitutions and high need for nutrition.

Children were a national treasure. I couldn't let them starve to death.

That said, even if I wanted to deliver food to all the starving people of the country, there were limits to how much support the country could offer. That was why, alongside longer-term strategies, short-term countermeasures with immediate effects would be necessary.

"And that's these ingredients we don't have a custom of eating?" Liscia asked.

"They're eaten in other countries, but we don't have a custom of eating them here," I said. "If we develop those customs, it will make it harder to starve. It simply increases the food supply, after all."

"Is there going to be anything so convenient?" she asked doubtfully.

"That's what we're checking. Now then, let's change locations."

"Change locations? Where to?" Seeing Liscia tilt her head to the side quizzically, I responded with a laugh.

"We're deciding whether we can use these ingredients or not. We're off to the cafeteria, obviously."

"Hey, Souma. I understand why you want to use the cafeteria, but...don't we have too many people?" Liscia asked.

As she had pointed out, the cafeteria was noisy, but in a different way than usual.

In the cafeteria which was used by the guards and maids (and recently, even the king), there were usually more than thirty long tables set up to accommodate many people eating at the same time. However, at present, all but one of the long tables had been taken away to make a wide-open space. Despite this, the cafeteria was full of people and equipment, and there was only a little free space around the long table.

The massive jewel floating in the room took up a particularly large amount of space.

"*Another* Jewel Voice Broadcast?" Liscia asked.

"It's a horrible waste that they only used a handy thing like this to read out declarations of war," I said. "I've got to put it to better use."

This Jewel Voice Broadcast was kind of like television. It could relay information to the people immediately, so airing some entertainment programs was bound to help win the support of the people. I supposed it did have a couple of faults in that the lack of recording technology meant all broadcasts had to be live, and that the video was only available in larger towns and cities (though apparently sound-only broadcasts were available in even the smallest of rural villages). That was just one thing where I would have to wait for the technology (magic?) to advance.

I had been thinking of starting with *Nodo Jiman*, the amateur singing contest, as our first entertainment program. Through the singing café where Juna worked, I had been calling out to the people who had come to show off their "gifts of singing" during my gathering of gifted people, and we were preparing to have them debut as singers and idols.

Elfrieden's first public broadcaster, huh... I thought. *The dreams are limitless.*

"What're you grinning for?" Liscia asked coldly while I imagined the possibilities. "You look creepy."

I coughed. "Ahem...for our current project, the goal is to introduce the custom of eating foods that are not commonly eaten in this country. Advertising them to the people at the same time will be more efficient, right? That's why I brought some beautiful ladies here, as well."

"Like Juna?"

"You too, Liscia. Oh, and Aisha and Tomoe, as well. They say the ABCs of drawing viewership are animals, beauties, and children. That's why I have Liscia the orthodox pretty girl, Juna whose mature charm belies her young age, Aisha with her healthy dark skin, and Tomoe, who is animal-eared, a beauty, and a child, as well. With this many beautiful specimens here, the people's eyes will be glued to the screen."

"M-me, too..." Liscia blushed scarlet. As for the other three...

"It's an honor, Sire," said Juna.

"Yes, Your Majesty! I will endeavor to meet your expectations!" Aisha added.

"Yesh! I-I'll do my best!" Tomoe cried.

Each of them showed their enthusiasm. Meanwhile, Hakuya was quickly getting things in order for the broadcast, and Poncho was hastily double-checking the ingredients. When I saw them like this, I felt like I had gotten a good group of people together. Of course, I still wanted more.

I gave the order to everyone. "Okay, let the broadcast begin."

◇ ◇ ◇

That day, every city deserving of the name in Elfrieden was packed with people.

When word spread that the young king who had stirred up the country with his personnel gathering the other day would be using the Jewel Voice Broadcast to do something again, people rushed to the fountain plazas in the cities. (The systems which dispersed mist into the air to project the Jewel Voice Broadcast on were generally installed on the fountain in the central plaza.)

People who lived in villages that could only receive sound went out of their way to come to nearby cities so they could see the video as well, so there were even more people gathered around than usual.

In this world where the only forms of entertainment to speak of were exhibitions, drinking, and gambling, the Jewel Voice Broadcast was beginning to be recognized by the people as a form of show business.

When people gather, money moves. There were already stands out in the plazas of each city. It was beginning to take on a festive atmosphere. Everyone laid out mats or sheets in front of the fountain, waiting impatiently for the broadcast to begin.

"Hey, hey, ith jewel voith going to do thomething again?" a child lisped.

"Yes, darling. I wonder what it will be," a mother smiled, answering her little girl with the slight lisp.

"Everyone seems to be having fun. Times sure have changed," another person said.

"They certainly have. Why, back in our day, we would never have thought of the Jewel Voice Broadcast as something enjoyable."

The elderly people, who knew the Jewel Voice Broadcast had only been used by generations of kings for declarations of war and public announcements of the current military situation, closed their eyes in silence. In those times, the country had had nearly twice its current territory but only half its current population.

The Jewel Voice Broadcast had always been things like "We have won the battle of X" or "We must overcome the brave death of X and continue to fight!" For those over a certain age, the Jewel Voice Broadcast carried an association with death.

"May our new young king be a man who will not make that image—"

"Wooooooooooooooooooooooooooooo!"

The old man's voice was drowned out by raucous cheering.

A man and a woman in uniform appeared in mid-air.

"Hello, people of Elfrieden," the woman said.

"H-hello," the man added.

"Coming to you with the latest from Parnam Castle is our new program, *The King's Brilliant Lunch*, or *The King's Brillunch* for short. We are your hosts, Juna Doma..."

"...a-and P-Poncho Ishizuka Panacotta, yes!"

"...Poncho, there's no need to be so tense."

"W-well, you see, I don't have any experience doing this... Madam Juna, you're so confident at this. I'm envious, yes."

"Well, I sing in front of customers all the time. If you visit Parnam, please come see our singing café Lorelei."

"Don't blatantly advertise, please!"

"Ha ha ha ha ha ha!" The contrast between the playful beauty and the flustered fat man brought laughs to fountain plazas around the nation.

"Now then, this gentleman will explain the purpose of our program."

"Th-the (provisional) fourteenth king of Elfrieden, His Majesty Souma Kazuya, yes!"

"Ohhh!" A cry went up in the plazas.

The young king they had seen during the gathering of personnel appeared on the screen. "I haven't been crowned, so I'm not king yet, strictly speaking, but...oh, hi. I'm Souma Kazuya, the guy who's currently acting as king. Now, to cut to the chase, I'd like to speak about the state of this country."

"He's not very kingly," said someone. With the way he was acting, you could hardly blame them.

Not seeming to realize this at all, Souma stood in front of a board that had been prepared for the occasion, explaining things with charts and maps. He was especially thorough about the causes of the food crisis.

"...In response to this increase in demand, it created conditions where you could sell as much as you could produce, so farmers shifted from growing food crops to growing cotton, and that is the cause of our current food crisis. Of course, this isn't solely the fault of the farmers. Responsibility also lies with the merchants who coerced them to do it in order to sell their products, the soldiers who benefited from those products, and the royal family for ignoring this until it became a problem. For this, I deeply apologize." With those words, Souma bowed his head.

For a king to bow to his subjects and retainers...this was unheard of. The situation hadn't even been caused during Souma's reign.

"At present, our kingdom is making the switch from cash crops back to food crops. However, I don't expect to see the effects of that until autumn or later. We are considering the importation of food from other countries, but the situation there is not favorable, either. One reason is that we have nothing to replace our primary export, cotton, and so we can't secure foreign currency. The other reason is that every country is in a similar situation. They can't sell us what they don't have."

Souma's words were more than enough to depress the people, but they were more surprised that Souma had released this information to the public. Normally, those who stood at the top didn't disclose such information to those beneath them. Sometimes it was because that information included mistakes they themselves had made; many times, they also believed that those below them wouldn't understand even if they were told about matters of national policy.

As a matter of fact, the king's explanation had been simple enough that a junior high student from Japan could understand it, and yet only around three-tenths of the people of this country could. However, this young king had disclosed the information.

The more educated a person was, the greater their surprise. Why had he exposed such a national disgrace, one that could lead to his own loss of power, to the people?

"Um, er...is that something that's okay to tell the people?" Poncho hesitantly asked the question everyone was thinking. However, Souma's expression didn't change in the slightest.

"The more you hide, the more people doubt you. There are things we need to hide when it comes to foreign affairs, but for internal policy, I intend to continue disclosing such things. You see, I want my fellow countrymen to use their heads. What is best for this country? Are my policies correct? I want them to think along with me."

"I've never seen a king like this before..." someone whispered.

It was unheard of for a ruler to ask his people to think about politics with him. Technically, even in this country, there was a Congress of the People which represented their will, but it was, to put it simply, "a place to decide on the people's pleas to the king." The king was free to implement them or not as he saw fit, and the content of these congresses was limited to things like requests to correct the inflation in prices for X or requests for public works spending. It was about as useful as having a suggestion box, and it was not a place for debating political decisions.

The feudal system was also still strong in this country. To put it at its simplest, the political system in this country was "Those below pay their taxes. Those above protect the lives and property of those below." That was all there was to it.

Commoners paid taxes to their lords, and the lords guaranteed their lives and property. Their lords (the nobility) paid taxes to the king, and in exchange for them serving in the military in times of crisis, the king guaranteed their lives and property. It was a society with a complete class system.

When there was rot at the top, the rot risked spreading throughout. However, to look at it the opposite way, so long as the people above them were on the level, the people didn't need to think about national policy; they could think about nothing but themselves. So it was an easy system to be part of in that way.

However, this young king had asked the people to use their heads. He had asked them to think about his policies with him.

There was no clear path yet for political participation from the people. Even if they were to be given that right, it was clear that the uneducated citizenry would descend into mob rule. However, even so, he sowed the seeds.

"This country's going to change..." someone said.

"I envy young'uns who'll be able to see that change," an old man added.

"Oh, we're not done yet," another one said.

While looking at the young king, the elderly squinted their eyes, as if blinded by his radiance.

Without any way to know this, Souma continued his explanation.

"As you see here, we will have to wait until autumn for a fundamental solution to the problem. It goes without saying that we intend to provide support, but there are issues of volume and geography preventing us from reaching every person in the kingdom with it. Not everyone lives in the flatlands, after all."

This was a country with many races living together. From the dark elves who lived in the forest, to the dragonewts who preferred to live at high altitudes like the mountains, to the dwarves who lived in underground caves, there were those who lived in places supply lines did not pass through, and it would be difficult to deliver relief supplies. It was the same for those who lived in marginal villages deep in the mountains.

"That is why I come to you, my countrymen, with a request— no, an order." Here, Souma stopped. Then, after a breath, he said clearly, "Everyone, survive until autumn."

When they heard those words come from the young king's mouth, the people gulped. The words' meaning was simple. However, his intent behind them was inscrutable.

"Because we have no cards to play, you will all need to survive for yourselves," the king said. "Go into the mountains, into the rivers, into the sea, in search of food. Cooperate with each other and bow your heads to others if necessary, no matter how humiliating it is, because I want everyone to survive until autumn."

Those words could have been heard as an abdication of responsibility. He was telling those who were suffering to go work hard on their own, after all. However, it was also true that only those who worked hard would be saved.

The young king bowed his head sincerely. "Please. When I say everyone, I mean every last one of you. Don't lash out at others because you're suffering; don't send away children because you have too many mouths to feed; do not throw away the old and frail. I want you all to greet the bounty of autumn together. This broadcast is something we've put together in the hopes that it will be some help with that."

Souma went into the objectives of the current broadcast. As a means of buying time until the food crisis could be solved, they would introduce ingredients not commonly eaten in this country and show the ways to prepare them. These ingredients could be obtained cheaply (or freely where they grew in the wild). Furthermore, by eating those ingredients live on-air, they would demonstrate that they were edible.

Even those citizens who had been indignant at his earlier statement, which had seemed to abdicate responsibility, felt their anger cooling as they listened to Souma's explanation. Because this king truly was thinking about them. They could feel that keenly.

"So, there you have it. Now then, I'll hand the show back over to your hosts, Poncho and Juna." With his explanation complete, Souma returned to his seat.

Souma couldn't have known this, but at that moment, roaring applause erupted through plazas around the country. It was spontaneous applause from those citizens deeply impressed by Souma's words. Without knowing it, Souma was slowly beginning to gain recognition as their king.

The video returned to Poncho and Juna hosting once more.

"Now then, let's get right to it," Juna said. "Poncho, what's our first ingredient?"

"Y-yes! Our first ingredient is right here!"

With that, Poncho brought over a cloth-covered box, placing it on the table where Souma, Liscia, Aisha, and Tomoe were seated like guest commentators.

It was a box big enough to hold a largish aquarium.

Pausing a moment for dramatic effect, Poncho pulled back the cloth.

◇　◇　◇

We were in the cafeteria at Parnam Castle for the live broadcast.

"Urkh..."

"Eeeeeeeeek!"

"Wai— What?!"

When they saw what had appeared on the table, Aisha, Tomoe, and Liscia each let out their own cries of shock.

Juna, on the other hand, looked at it and seemed to be thinking, "Ohhhh, so that's it."

"That's an octopus."

"It sure is an octopus."

The thing in the box in front of them was the eight-legged, wriggly, soft-bodied creature you all know to be an octopus.

While many of the creatures in this world had a touch of the fantastic about them, such as even the cows and chickens having armored carapaces, this was just a straight-up (though rather large) octopus. Well, even in fantasy worlds, giant octopi are often a thing, so I guess it's okay?

By the way, in this country, they called octopi "ocatos," but that's just confusing, so we'll stick with octopi. I mean, with my mysterious translation ability, the word sounded like "octopus" to me, anyway.

"Huh? You people don't eat octopus in this country?" I asked.

"We do not! Hold on, Souma, have you actually eaten one of those creepy things before?!" Liscia looked at me incredulously.

Come on, it's just an octopus, you know? I'm having a hard time accepting this reaction.

"Well, considering how they look, I'm sure they're only eaten in some coastal regions. My hometown is one of them, though," Juna gently explained.

Well, even back on Earth, in Europe (excluding Italy and Spain) they're called "devilfish," and in some countries people refuse to eat them...I guess? I thought.

"But they're so tasty..." I said.

"A-are they?" Liscia asked.

Once she heard they were delicious, Aisha was ready to dig

in. Her being my bodyguard meant we often ate together, so I already knew this, but the girl was quite the glutton. She had a special weakness when it came to sweet foods (like the snacks that came as offerings for the king and maids), and she would munch away at them to the point that the maids jealously grumbled, "How does she eat so much and still maintain that figure...?"

"Yeah. There are divergent opinions about how good it is raw, but if you just rub salt into it, wash off the mucus, and boil it, it's good like that. Cooked, fried, served with rice, it's delicious any way you like it."

There was silence.

"Aisha, you're drooling," I added.

"Whoops...pardon me."

"Honestly, it's high protein, low calorie, so it's great if you're on a diet, too."

"High-pro? I-I'm not sure what that is, but my ears pricked up when I heard the word 'diet'..." Liscia seemed to be ready to dig in now, too.

Honestly though, I thought Liscia could stand to put some more meat on her bones. Maybe it was because she was in the army, but she was very slender.

"I don't think you need to worry so much about your weight," I told her.

"Souma...a girl stops being a girl the moment she stops caring about her weight," Liscia admonished me with eyes that seemed to be staring off into the distance.

Since Juna and Tomoe gave firm nods as well, I guessed that

was just how it was. Aisha was the only dissenter, with a face that seemed to say, "Forget that, I want to eat already."

"Okay, then...for now, shall we get to cooking?" I asked.

We moved to the kitchen attached to the cafeteria and began to prepare the octopus. The cooks who worked there protested, "If you had just said something, we would have done it for you ourselves..." but I liked cooking, so I decided to do it.

First, I put the octopus in a large bowl, cutting out the guts, ink sack, and eyeballs with a kitchen knife. (This elicited an "Uwah..." from the girls, but I ignored them.) Then I rubbed salt into it, waited for the slimy surface to harden, and washed it well with water. I cleaned the suckers thoroughly as well because there could be mud in them sometimes.

After that, I brought water to a boil, dropped the octopus into the pot legs-first, and then that very octopus-shaped creature (I mean, it *was* an octopus) boiled up. Watching until its yellowish-brown flesh turned a firm reddish-purple, I pulled it out, and a fine example of a boiled octopus was ready. After it had cooled a little, I cut the legs into bite-sized pieces. It would already be delicious like this.

"Eh, good enough. Time to eat," I said.

"Wha?!" Liscia and the others were shocked to see me nibbling at it already with zero hesitation.

When I popped a bite in my mouth, yep, it sure tasted like octopus. That slightly salty taste was great, and because it was so great, I couldn't help but lament that there was no soy sauce in this world yet!

"Is that really edible?" Liscia murmured.

"Come on, Liscia. You could just try it and find out, you know?"

"Uh, no...I'm not emotionally prepared just yet..."

"You sure? It's delicious."

Ignoring the hesitant Liscia, Juna popped a slice in her mouth.

"Ahh, no fair, Madam Juna!" Aisha cried. "Fine then, me too!"

Seeing that, Aisha went *chomp*, and—

Hey, wait! Don't just bite right into the head! Just how much of a glutton is this dark elf?!

"Oh! It's crisp and delicious!"

"...Is it now?"

Okay, time to get back in control of things.

I coated the bite-sized pieces of octopus in wheat flour, egg, and white flour, putting them on skewers three at a time. Then I put the whole skewers into a pot of hot oil. I let them fry until the batter was light brown and crispy. I pulled them out of the pot, and once I had put on the finishing touches with Worcestershire sauce, which they had even in this world, and a homemade mayonnaise I had made with eggs, vinegar, and other things, they were done.

"'Fried octopus skewers' is what you'd call them, I guess. Go on, try eating them." I offered each person one skewer.

Liscia and Tomoe timidly brought them to their mouths. The moment they took a bite...

"What is this?! It's delicious!"

"It really is...very delicious, Brother."

Their eyes went wide at how good it was.

Nice! I thought, giving myself a mental thumbs-up.

"It really is delicious. The octopus hidden inside the crispy batter is very juicy," Juna said.

"I-it really is! Even I didn't know octopus would go this well with Worcestershire sauce!" Poncho cried.

"This white sauce goes well with the octopus, too. Splendidly done, Sire," Juna added.

"Y-you can cook, too, Sire! That surprised me, yes."

Juna and Poncho gave commentary like professional food critics. Since both had eaten octopus before, they could both take the time to properly savor it. Meanwhile, Aisha was chomp, chomp, chomping away and producing a massive pile of empty skewers.

There's nothing more I can say about that.

◇ ◇ ◇

"It really is delicious," the broadcast said. "Wrapped outside in a crispy batter, the octopus inside is very juicy."

"Hey, Daddy?" a child asked.

"Yeah. If you want octopus, a lot of them got caught in our nets today," the father answered.

"Really?! I want to try it!"

"Sure thing. Normally I throw them back, but let's try it."

It seemed there were a lot of conversations like this one in many villages by the sea.

◇ ◇ ◇

"Our next ingredient is this."

After we finished eating the well-received octopus skewers and returned to our seats, Poncho opened a new box in front of us. When we saw the thin brown ingredient covered in dirt inside...

"Are these...roots?" Liscia said.

"I think they're roots," Juna added.

"They don't look so good... are they really edible?" Tomoe asked doubtfully.

Liscia, Juna, and Tomoe all acted like they had question marks floating above their heads. Aisha and I, on the other hand, were completely unsurprised.

"Oh, burdock root, huh?" I said.

"That's burdock root," Aisha agreed.

Well, I had heard burdock root was a strange thing to eat in the West, so I didn't find it odd that it wasn't eaten here. That Aisha knew about it surprised me, since she looked like a Westerner.

"In the forest, we must eat everything we can, otherwise we would succumb to malnutrition in no time," Aisha said, staring off into the distance.

Perhaps that food situation was what had made her the hungry dark elf she was today.

"Since they're being introduced here, that means you can eat them, right?" Liscia asked, to which I nodded.

"You can eat them. But rather than enjoy them for their own flavor, you enjoy the flavor of the broth they were stewed in, or their texture. They're mostly dietary fiber, which you can't digest, but they have a medicinal effect and can help keep your bowel movements regular. They're a good friend to those who are constipated."

"I wish you wouldn't talk about bowel movements and constipation while we're eating," Liscia said.

"It helps expel waste products from the body. Of course, it's good for your health and beauty."

"Urkh. When you say that, it sounds tempting, but..."

Well, now that Liscia's been talked into it, shall we get down to eating? I thought.

This time, I kept it simple. After scraping off the dirt using the back of a knife, I cut the burdock into long, thin shavings, coated it with potato starch, and put it into the pot of oil we had used earlier. Once it was properly fried, I took it out of the pot and split it into two bowls. On one of these, I sprinkled salt, while the other I sprinkled with sugar. With that, the burdock chips (potato chip-style and rusk-style) were complete.

As for everyone's reactions after eating them...

"Huh, they're crunchy and delicious." said Liscia.

"These...would probably go well with beer," Poncho said.

Liscia and Poncho were munching away at the salted ones like a snack.

"The oil that comes out when you bite into them melts the sugar, and the sweetness spreads through your whole mouth," said Juna.

"I'd sure like to let both my moms try this," said Tomoe.

Juna and Tomoe, who were eating the ones with sugar, gave comments that were worth full points as a food critic and a child respectively.

As for Aisha...

"If you eat them together, they're salty-sweet and delicious!" she announced, munching away at both.

Yeah, sure, I guess it's okay to eat them that way, too.

◇ ◇ ◇

The next edible ingredients were red bear's paw (bear paw), sword tiger's liver (tiger liver), and whole cooked salamandra (whole cooked giant salamander), but we only went as far as introducing them.

It was true they weren't customarily eaten in this country, but rare delicacies that only an adventurer could hope to catch weren't something I wanted people going out of their way to acquire. If they happened to get their hands on them by some chance, I just wanted them to know to please eat them, not throw them away. Besides, even I don't know how to prepare bear paw.

Ah, by the way, at the ingredients selection stage I removed blowfish, poisonous mushrooms, and anything else poisonous from the list. I knew they could be eaten if prepared properly, but if starvation-stricken amateurs were to try their hand at them, it was clear it would only end badly.

Mind you, even the poisonous parts could be eaten if you really wanted to. In Ishikawa Prefecture, there's "blowfish ovaries pickled in rice-bran paste," and in Nagano Prefecture, there are regions where they eat the famously poisonous fly amanita mushroom.

The human appetite sure is something, huh?

Getting back to the story, the next ingredient shocked all of us.

"This here is our next ingredient, yes."

"Th-this is..."

This time, all our eyes went wide.

Inside the box Poncho opened, there was a bluish-green gelatinous object.

"That's...a gelin, right?" I asked.

It was one of the soft-bodied slime creatures that could be found in fields everywhere. They looked and acted just like the enemy from RPGs. Their defining characteristic was how weak they were. If you cut them, they'd die. If you smashed them, they'd die. They attached themselves to living (or dead) creatures and sucked nutrients from them. There was no male or female; they multiplied by division. They were probably what you'd get if you had an amoeba or other single-celled organism grow to a gigantic size.

Huh? We're eating that? Or, rather, can we even eat that?

Then I noticed Aisha seemed to be cocking her head to the side in confusion.

"Hold on. Is that gelin dead?"

"Yes. This gelin has already been finished off," Poncho said.

"That can't be. I've never heard of a gelin corpse before."

"Oh, that's right. Now that you mention it, it *is* strange," Liscia agreed, seeming to have noticed something.

I, on the other hand, didn't get it. "Liscia, could you just tell me what's up already?"

"What's with that tone...? Gelins are weak. They have a thin membrane, and if you cut them just a little, *gush*, out flows all their bodily fluids. It's the same if you splatter them with a club. All you have left is a bluish-green puddle."

"Is that how it is?"

Aisha nodded, as well. "Yes. That's why such a neatly pre-served corpse seems impossible."

I see...Aisha as a warrior and Liscia as a soldier have experience fighting gelins, so they noticed something was odd here.

"So, what did you have to do to get the gelin like this?" I asked.

"Well, you see, there's a slight trick to it. This is a technique I learned from a tribe that lives far to the west, in the Empire. They use a thin pole-like object to strike the nucleus without breaking the membrane. If you do that, the gelin will maintain its shape in death. In that area, they called it 'ike-jime for gelins.'"

Ike-jime? Come on, this isn't like draining blood from fish...still, that makes sense now. It looks like I wasn't wrong to think of them like single-celled organisms.

"The fluids of a gelin gradually lose liquidity and harden once the core is destroyed," Poncho added.

"Like rigor mortis, I guess," I said.

"Yes. If you leave it longer, the fluids will evaporate, and it will turn into a dry husk, but around two hours after death, while it has hardened somewhat but the flesh is still supple, it is possible to cook it. That would be the state this one is in, yes."

Hmm...I get that you can cook it, but isn't that a separate issue from whether you can eat it? As I was thinking that, Poncho took out a knife and began making a vertical cut in the gelin.

"When the gelin is in this state, you can insert the knife vertically and cut it into pieces without the body collapsing. The fibers of the gelin's body run vertically, so doing it this way gives it the best texture, yes."

Poncho skillfully cut the gelin into long thin strips, like making ika somen. It was turning into noodles with an udon-like thickness. Poncho took those and put them into a pot of boiling water.

"Now, if we boil them in a pot of water with a little salt, the flesh will firm up more."

Now it was seriously starting to turn into something like soba or udon. As they were boiling, that vibrant bluish-green color had darkened, starting to look something like green tea soba, too. Then Poncho added things like dried mushrooms and kelp to the pot with the boiling gelin.

Is he boiling those to get broth out of them?

Lastly, after adding more salt to adjust the flavor, he served them to each of us in a bowl of soup.

"Here you go. This is 'gelin udon.'"

"He's even calling it udon!" I exclaimed.

"I-is something the matter, Sire?" Poncho asked.

"Oh, no, nothing."

I heard this country's language as Japanese. "Udon" was probably some other word that had gotten translated into that. How confusing. Setting that aside, what was laid out in front of us looked exactly like Kansai-style green udon in a clear broth.

Red Fox and Green Gelin, is it? I thought. *Yeah...now's not the time to escape reality by remembering old commercial jingles for instant udon. Huh? Wait, I seriously have to eat this?*

When I looked around, everyone was looking at me as if to say, "Go ahead, go ahead."

I haven't put up my hand and said "Okay, I'll eat it," yet, you know! Well, I guess I've been making Liscia eat things she's not used to. It wouldn't be fair for me to be the only one who runs away! Time to dig in!

I took a slurp.

"?!"

"W-well, how is it, Souma?" Liscia asked with a worried look.

"...This is surprisingly good," I responded.

Yeah. I wonder what it is. This is completely different from what I imagined.

I had been imagining something like ika somen, with a slimy texture and fishy flavor, but these were smooth and chewy, no fishy flavor at all. Rather than udon, it was like kuzu-kiri that you cook in a pot, or Malony noodles. However, when you bit into it, there was a unique squeaky texture. Was that fiber, maybe?

If I were to describe it, I would say, "It looks like udon, tastes like kuzu-kiri, and has the texture of a regional dish from Kyushu."

Yeah, it's not bad. Not bad at all.

"You're right...it's surprisingly good," Liscia said.

"It's delicious the way they've absorbed the flavor of the broth," Juna agreed.

"Is this really gelin? I'm shocked," Tomoe said.

"*SLURRRRRP.*"

That was Aisha.

It seemed everyone who ate after me had a good impression of it, as well. Well, of course they did, because it was delicious. If you were to ask which tasted better, this or normal udon, I would say the question was nonsense. It would be like asking which was more delicious, soba or udon. It's just a matter of personal preference.

"By the way, what sorts of nutrients are in this stuff?" I asked.

"Nutrients...I don't know what those are, but I suspect that it's like the gelatin you can extract from bones," Poncho said.

"Collagen, huh?"

So, they have the protein you find in animal bones with fiber like you would find in plants, huh. It really is hard to decide whether gelins are plants or animals.

"Anyway, it sounds like it should be fine nutritionally," I said. "Gelins are everywhere. If people eat them, it should alleviate the food crisis a fair bit, don't you think?"

"Yes, I suppose so. Raising gelins is easy. If you just give them raw garbage as food, they'll grow and multiply on their own," Poncho said.

"Uh, no, I don't want to give weird stuff to something I'm going to be eating," I said. "I don't want to eat a gelin that's absorbed toxic chemicals and have it give me food poisoning."

"I-I suppose not."

"Anyway, let's try raising them as an experiment. Hunting them in the wild is fine, too, but I wouldn't want to reduce their numbers too much and have it impact the local ecosystem..."

"I think that would be for the best," Poncho agreed.

All that aside, we greatly enjoyed the rest of the gelin udon.

◇　◇　◇

"Are they really edible?" someone asked.

"Well, the king and the others seemed to be enjoying them," another person responded.

"I think I'm going to request a gelin capture quest at the adventurers' guild."

"Oh, me too, then."

There were conversations like this in fountain plazas everywhere.

"Elfrieden's signature dish is gelin." Who could have predicted that people would be saying that in the not-too-distant future?

◇　◇　◇

"Now then, on to our last ingredient. I have something already cooked and prepared."

When we saw what was inside the container Poncho opened after saying that...

"Uwah...?!" was our universal response.

Because inside it were insects. What was more, this sort of dish existed in my world...in Japan, even.

"This is inago no tsukudani, isn't it?" I asked.

"Yes. This is large locust tsukudani."

"Yeah...they certainly are large."

With the inago no tsukudani, I remembered, each one was about the size of a cricket. With these, on the other hand, each one was the size of a kuruma prawn.

Though the color suggests they have that spicy-sweet flavor boiled into them and the flavor has properly seeped all the way in...wait? Tsukudani?

"If these are tsukudani," I said, "that means..."

"Huh? Souma, you're going to eat them?"

Since I had suddenly stabbed my fork into one of the big locusts, Liscia was now looking at me, shocked. Fair enough; they did look like the sort of thing you'd normally hesitate to eat. If I were calmer, I might have eaten it a bit more timidly. But right now, there was something I was more interested to find out.

Munch, munch...

"?!"

The texture was like shrimp with the shell on, but there was something more important.

This taste...there's no mistaking it!

"This tsukudani...is made with soy sauce!"

"Soy sauce?"

Soy sauce.

Yes, soy sauce. The heart of Japanese flavor.

You can't have sashimi or nimono without it. It's the magic sauce that can turn ramen, steak, spaghetti, and any other foreign dish into a "Japanese" one. It was the flavor I had probably most longed for since coming to this country. The mystic sauce that, due to its fermentation process, I couldn't recreate as easily as I had mayonnaise. Now, a dish made with it lay before my very eyes! Locusts or not, they were looking like fine cuisine to me.

"What? No way, Souma, are you crying?" Liscia exclaimed.

"How can I not?! This is...the taste of my homeland."

"The taste of your homeland..."

"Brother, they have large locust tsukudani in your homeland, too?"

When I looked over, Tomoe was crunching away at the large locust tsukudani and clearly enjoying them. Come to think of it, when everyone else had been recoiling in shock, this kid had been the only one who was unsurprised.

"Could it be, this dish is...?" I said.

"Yes. I ate it a lot back in the mystic wolf village."

"Then do the mystic wolves make soy sauce?!"

"Soy sauce...do you mean hishio water, maybe?"

"Hishio water?"

"Hishio water is a sauce the mystic wolves are fond of using, yes," Poncho jumped in to explain. "Originally, the mystic wolves would coat soybeans in salt and allow them to ferment, creating a sauce called 'bean hishio.' When they take the clear liquid that is created in that process and let it ferment, that produces hishio water. Both are sauces with a unique flavor not found in this country, yes."

"I see."

After that explanation, I was certain of it. I had read in a book somewhere that soy sauce was born from the process of making miso. So, basically, bean hishio was miso and hishio water was soy sauce. (The reason I didn't hear those words as miso and soy sauce may have been because they were similar to, but distinctly different from, modern soy sauce.) Maybe the mystic wolves had eating habits like the Japanese. *Wait, hold on. This flavor permeating through the locust is...*

"Hey, Tomoe. Alcohol is used in making these, too, right?"

"Ah, yes. It's an alcohol made from the seeds of a plant."

"What kind of seeds?"

"Let's see...it's a plant that grows in marshy areas, it has ears that look like the end of a broom, and on them, there are lots of little seeds like wheat."

No doubt about it! Those are rice plants! My hope for the future!

For the transition from cash crops to food crops, I had wanted to grow rice, because I had heard that paddy fields didn't degrade the fertility of the soil, unlike wheat in dry fields. But because the all-important rice plants didn't exist in this country, that plan had ground to a halt.

Now I see. It grows further north, huh? I'd very much like to bring some here and try cultivating it. Still, these mystic wolves... between the soy sauce, miso, and now rice, their race has a lot of the things I've been wanting.

I paused.

"Okay, that settles it! I'll give the mystic wolves among the refugees a district in Parnam."

"Whaaaa?!" Tomoe exclaimed.

I wanted them to produce this bean hishio and hishio water there. We had plenty of soybeans, since we had planted them as part of the soil restoration process.

"Hold on, Souma, are you serious?!" Liscia seemed confused and flustered, but I was as serious as serious gets.

"With soy sauce and miso...I mean, hishio water and bean hishio, I can recreate most of the dishes from the country I came from. It sounds like there's rice here, too. Don't you want to try the tasty foods of another world?"

"Th-that's..."

"Yes! I really want to try them!" Aisha raised her hand with gusto.

"Ha ha...while they may not feel as strongly as Aisha, I'm sure our people would like to try them. If I publish the recipes, they'll either gather the ingredients and make them themselves or go to a restaurant that serves them, I'm sure. Either way, it will cause a lot of movement in the economy."

Huge market liquidity would bring prosperity to this country. That, I firmly believed. That was why I said this to the people watching:

"My search for the gifted is still ongoing. If people have a gift, I will use them even if they are refugees. This race has superior food production techniques, so I have no reason not to accept them. Oh, I know...for the next five years, I will grant the mystic wolves a monopoly on bean hishio and hishio water. We will clamp down on illicit production by any other parties. However, five years from now, I will lift the monopoly on bean hishio and hishio water to create a free market, so I recommend the mystic wolves create a firm economic base for themselves in that time. That is all."

◇ ◇ ◇

After this pronouncement, a mystic wolf quarter was built in the capital of Parnam, and bean hishio and hishio water were produced there with assistance from the country.

In this world, there had been many cases where refugees had been given a district of their own and it had turned into a slum. That was because the refugees faced economic limitations (lack of jobs, being used for cheap labor, and more) and struggled with poverty.

However, in the case of the mystic wolves, because they had been given a monopoly on bean hishio and hishio water by the king, they were able to build an economic base for themselves, and so their quarter did not turn into a slum. Instead, it became an integrated part of the capital by the time the five-year limit was up.

Furthermore, even after bean hishio and hishio water had been renamed to "miso" and "soy sauce" and the monopoly had ended, they continued to study it. The miso and soy sauce that the mystic wolves put out under the Kikkoro brand, marked with a hexagonal logo with a wolf in the center, would continue to be loved for a long time after that.

◇ ◇ ◇

Cheery background music and the soft voice of Juna Doma echoed through the fountain plaza.

"Now, it is time for this program, *The King's Brillunch,* to end. How did you feel about hosting, Poncho?"

"Y-yes. If my knowledge has been able to help our countrymen in the slightest, that would make me very happy. Still, I think hosting was too great a burden for me, yes. Please, have someone else take my place next time."

"I wonder, will there be a next time? What do you say, Sire?" Juna asked.

"If the people demand it."

"Well, there you have it. I hope they do demand it, Poncho."

"I-I don't think I want there to be a demand for me, yes!"

"Oh, don't say that. Do this with me again sometime!" Juna cried in a singsong tone.

"Eeek! Please, spare me!" he yelped.

"Now then, thank you all for watching. This is your hosts, Juna Doma..."

"...and Poncho Ishizuka Panacotta, signing off, yes."

"Now everyone, I bid you good day."

The music cut out, and the video faded away. It seemed that the program had ended.

From here and there around the plaza, sighs could be heard.

"Aww...it's over, huh."

"That was more interestin' than I expected. Wish I coulda watched it a bit longer."

"Yeppers. It don't hafta be every day, but I do hope they'll make the broadcasts semi-regular."

"If there's demand, they'll do more, yeah? Well, how's about we send in a request to the Congress of the People?"

"Oh! Now that there's an idea that wouldn't've occurred to me! I'm gonna go talk to the mayor about it right now."

Conversations like this one happened in towns everywhere.

The people were completely taken with this new form of entertainment called the "variety program." Souma had intended it as an "information program" about the food crisis, but with Juna and Poncho playing off one another, the cooking program-like aspects, and pretty girls squealing over and then eating bizarre ingredients, you couldn't blame them for seeing it that way.

Later, the Congress of the People submitted a "request for the regular holding of Jewel Voice Broadcast programs." With Souma's assent, a time for a public broadcast that would take place every evening was established.

There were those who took a different view of this from society at large.

"When the new king suddenly took the throne, I suspected usurpation, but that young king seems to be a surprisingly affable fellow," said one old man.

"You're right," another responded. "I can see why King Albert chose to abdicate in favor of him."

"The princess seemed to be in good spirits, too. I had suspected she was forced into the betrothal."

"They were very natural together. They didn't seem to be on bad terms."

"Ho, ho, ho, we may have an heir by next year, I reckon."

"A child from the wise and gentle king and the dignified princess, huh? The next generation will be one to look forward to."

"It really will. Ho, ho, ho."

The old men laughed quietly together.

A wise and gentle king...that was how they had evaluated Souma. However, about half of that evaluation was wrong.

Souma was not purely a gentle king.

◇　◇　◇

Sitting in my chair in the king's governmental affairs office, I spoke to Hakuya, who stood across from me.

"Give me your report on the surrounding countries."

Right now, Hakuya and I were the only ones present in the room. Liscia and the others were elsewhere, probably having a great time at the party to celebrate the launch of the Jewel Voice Broadcast. Even Aisha, who usually stayed at my side at all times, claiming it was to guard me, was busy with the food that had been prepared for the occasion.

We had left the celebration partway through, coming to the governmental affairs office for a secret meeting.

Hakuya spread out a map of the world on my desk.

"I will now make my report. First, I will review the surrounding countries. Our country, which is situated in the southeast of the continent, shares a border with three countries: the Union of Eastern Nations to the north, the Principality of Amidonia to the west, and the Republic of Turgis to the southwest. Also, across the sea to the southeast there is the Nine-Headed Dragon Archipelago Union. In addition, to the west of Amidonia, the mercenary state Zem could also be called one of our surrounding countries. Of these, zero are friendly, four are neutral, and one is hostile."

"We're pretty isolated, huh," I said.

"With all due respect, given that these are troubled times with the Demon Lord's Domain expanding, this is normal. In these days where each nation eyes the others with suspicion, the only countries on friendly terms are those in the relationship of suzerain and vassal state."

"You call that a friendly relationship?"

"If there is no fear of betrayal, it is friendly enough."

He said the most outrageous of things with a cool face. What he had said meant, basically, that he felt a relationship of control and subordination which allowed no room for complaint even if one nation was used like a tool and then thrown away still qualified as friendly, didn't it? Sort of like the alliance between the Matsudaira and Oda clans when Oda Nobunaga had still been alive.

"So, which is the hostile one?" I asked. "Amidonia? Zem?"

"Not Zem. Certainly, *that matter* has worsened their impression of us, but not to the point where they would be considered hostile. That said, if Amidonia requested reinforcements from them, I have little doubt they would dispatch mercenaries on their behalf."

"Amidonia, huh...if I recall, they sent us an 'offer of assistance,' right?"

"Yes. 'The stability of our neighbor Elfrieden is directly tied to our own national defense. If a request is made, we will dispatch forces to help subdue the Three Dukedoms,' was what they offered."

"Ha ha ha ha...that's pretty straightforward."

It was plain to see that they wanted to take advantage of the discord between the Three Dukedoms and myself to expand their territory.

"It is. The Three Dukedoms have likely been told something similar."

"'Let us strike down the usurper Souma together,' is it? Hard to laugh at that."

Well, I could probably count on the Three Dukedoms to see through Amidonia's scheme. They wouldn't let foreigners run roughshod over this country just because they didn't like me. Of course, Amidonia knew that too, so basically...

"By making offers of aid to both sides, they want to give themselves a cause to mobilize their troops," I said.

"While seizing cities in the west, they'll send reinforcements to the side that 'wins,'" he agreed. "Then, they'll come up with some reason to assume de facto control of the cities they occupied, integrating them into their country. It's an orthodox strategy, but an effective one, I would think."

Well, yeah. There were many examples of it in my own world's history. Like So'un Hojo with his "Borrow a deer hunting trail, steal a castle." The simpler the strategy, perhaps the more likely people were to be deceived.

Amidonia was blatantly trying to deceive us, Zem was tilting towards hostility, and the Elfrieden Kingdom was unable to achieve national unity because of my conflict with the Three Dukedoms. Difficult problems to solve, all of them.

"However, this is all part of the scenario you wrote, isn't it?" I asked, staring hard at Hakuya.

Hakuya remained unperturbed.

"Yes. At this moment, everything about the situation is shifting as it should," he declared. That cool expression of his made me scratch my head vigorously.

"You...do realize, right?" I asked, referring to the number of people who would be sacrificed by Hakuya's plan.

The scenario Hakuya had laid out would mean great losses for our foes, and great gains for our allies. It was true that I needed a move, no matter what it was, that would let this country rise to be a strong nation. However, to bring it to fruition, this country would also need to shed a fair amount of blood.

Despite that, Hakuya declared this without showing any guilt: "Yes. I believe we should take everything that this opportunity offers us."

I was silent.

"Sire, you should understand, the result will save many of your countrymen."

"I know that. But, still, I'm only going to accept doing 'this' once." I looked Hakuya straight in the eye. "A political thinker from my world, Machiavelli, wrote about it in *The Prince*. If a ruler does 'this' just once, and in doing so finishes everything, never doing it again, he will be regarded as a great ruler. On the other hand, should the one time he does 'this' fail to be decisive, he will sooner or later face his end as a tyrant."

"This Machiavelli had a terrifyingly realistic view of things." Hakuya was slightly taken aback.

Yeah. That was why I liked him. I had been enthralled by the endless realism of Machiavelli and reread *The Prince* many times, though I had never expected the knowledge to come in handy like this someday.

"Regardless, I have deemed your plan to be an example of doing 'that,'" I said. "So..."

If we are to do it, let it be in one stroke.

Serina and the Death Spirit Panic

PARNAM CASTLE in the kingdom's capital, Parnam.

You are already aware that this was the royal palace where the king resides, but, recently, there had been a ghost story making the rounds in the castle.

It happened one summer evening, in the witching hour, when even the grass and trees slumbered.

One of the castle's live-in maids was sleeping in her room when she awakened due to the summer heat. She tried to go back to sleep, but just couldn't seem to.

Accepting that she was going to have to stay awake, she decided to at least get herself something to drink and headed towards the cafeteria used by the guards and maids. Water was drawn from a nearby mountain for the castle's cafeteria, and the maids were welcome to take a drink whenever they pleased.

Then *it* happened when the maid entered the cafeteria. She saw something that looked like a faint light by the kitchen oven. When she squinted, she could also see what seemed to be the outline of a person.

Oh...one of the cooks is still here. The maid was relieved to see another person. This being the royal palace, security was very tight. It wasn't the sort of place intruders could get into.

That was why the maid thought it was simply one of the cooks still in the kitchen. When she approached, it appeared that the person was mixing something in a pot. The maid was about to call out to them, but the next moment, a chill ran down her spine...

"Heh heh heh..."

The person let out a creepy laugh.

The maid felt something abnormal in that laughter, and, despite herself, looked into the pot the person was stirring. In the pot, floating in its oily mud-like brew, there were several bones, bones, bonesbonesbonesbonesbonesbonesbones....

There, the maid lost consciousness.

"...So, there you have it. A necromancer appeared in the castle and may have been trying to summon something. Everyone's been talking about it! What do you think, Head Maid?" one of the coworkers of the maid who had collapsed asked Serina.

Serina didn't let her usual beautiful poker face slip. "I see. And what happened to this maid?"

"Huh? What do you mean?"

"Did it not turn into something like, 'Stop! You're going to do perverse things to me, aren't you?! Like in shunga prints!'?"

"No?! Instead of tearing off her clothes they laid a cloak over her, and she was discovered sleeping there by the cooking staff the next morning."

"Well, that's bor—I mean, good."

"Did you just start to say 'boring'?!"

Serina let the maid's question pass with a vague smile.

Serina was the personal attendant of this country's princess, Liscia, as well as being capable enough to be placed in charge as the head of all the maids in the castle, but there were issues with her personality. She was a bit of a sadist.

What was more, when it came to cute girls, she always wanted to "buwwy" them. Not "bully," "buwwy." To toy with them a bit psychologically, nothing insidious; she just liked to do things like make them wear risqué outfits to stir up their sense of shame a little. That her number one target now was her own mistress Liscia made it all the more incredible.

Still, a necromancer, is it...? she wondered.

At her core, Serina was a woman who was good at her job. If ghost stories were spreading in a castle which had been left in her care, she wasn't so irresponsible that she could ignore them.

The witching hour, is it...? They say late nights are the enemy of your skin, but... While thinking many thoughts that called for a witty retort, Serina let out a sigh.

Then, in the witching hour...

Lantern in hand, Serina headed towards the cafeteria. She walked with such a bold stride that you would never imagine she was walking around a castle in the middle of the night. Soon, she arrived in front of the cafeteria.

It's a little late to think about it now, but...if this necromancer doesn't appear tonight, I wonder just how many nights I will have to stay up late.

With a little sigh, Serina stepped into the cafeteria. Fortunately for Serina's beautiful face, she soon spotted the person in question.

Near the oven in the kitchen there was a light, and by it, someone was doing something. Serina approached silently, peeking into the pot over that person's shoulder. Inside the pot was an oily burbling liquid and a large number of bones floating in it.

"Heh heh heh...soon...soon it will be complete..."

The person stirred the pot, letting out little laughs like that as they did. It was a sight that would have caused other maids to faint, but the capable Serina was able to identify the bones for exactly what they were.

Those aren't human bones. They're from a giant boar, perhaps? I see several bird and large fish bones mixed in, as well. Also, while it looks unappetizing, that muddy liquid has a tantalizing smell.

Serina resolved herself and tapped the person on the shoulder. "What are you doing there?"

"Wah?!"

She must have startled the person, because the big round body leapt into the air. When they turned around, she was able to see their face clearly.

"M-Madam Serina?! What are you doing here?!"

"I ought to ask you the same, Sir Poncho."

Stirring the pot was the man who had received the name of the food evangelist "Ishizuka" from Souma the other day, and who had been appointed as Minister of State for the Food Crisis, Poncho Ishizuka Panacotta.

"What, pray tell, are you doing in the cafeteria at this hour?" she demanded.

"Th-this is...well..." Poncho flailed his arms about anxiously. He was entirely too suspicious.

Serina was about to press him further, when...

"What're you two doing?"

Caught by surprise, she turned around, and there stood King Souma Kazuya.

"There were ghost stories like that going around?" he said. "Liscia is going to get mad at me again."

After Souma heard about the rumors from Serina, he stood there scratching his head.

"In the end, what was it you were doing, Sire?" she asked.

"Oh, well...we were making exactly what you see here," he said. There were three bowls sitting on the table Souma pointed to. "In the world I come from, it's called ramen."

"Ramen...is it?"

As Souma had said, the three bowls were filled with ramen. What was more, it was the oily kind made with seafood and pork bones. Souma offhandedly thrust his chopsticks into a bowl and began slurping the noodles noisily.

"Yep...the soup is almost perfect. But since we're using gelin udon, it's a little bland."

"There's no helping that. Right now, wheat is precious, yes."

"All the more reason to resolve the food crisis quickly..."

While watching Souma and Poncho talk, Serina tried her own ramen. Wrapping the noodles around her fork like pasta, she put them into her mouth.

When she did, the rich, savory flavor of the seafood and pork bone broth surged forward. It was thick, rich, and had punch, yet the taste of the vegetables had melted into the broth, keeping it from being too rich. What a complex flavor this was. It was greasy, yet her instincts demanded another mouthful.

Souma and Poncho watched Serina, smiling.

"I was wondering if we might be able to use the bones and vegetable scraps we would otherwise throw away to make a soup, you see," Souma said. "I had Poncho studying it. He did it late at night like this, so we wouldn't disturb the cooks."

"Oh, it was a lot of hard work, yes," Poncho said. "It was a dish I had never eaten for myself, after all."

"I see...so this was the truth behind the necromancer, then," Serina said, wiping her mouth with a napkin. "Still, this is delicious. Sir Poncho?"

"Y-yes. What is it?"

"Could I trouble you to teach me how to make this soup?"

"Of course you can, yes."

It seemed that Serina, too, had been charmed by the magic of this oily soup.

After that, a ghost story spread saying that there were two necromancers.

At almost the same time, Serina, whose skin had become oddly smooth (an effect of the collagen?) said, "Sir Poncho, about the bones you use in that soup, why not burn and crush them to powder before putting them in?"

"Th-that makes sense! I'm impressed, Serina! You look at things differently, yes!"

"Tonight...if you have the chance to try it, let me taste some."

"Of course I will, yes."

When the maids saw the two of them speaking intimately like this, their imaginations ran wild, but that is a story for another time.

HOW A REALIST HERO REBUILT THE KINGDOM

CHAPTER 4
A Day Off in Parnam

IT WAS A FEW WEEKS after the first episode of *The King's Brillunch* had been broadcast.

That day, a petition was delivered to Prime Minister Hakuya Kwonmin.

The personnel department had been the ones to organize it, but it included names from the royal guard, the maid force, and every other group within the palace. Marx, who was now the chamberlain, and Ludwin, the head of the royal guard, had put their names on it, as well.

Wondering what it could be, Hakuya quickly perused the contents to find...

"...Ah, I see."

Hakuya agreed with the petition despite himself.

◇　◇　◇

"So, there you have it. I will be insisting you take time off, Sire," Hakuya said.

"There I have what, exactly?" I asked. "I still can't make heads or tails of what's going on."

While I had been working in the governmental affairs office, Hakuya had suddenly come in and said, "Take time off." Then he'd casually dropped the bundle of papers he was holding onto the desk I'd been working at.

"This is a petition I received from the personnel department," he informed me. "According to it, 'When those at the top do not rest, those below them find it difficult to take time off.' You will find Sir Marx and Ludwin's names on here, and I, your humble servant, have added my own name, as well."

Ah...now that he mentions it, I haven't taken time off since being summoned here, have I? I thought.

It wasn't that I wasn't resting at all. Recently, now that I had gotten used to using Living Poltergeists, I'd sometimes left the paperwork to my ability and gone to do things like make dolls in Liscia's room. If I let part of my mind work while part of it rested, I could work 24/7 without feeling the slightest bit exhausted. However, according to Hakuya, it seemed that wasn't the issue here.

"Even if you are resting, you are always in the palace, correct?" he asked me.

"Yeah, just in case anything happens."

"I am telling you that it does not look like you are resting when you do that. And, because it does not look like you are resting, everyone else finds it difficult to rest themselves. Please, understand that."

"That's easy for you to say," I said.

"Normally, I would want you to take a large block of days off to rest," he said, "but..."

"Do we have that kind of time?" I asked.

"We do not."

"I figured."

As a matter of fact, there was a mountain of things that needed doing. Expanding and strengthening the military, meeting with VIPs, creating documents for external use, pushing forward all sorts of reforms...the list could go on forever. Even Aisha's request that I go to the God-Protected Forest as soon as possible was on hold at this point, though I had at least told them how periodic thinning worked. In this country beset by internal and external issues, there was no time we could afford to waste.

"However, if this lowers morale, and as a result work efficiency, I believe your hard work may be self-defeating," Hakuya explained.

"Well, what do you want me to do, then?" I asked.

"Somehow, I will find time to give you a day off," he said. "Why not use it for an outing somewhere?"

An outing, huh...?

"Since I don't get many days off, what if I said I want to use it to lie around in my room?" I asked.

"That request is rejected. I must ask you to take your vacation in a way that your subjects can see you enjoying it."

"You still call that a vacation?"

In my opinion, it's only a day off if you're able to do what you want with it. I gave Hakuya a meaningful glance to try to convey that, but it was met with utter indifference.

"Is this not the perfect opportunity? You can use the time to see the castle town with Princess Liscia."

"You're sending me out on a date?" I asked.

"You two are betrothed, so please go out and show the people how close you are."

"Oh, come on now, this is just turning into part of my official duties," I protested.

Do you want us to do stuff like they do on the Imperial Family Album TV show?

"And what'll we do about guarding me?" I added.

"Is that not what you have Aisha for?" he responded.

"First you tell me to go on a date, now you're telling me to bring another woman along?!"

"Why, it will be like having a flower in each hand," Hakuya commented. "I am most jealous."

"You don't mean that."

Sigh...well, it's definitely some long-awaited time to rest. I guess I can enjoy it with the mindset that I'm going out to have fun with friends. I can go around to all the places in the capital I've been interested in. Let's see...checking out that singing café where Juna works might be nice.

"Okay. Fine. I'll take a day off," I said.

"Your understanding is appreciated."

As Hakuya bowed reverently, I gave him a cold look.

"Now then, where's Liscia at?" I wondered.

I wanted to let her know we had a day off, but she wasn't in her room. Usually, that meant she was somewhere in the palace's training facility. When I had ascended the throne, Liscia's position as royalty had gone up in the air. Now all she was left with was her military rank, so acting as my advisor (which, mind you, was pretty hard work) was the only job she had now. Hadn't she been complaining lately about how she had nothing to do other than join the royal guards for training?

First, I visited the shooting range, then the indoor training grounds. Finally, when I visited the inner garden, I found Liscia in the middle of crossing blades with Aisha.

"Hahhhhhhhhh!"

With a loud cry, Aisha swung a sword that was as tall as she was.

In contrast, Liscia silently read her opponent's attacks, striking with her rapier.

It was hard for an amateur to tell which of them had the advantage. Was it Aisha, who was unleashing an attack that would be crippling if it landed? Or was it Liscia, who dodged that attack, unleashing three sequential thrusts with her rapier?

Was it Aisha, who knocked those thrusts aside using nothing more than the gauntlet she wore? Or was it Liscia, who used the opening that left her with to step on Aisha's great sword, preventing Aisha from lifting it up?

Is this really a practice match? Their swordplay was so intense, I couldn't be sure how serious they were.

"Sonic Wind!"

"Ice Sword Mountain!"

Now they've started using magic and skills!

Aisha's Sonic Wind was apparently a skill that released a "cutting wind" from her great sword. When Liscia dodged, it cut the tree that had been behind her in half with a diagonal slash.

Meanwhile, Liscia's Ice Sword Mountain seemed to be a skill that instantly froze the ground like a skating rink and shot icy spikes out of it, but Aisha cut down all the spikes that looked like they might hit her using her great sword.

What's with this battle to the death?

I had already seen magic in this world. Recently, to practice my ability to manipulate dolls, I had been using a mannequin to go out and hunt monsters, so I had often seen the adventurers it encountered use magic (though it was usually when my mannequin got attacked after being mistaken for a monster).

However, with the magic ordinary adventurers used, the most they could do was shoot flames or ice, or heal minor wounds. I'd never thought magic used by someone experienced would be this incredible.

Aisha was strong, but Liscia seemed quite capable herself. As the two fought, their eyes were filled with life, sparkling even, as if they had discovered a worthy rival.

So, these are warriors, huh... wait, if I let them keep going, they're going to wreck the castle!

"Both of you...cut that out!"

"Yes, sir! Wait, wha—?!" The two of them returned to their senses, landed on the ground, then both slipped on the ice and fell on their rumps in unison.

"A-a date?!" Liscia exclaimed.

"Yeah."

When I explained to her that I had a day off, and that Hakuya had recommended I spend it going on a date with her, Liscia looked dumbstruck.

"Wait...is that something we should be doing because someone else told us to?"

"I feel the same way, but...in Hakuya's mind, royal dates are probably a part of our duties."

"What an inhumane way of thinking," she muttered.

"'Before I am a human being, I am the prime minister.' That's probably something he'd say."

"Ha ha ha!" she giggled. "He would."

"So, before we're human beings, he wants us to be king and queen, basically."

"Sorry. That one I can't laugh at."

The two of us sighed in unison.

Hakuya was sharp, reliable, and he took his work seriously, but he could take loyalty to his post too far sometimes. That wasn't to say he didn't have a soft side. Recently, he had started tutoring Tomoe at her request.

"Well, I'm happy for the day off, and I figure heading out somewhere is okay, right?" I asked.

"I suppose so," she agreed.

"Oh, oh! In that case, please, come to my forest!" Aisha raised her hand, trying to get our attention, but I shook my head.

"I still have a pile of official work to get through. It has to be somewhere we can make a day trip to."

"Ohh...even by horse, it takes three days each way to get to the God-Protected Forest..."

Yeah, that's out of the question.

"You'll have to give up on it this time. But I did teach you how to do periodic thinning, didn't I?"

"Yes. However, there are some among the dark elves who are blindly stubborn. 'What is this nonsense? How can you suggest that we dark elves, protectors of the forest, cut down trees?' they say."

Ah. Yeah, you get types like that in every world.

I respected their desire to protect nature, but when that desire goes too far, it reaches a level of arrogance, and it can actually be a problem. Nature isn't so weak that it needs humans to look down on and "protect" it. If anything...

"That's why I want you to come, Sire," she explained. "To give them a good shouting at."

"I get it. The moment I'm free, I'll go."

It feels like the number of things that I need to do is only going up, but...saying that won't help matters, will it? I thought.

"Please do. If it will help, please, use my body, my life, in any way you see fit," Aisha said, bowing her head.

"Well, then I've got a favor to ask right now..."

"Yes, Sire! You want me to see to your needs?" she asked immediately.

"Why is that the first thing that comes to mind?!"

"Well, I did just finish pledging my body to you."

"Souma..." Liscia said dangerously.

"Of course, I'm not going to ask for that! Liscia, stop giving me that look!"

When Aisha got worked up, it seemed she had a way of letting herself run wild.

"I just wanted to ask you to be my bodyguard while we go into the castle town," I explained.

"Y-you want me to join you two on your date?" she asked.

"Well, if it were just me and Liscia, we'd be in trouble if anything happened," I said. "We may be calling it a date, but really we're just walking around town together, so you don't need to let that bother you."

"It bothers me, though." For some reason, Liscia was pursing her lips.

Maybe she'd wanted to go on a date alone together...? Nah, that couldn't be. I mean, even though we were betrothed, that was just a formality.

"Well, that's how it is," I said. "I'll be counting on you two when the day comes."

"Yes, Sire! Understood!" Aisha said enthusiastically.

"Fine, I get it." In contrast to Aisha's enthusiasm, Liscia seemed dissatisfied somehow.

And so, our day off came.

Liscia, Aisha, and I were walking along a shopping street in the castle town of Parnam. Hakuya had said, "Please go out and show the people how close you are," but apparently that had been a joke, because when the day came, he asked us to be discreet. Well, for the king going down into the castle town, Aisha alone probably wasn't enough security, after all.

So, I wore a uniform from the Royal Officers' Academy in Parnam and passed myself off as a student...which I was, given that I had been in university back home.

By the way, Aisha and I were just wearing school uniforms, but we'd realized people would recognize Liscia, so she had her hair in braids and was wearing vanity glasses, giving her an honors student look as a disguise. With this, if anyone looked, all they would see was three students out on the town for their day off.

"Heya, buddy, you've got some real beauties there with you! If you're a real man, how 'bout buyin' them some of my wares as a present and showin' off how generous you are?" a middle-aged guy at a stall with accessories on display called out to me in a Kansai accent. Apparently, the merchant slang from this world got translated as a fake Kansai accent to my ears.

While turning the man down with a tactful smile, I talked to Liscia. "Liscia, you sure do look good in glasses."

"I-I do...? Thanks."

"Sire! What do you think of me in a school uniform?" Aisha quickly raised her hand. Lately, she'd been downright aggressive about doing that.

"Uh, yeah, it doesn't really suit you," I said.

"Why not?!"

Yeah...the Officers' Academy's uniform was something like a blazer, and that didn't go with her brown skin and silver hair at all. I don't know how to say it, but it felt like I was looking at someone cosplaying as a character from a school anime. Like how there aren't pink-haired girls in real life, and even when girls dye their hair that way it just looks completely unnatural. There was a clash between the realistic and the fantasy here, you could say.

"Personally, I don't think it looks that bad on her, you know?" Liscia said.

"Princess!" Aisha exclaimed.

"Yeah. Well, I'm sure it's probably just because I was judging her by the standards of my own world," I said.

Really, this is a diverse world with many races. I should try to get used to it as quickly as I can.

Rattle, rattle, rattle...

"And, anyway, Souma, it's not Aisha that's bothering me, it's that thing you're dragging behind you," Liscia said.

"Hm? This rolling bag, you mean?"

"That's a bag? It has wheels on it!"

"Yeah," I said. "There are caster wheels underneath, which makes it easy to carry heavy things."

"My word, what a convenient thing to have." Aisha's eyes were wide. Not surprising, since these weren't common in this country yet.

I had special-ordered this one from a craftsman in the castle town. The person who'd made it for me had said he wanted to sell them himself, and I'd allowed it so long as he didn't try to keep a monopoly on the concept. If there turned out to be demand for them, they might not be so unusual a few years from now.

"But Sire, if you want your luggage carried, you need only ask..." Aisha protested.

"We're supposed to be disguised as school friends. It'd be out of place for the guy to be making a girl carry his stuff," I said. Besides, a bunch of my self-defense equipment was in there. I couldn't let go of it. "Also, Aisha, stop calling me Sire. Technically, we're supposed to be incognito here."

"Yes, Sire! But what am I to call you, then...?"

"Just address me normally, no formal title. If you'd like, you can even use my given name, 'Kazuya.'"

"Huh?" both girls exclaimed.

Huh? Why is Liscia confused, too?

"But...Souma, isn't your given name 'Souma'?" Liscia asked.

"Huh? Souma's obviously my family name. Kazuya's my given name."

"But you said you were Souma Kazuya, didn't you?"

"...Ah."

Shoot. In this country, they follow the European style, where the given name comes first. I should have given my name as Kazuya Souma. Oh, I see! That's why everyone's been calling me King Souma. Now that I think of it, it's weird to have "king" attached to a family name. In a hereditary system, you'd have many kings with the same name if you did it that way.

"I-is it too late to correct it?" I asked.

"Probably? Everyone thinks you're Souma, and I think all your external correspondence has been under the name Souma Kazuya."

"Augh! To think I was making such an awful mistake..." I moaned.

"Well, maybe it's not so bad?" Aisha asked. "Why not use one name in public and the other in private? So, on private occasions like today, I'll call you 'Sir Kazuya.'"

With Aisha finding ways to cover for my mistake, I just got more depressed about it. "Now I have Aisha, of all people, having to cover for me."

"Just what do you think of me as, Sir Kazuya?!"

"What are you, you ask...? A disappointing dark elf?"

"That's just mean!" she exclaimed.

"Honestly, cut the stupid banter, you two, and let's get going," Liscia urged while I was still dealing with the teary-eyed Aisha.

Yeah...it's fine to say let's get going, but we haven't chosen a particular destination, I thought. "Is there somewhere you girls want to go?"

"No," Liscia said.

"Wherever you go, I will follow, Sir Kazuya," Aisha added.

"Yeah. At least pretend to think about it, you two."

If they pushed the decision off on me, I wouldn't know what to do. Now that I thought about it, this was my first time walking around the castle town. The last time I had come here, we had just galloped straight through on horseback, after all.

Hmm...in that case, maybe that's all the more reason why I should take a good look around. Even if we just meander around, it'll still be new to me.

"Well, let's just take it easy," I said.

Parnam Central Park was a large park in the center of the royal capital.

Although it was called a park, there wasn't a playground or anything like that. There were just trees, shrubs, and flowers that had been planted there, but the grounds were three times the size of Tokyo Dome. In the center of the park was an impressively large fountain with a Jewel Voice Broadcast receiver. When there was a broadcast happening, it could project a massive image that was large enough to be seen from a hundred meters away. There was amphitheater-style seating around the fountain, and during the last Jewel Voice Broadcast, a crowd numbering in the tens of thousands had apparently gathered there.

You know, it might be interesting to hold a live concert here, I thought. *As soon as Juna's broadcast program using the Jewel Voice Broadcast gets up and going, I'd really like to plan something like that. Someday, this fountain plaza might become a stage that singers from across Elfrieden aspire to stand on, like the Budokan or Hibiya Outdoor Theater.*

Well, that's enough of my idle fantasizing. Anyway, we had come to Central Park.

"This is a lovely place full of natural beauty," Aisha said.

"Even though it's in the middle of the city, the air is so clear," Liscia commented. "Mmm."

Aisha looked around full of curiosity while Liscia stretched widely.

"Huh? But I don't remember the air being this clear before..." she murmured.

"Well, yeah, I worked hard to arrange that," I said.

"You arranged it? Did you do something to this park?"

Liscia seemed puzzled, so I puffed out my chest and explained. "Not just to the park. I prepared infrastructure all over the underground of Parnam, and I could go further and say I prepared the laws, as well. If you compare things to a few months ago, I think you'll find environmental hygiene has improved considerably."

To be blunt, before my preparations, the environmental hygiene in this country had been on the same level as Middle Ages Europe...which is to say, it'd been disgusting.

Horse dung had been left lying out in the streets as if that were perfectly normal, and people had just poured their domestic sewage into ditches along the roadside. I'd heard it had smelled absolutely foul in summertime.

Because the concept of hygiene hadn't existed, these problems had just been left alone. But when horse dung dries out, it turns into dust which is lifted into the air. When that gets into people's lungs, it causes a variety of respiratory diseases.

That was why the first thing I had done was set up an aqueduct and sewer system.

"An aqueduct and sewer system," Liscia gasped. "When did you have the time to make those?!"

"Actually, there wasn't that much effort involved," I shrugged. "There were underground passages running all over Parnam to begin with, you see. All I had to do was run water from the river through them."

"Wait, those were escape tunnels for the royal family!" she cried in outrage.

As Liscia had said, in the event that the capital came under attack and the fall of the royal family became unavoidable, those tunnels had been meant for the royal family to escape through. Even if the enemy discovered them, they had been built like a maze to hinder pursuit, and they covered the entirety of Parnam. What was more, they had been built in three layers. All of that had been very convenient for repurposing them as an aqueduct and sewer system.

First, water from the river that ran near Parnam had been drawn into the first layer, which served as an underground aqueduct. That water was now being used in wells and public bath houses that once relied on underground water. The third layer was used as a sewer, ultimately emptying out into sedimentation ponds outside the capital where the sewage would be filtered before being returned to the river once more. The system had been designed so that the water that made the full trip around the city in the first layer would ultimately drain into the third layer. We had filled in the second layer and set things up in a way that bad smells from the third layer wouldn't rise into the first.

"If you've turned them into an aqueduct and sewer system, what do you plan to do if there's an emergency?!" Liscia demanded.

"If we get to the point where the royal family needs to flee the capital, the country's already finished, isn't it?" I asked. "If it were up to me, I'd probably surrender at the point when the enemy was closing in on the capital."

"That easily?" she exclaimed.

"Liscia, so long as a king has the people on his side, he's safe."

This was another lesson from Machiavelli. According to him, "the best possible fortress is not to be hated by the people."

A king has two types of enemies. Traitors within, and foreign enemies without.

If you have the support of the people, traitors can't gather supporters or incite the people into rebellion, so they'll just have to give up. On the other hand, if you're hated by the people, there will be no shortage of foreigners willing to assist them in your eventual downfall, so Machiavelli says.

"Even if I lose my title, so long as the people are still there, there's a chance for revival," I said. "On the other hand, if the king is the only one to survive, without any people left to support him, he'll just be eaten up by another foe himself."

"It's a hard world, huh," Liscia murmured.

"That's reality. Well, anyway, the aqueduct and sewer systems were easy enough to make, but when it came to the sedimentation ponds...ah, let's go sit over in the shade."

There wasn't much point standing around while we talked, so we went over to sit in the shade provided by some trees in the park.

Not long after we sat down, Aisha leaned against a tree and began to nod off. She probably couldn't keep up with the complicated subject matter. I had to question whether it was okay for someone who was supposed to be my bodyguard to be doing that, but, well, knowing Aisha, she could probably protect me in her sleep. I kept talking.

"I couldn't let raw sewage drain into the river. Domestic sewage often has pathogenic bacteria and parasites in it, you see. To protect against those, we need to let the water sit in a place where it can filter through sand and pebbles...in other words, a sedimentation pond."

"P-pathogenic bacteria?" Liscia cocked her head to the side. It seemed that those were unfamiliar words for people in this world.

Well, there was probably no need to get too sensitive about it just yet. The people of this country had no concept of pollution. That was because, with this country's standards of living and level of technology, even if they dumped untreated sewage into the river, it wouldn't make much of a difference.

However, as the country grew and its technology advanced, there were sure to be problems with pollution. The sooner I tackled that problem, the better. The Japanese people had learned about pollution by experiencing Minamata Disease, Itai-itai Disease, and Yokkaichi Asthma. There was no need for the people of this country to experience anything like that.

"So, did something happen with these sedimentation ponds?" she asked.

"Right, so I used the Forbidden Army to dig holes for the sedimentation ponds..."

"What are you making Sir Ludwin and his men do?" she exclaimed.

Well, if I'd hired workers, that would have been expensive, and I'd wanted to teach the soldiers of the Forbidden Army "combat engineering" skills. Digging holes, filling them up, reinforcing them. It was the perfect practice for digging trenches. It seemed battles in this world were still fought on the open field, so a group that could use trench warfare tactics like in World War I would stand head and shoulders above the rest.

Anyway, I digress.

"While I was having them dig, we came across a large pile of monster bones."

"Bones?" she asked.

"Yeah, bones. Dragon bones, giant bones, all kinds of bones."

It's like a monster graveyard, one of the soldiers doing the digging had said.

There had been a large quantity of clearly non-human bones just scattered around haphazardly: dragons, giants, gargoyles, and more.

By the way, of the creatures I just listed, dragons were the only ones that weren't monsters.

Dragons had a degree of magical power that was incomparably higher than wyverns. They were also intelligent, and, apparently, they could even take on human form. They had a pact of mutual non-aggression with humans and had built their own country in the Star Dragon Mountain Range. The chief of the Star Dragon Mountain Range, Mother Dragon, was strong even by dragon standards. She was said to be an incredibly beautiful specimen and was even worshiped by some people. Basically, dragons were terrifying god-beasts, but they were also another race, just like humans and dragonewts were.

Anyway, according to the scholars who investigated those bones, they were in a geological stratum from thousands of years ago.

"So, there was a dungeon there?" Liscia tilted her head quizzically, but I shook my head.

"I said they were in a certain geological stratum, didn't I? Thousands of years ago, that place would have been the surface."

"The surface...? No, you can't mean...sometimes monsters do come out from a dungeon but never on so large a scale. Outside of the Demon Lord's Domain, monsters never swarm over the surface like...ah!" Liscia gasped, shaking her head as if trying to clear it of the thought that just occurred to her. "Hold on! The Demon World only appeared for the first time ten years ago!"

"In other words, this means, even before that, there was an era when monsters roamed the surface," I said. "If you think about it, there are dungeons all over this continent with monsters living inside them. For some reason, the monsters that lived on this continent thousands of years ago vanished, and some small portion of them survived by secluding themselves in dungeons. That's the idea the scholars came up with."

This was like discovering dinosaurs still living in some unexplored region of the world. Or like seeing a pandemic of a virus thought to be eradicated. Whether that hypothesis was right or not remained to be seen.

"Well, what then?! The monsters and demons that destroyed the Northern Countries didn't 'come here,' they 'returned,' is that it?!"

"That, I don't know," I said. "It's dangerous to jump to that conclusion at this stage."

What were we trying to fight against? Who were our enemies? It was a question where choosing an easy answer wasn't going to cut it.

"Also, there's one more thing bothering me..." I went on.

"There's more?!"

"Even setting aside the issue of the bones, I needed to get that sedimentation pool made. So, I had the scholars keep archaeological records of the bones that were dug up. The thing is, a full skeleton's worth of the largest and best-preserved dragon bones has gone missing. Even though I know it was disassembled for display and sent to be stored at the Royal Parnam Museum..."

"So, it was stolen, then?" Liscia asked.

"That would be good news... well, no, not *good* news, but still. With a full, twenty-meter-tall dragon skeleton, even if you disassemble it, it's not going to be easy to transport. Despite that, there's no sign that it was taken out of Parnam. And yet, the bones are still missing now. It's as if the full set suddenly started to move, took wing, and flew away."

"Ah! No, it couldn't be! A skull dragon?!" she cried.

"That's what the scholars suspect."

A skull dragon. Apparently, there were monsters like that.

They say a raging dragon can level a kingdom. Dragons have vast stores of magical powers within their bodies, and those reserves remain in their bodies after death. Normally, the magic power gradually drains out, but when a dragon dies with regrets (or, rather, when its body is left in a bad environment for too long), on rare occasions, it may turn into a skull dragon.

These skull dragons are designated by the country as Special A-Class harmful creatures. Winged ones can fly, even though they have no membranes on their wings, and they spread a miasma that brings death to all living things. They can also use the Dragon Breath technique they had when they were alive, so when one appears, it is a living (unliving?) disaster which requires the full mobilization of a country's military to defeat. That alone was reason for smaller countries to go to the Star Dragon Mountain Range, where the dragons live, to seek assistance.

However, this time, things were different.

"If that were it, Parnam would already be enveloped in miasma," I said. "The scholars performed a magical test to make sure there was no risk of that happening, after all. There shouldn't have been any magic left in that fossil."

"I see... that's good."

"Still, that's why I don't get it. Where did those dragon bones vanish to?"

It had already been close to a month since the dragon bones vanished. Despite that, there was still no sign of them, so did that mean they had been carried outside the walls somehow, after all? If so, for what purpose? There was apparently little use for the bones once the magic left them. They had lost their value as a magic catalyst. The best that could be done with them was to put them in a museum (of course, I would need permission from the Star Dragon Mountain Range for that) and use them as a tourist attraction.

I didn't get it. That was why it bothered me.

I laid down on my side. Liscia frowned at me, but I didn't care.

"You're getting your clothes dirty, you realize?" she commented.

"They can be washed. Besides, considering my position, I can get someone else to wash them for me."

"A king can't let himself get dirty all over," she said.

"Yeah, I'm sure dignity is important and all, but...it's a pain in the butt."

"As one of the people who forced this on you, it's not my place to say it, but give up and accept it."

"Right, right. Whew, having time where I'm off completely sure is nice." I stretched my arms and legs wide. How relaxing it was to not have a single part of my spirit working.

Now that I thought about it, I had been working constantly since coming to this world. There were things to do, things I ought to do, things I had no choice but to do, piles and piles of them, and so I had been using my head all the time. Having this sort of time where I didn't need to think about anything was the best.

"I wish I could just melt away and return to the soil," I murmured.

Liscia was silent. After seeing me like that, she seemed to think for a moment, then hesitantly said, "Do you want...to rest your head in my lap?"

◇　◇　◇

I sat with my knees bent, resting Souma's head on my thighs.

When someone rests their head in your lap, they can either do it with their body lying horizontally or vertically from your perspective. This was the vertical variety.

When I peeked down at him, my face was reflected upside-down in his eyes. Souma's head was lying between my two thighs, and it tickled a little.

"Th-this is...kind of embarrassing, you know." Souma's face was a deep shade of red.

I was sure mine was, too.

"Who do you think this is most embarrassing for?" I asked him. "The person giving the lap pillow, or the person using it?"

"I don't know... maybe it's for the people watching, don't you think?" he said.

"Ha ha ha! You could be right."

If Aisha hadn't been asleep, what expression would she have had?

When she saw us looking like a couple who were engaged, would her face have turned red? Or would she have said, "Princess, I'll not allow you to do that! If anyone is to be his pillow, it will be me!" or something oblique like that?

When I saw the fondness that girl showed Souma, sometimes I felt there was something more than just loyalty there...

Somehow, I suspected that out of those two options, it would have been the latter of the two.

"Do you think we look like we're engaged?" I asked.

"Well, in name only," he said.

"In name only..."

Any time it came up, Souma always told those close to him that our engagement was just temporary, and he was only holding on to the crown for a little while. Once the kingdom was reasonably stable, he probably planned to abdicate the throne to me. I felt like that was the reason he always carefully explained the reforms he was carrying out to me. I think I understood enough of who Souma was as a person to figure out his intentions there.

Souma didn't desire excessive wealth or fame. He just wanted to live in peace and quiet. For Souma, being a king bound by *noblesse oblige* was the exact opposite of his calling in life. Even though my father had made the decision, I felt awful that we had pushed this burden onto him.

But right now, this kingdom was changing to center around Souma.

This country, which had been thought of by the surrounding nations as a moldy old kingdom that never changed, was now changing. It was thanks to Souma that we had been able to cope with the deepening food crisis. As for Hakuya, Poncho, and the others, they had only volunteered to serve because Souma was there. Even if the throne were abdicated to me, could I keep them all tied down here?

Besides that, more than anything, I myself wanted Souma to stay in the kingdom. So...

"Souma...does it bother you to have me as your fiancée?" Those words naturally came to my lips.

Souma's eyes went wide, and he turned his bright red face to the side. "It's not fair for you to put it like that."

"O-oh, yeah?" I stammered.

"Then are *you* fine with it, Liscia? Having me as your fiancé?"

"I don't mind." I was a little surprised myself that I was able to say it so clearly. Though, after I did, I felt just a little embarrassed. "You know, I think you're better suited to rule this country than I am, Souma."

"Even if I'm suited for it...are you going to get engaged to someone you don't love?"

"Isn't that what it means to be royalty?" I asked.

"I'm not royalty. Besides, I'd rather marry for love."

"Then...do you hate me, Souma? Can you say for sure that you'll never fall in love with me?" I asked.

"Urgh... I told you, it's not fair when you say stuff like that. The thing about men is, if a girl shows even the slightest hint of liking them, they'll fall for her. That's the sort of creatures we are. If a beauty like you says that to me, Liscia...there's no way I wouldn't start to feel conscious of you."

Souma had said something that sounded like an excuse. He was surprisingly calm and realistic in his duties, so it was funny to see him flustered in a situation like this.

I giggled. "You can make the country move, but you're hopeless when it comes to this."

"I lack the experience. In so many ways."

"I spend all my time in my studies and military duties, so I haven't had much experience either, you know?" I said.

"Don't act like it's the same for guys and girls. Our base specs when it comes to love are completely different."

While we were talking about that, a hesitant voice spoke up. "Um…"

When I turned around, Aisha had woken up at some point, and she was looking at us with a wry smile that looked like it had been concentrated to three times the usual intensity.

"How much longer do I need to pretend I'm asleep for?" she asked.

"…"

We both leapt into the air.

◇　◇　◇

After leaving the park, we walked around the castle town some more. It was noon and we were getting hungry, so the three of us decided to head to the singing café where Juna worked.

As we walked down a cobblestone path, Liscia said, "So, about what we were talking about earlier…you mentioned changing the laws, as well. What was that about?"

"Oh. What I did was convert the smaller roads into pedestrian paradises and nationalize garbage disposal."

"I'm sorry. I have no idea what that means."

Well, no, I suppose she wouldn't. They both tied back into the hygiene and sanitation problem, though.

"Well, first, let me explain the pedestrian paradise thing. This one's simple. I prohibited carriages from using anything but the largest of thoroughfares. Carriages that carry merchandise receive a special exemption, but only for a few hours in the morning. We've been walking in the middle of the street all this time, and nobody's run us over yet, right?"

"Now that you mention it..." Liscia looked all around, not spotting a single horse.

"This provides an easy reduction in the number of horse accidents, creating a safe environment for people to shop, which helps to stimulate the economy, but the main goal was to clean up all the horse dung."

"Horse dung?" Liscia repeated.

"When a horse is on the move, you generally just leave its droppings behind, right? Well, that dung dries out, gets picked up by the wind, and it harms the lungs of those who inhale it. The more unsanitary a place was to begin with, the more likely horse dung is to be left alone. If we limit the horses to the main roads, it makes collecting their droppings easy. This ought to bring down the number of people contracting pneumonia considerably."

"Huh?! That's all it takes?!" Liscia exclaimed.

"Yeah," I said. "'That's all it would have taken to save lives."

"Urkh..."

It may have been a harsh way to say it, but I couldn't have her writing off something that would mean the difference between life and death for people with a "that's all it takes."

"Well, in some ways, I can't blame you," I said. "The concept of hygiene doesn't exist yet in this country. In fact, only two of the medical professionals I've met with understood it."

I think I've mentioned before that because this country had magic, its technology was sort of all over the place. Well, that was true in the field of medicine, as well.

As you might expect from a fantasy world, this place had what was called recovery magic. By converting magic into certain wavelengths within the body, it heightened the body's natural healing ability. It was effective in treating external injuries such as scratches, cuts, and bruises. Really impressive practitioners could even reattach an arm that had just been severed.

If this was all someone saw of it, it would seem like a miracle.

On the other hand, recovery magic couldn't treat viruses and infections that the body's natural ability to recover couldn't treat on its own. All that people had to lessen those symptoms were medicine men and women who could brew herbal remedies. Furthermore, for the elderly, whose natural healing ability had declined, magic wasn't effective in treating external injuries, either.

Once you know how something works, it might be easy to think, "Oh, that's simple," but most people in this country didn't even know about microbes, let alone viruses. When people try to find answers to questions they don't have the necessary knowledge to answer, they're prone to finding answers that fall within what's common sense to them.

"Healing magic doesn't work," would equate to, "Even miracles can't cure it," and then turn into, "It's a devil's curse."

People put together these sorts of formulas in their heads, then end up using bizarre occult goods in their attempts to treat the illness.

"If you buy this pot, you'll never get sick," worked as a sales pitch in this world, so it was nothing to laugh at. If you're going to buy something like that, you might as well wrap a leek around your neck before you go to sleep instead.

However, there were buds of hope in the two doctors I just mentioned. If I could have those two lead a reformation of medical practice in this country...

"Hey, Souma, what are you mumbling to yourself for?" Liscia's voice snapped me back to reality.

"Sorry," I said. "I got to thinking for a moment there."

"Geez...okay, so what did you mean when you said you nationalized garbage disposal?"

"Exactly what it sounds like," I said. "Liscia, do you know how trash is generally disposed of in this country?"

"Garbage is sorted into 'burnable' and 'non-burnable,' then burned or buried accordingly, right?"

"Wow, you were able to answer that pretty easily," I said.

"Did you think I was ignorant of the peoples' lives just because I'm royalty? Don't insult me. I lived in the dorms when I went to the military academy, I'll have you know," she said indignantly.

I see. So, she's not as ignorant of the world as I thought...

"But you're still wrong."

"Huh?" she asked.

"I said 'generally,' didn't I? Your answer is still only representative of upper-class thinking. It's a world away from the common way of thinking."

"W-well, what is the common way of thinking about it, then?" she asked.

"Aisha, how do your people dispose of garbage in the God-Protected Forest?" I queried.

"Hm? Garbage?" Aisha's eyes went a little wide when I suddenly turned the conversation to her, but she was able to come up with an answer right away. "Let me think... we burn it."

"Is that all?" I asked.

"That is all."

"That can't be right! What do you do about the things that won't burn?!" Liscia objected, but Aisha just stared blankly back at her.

"Why would you even throw out things that aren't burnable to begin with?" Aisha asked.

"Of course you would! What else would you do with broken tools?" Liscia demanded.

"We fix them and keep using them."

"Huh?"

"We use kitchen waste as fertilizer. With pottery that is too broken to repair, we break it into fine pieces and scatter it over the ground. If metal tools break, we fix them so they can be used again. If they can't be fixed, we sell them to a used metal dealer." (A type of merchant who collects scrap metal.) "The only things we throw out are splintered wood and damaged leather armor, but...we burn those in our campfires."

This time, it was Liscia's turn for wide-eyed surprise. I couldn't help but laugh a little at their exchange.

"Ha ha! Aisha's got it right this time."

"Soumaaaa..." Liscia moaned.

"Don't let it get you down so much," I said. "For the upper classes who must keep up appearances, and for the military whose equipment can mean the difference between life and death, it's probably best for them if the things they have are practically brand new. However, for ordinary households, that isn't the case. Now, Aisha's example takes it to an extreme, but people in the capital handle things in a similar fashion. The main difference would be that they burn their kitchen waste, too, I guess? Also, for oversized trash, like wooden furniture, they customarily gather it all in the main plaza once a year for burning, don't they? So, they're the same in that they only have burnable trash."

In this world, there was nothing like plastic or styrofoam that needed special treatment before it could be reused. Most tools were made of iron, stone, soil (which included glass and ceramic), or wood. They could reuse iron by melting it down, and if they just left stone lying around, it would blend in with the natural scenery around it. The one exception was artificial substances that were created by mages using magic (magic substances), but these were valuable in and of themselves, so they were almost never thrown away.

As for things made of metal, they could be expensive, too, so the common people did everything within their power to repair them. Beating iron back into shape was easy, after all. When there was really nothing they could do, and it seemed cheaper to just buy a new one, they would sell it to a used metal dealer for small change. Used metal dealers collected this metal and melted it down, recasting it into other metal products.

However, this was being done by individuals, so they didn't have good facilities for it or the ability to devote a large amount of time, so they could only produce low-quality metal as a result. All they did was melt it down and then let it harden, so impurities got mixed in in the process. As a result, low-quality metal ended up circulating in the country.

This country was resource-poor. If low-quality metal was all that could be obtained locally, people would be forced to import high-quality metal from other countries. I wanted to limit that spending as much as possible. However, if I tried to tell the used metal dealers, who were acting as individuals, to reuse the metal in high-quality impurity-free metal, it wasn't going to happen.

"So, that's why I've nationalized garbage disposal. Basically, I had the country take over handling it. Even if it's difficult for an individual to do, when the state does it, we can afford to spend money on it, arrange for specialized facilities, and we can take the time to do it right, too. We can pull every last nail out of the wooden boards people throw out, then reuse the iron."

"That's amazing and all, but what about the used metal dealers? Aren't you stealing their jobs?"

"Oh, that's fine," I said. "For that work, I'm retaining the used metal dealers as civil servants."

They were low-wage workers, anyway. They paid a small amount to buy up scrap metal, then melted it all down to sell to the trade guilds wholesale. However, since they could only produce low-quality metal, their prices got haggled down to almost nothing, and they saw very little profit for themselves. As a matter of fact, used metal dealers were at the very bottom of this world's hierarchy. Because they dealt in garbage, people looked down on them.

"However, now that it's a public-sector undertaking, the cost of buying the metal will be footed by the country," I said. "The items to be melted down can be recast as high-quality metal in good facilities provided by the country, and the country will negotiate with the trade guilds, so there's no need to worry about their prices being haggled down to nothing. What's more, they will be paid a monthly salary that's equal to the average monthly income in this country. If you compare that to what they were making before, it's probably a ten-fold increase, don't you think?"

"Well...I can't see them complaining about that," Liscia admitted.

As a matter of fact, we hadn't received a single complaint. Quite the contrary: when the minister of state who had been given the garbage disposal portfolio had gone to survey the reprocessing facility, he had been greeted with tearful thanks by all the workers.

"But, if you aren't careful, couldn't that be more expensive than importing it from another country?" Liscia asked.

In response to Liscia's point, I nodded and said, "Yeah, kinda."

Elaborating, I added: "At this stage, we're probably a little worse off doing it this way. However, money spent inside the country has a completely different meaning from money spent outside the country. If we spend money outside the country, that's an outflow of capital, but if we spend it inside the country, it stimulates our own economy."

"Th-the economy again, huh..." For Liscia with her military background, it seemed she wasn't as strong with this sort of topic. The military had its own bureaucracy, so officers probably only needed to think about maintaining supply lines.

"Okay then, I'll give you the military angle," I said. "Let's talk diplomacy. If we can conserve the resources in our country, other countries can't use the resources we import from them as a card in their diplomacy. For instance, what would we do if the Principality of Amidonia, which has been eagerly eyeing our country, were to halt their export of iron to us?"

"We'd be in trouble," Liscia said. "There's no telling what demands they might present us with to reopen trade."

"That's right. I did it with an eye to preventing that sort of situation, too."

I'm not going to name names, but in my world, there had been a country which used the rare resources they produced as a diplomatic tool to pressure other nations. Although, once a certain island country got serious, they found new import routes from other resource-rich countries, and they developed alternative technologies, which caused the other country's rare resources to plummet in value.

"If we can be frugal with our resources, that will limit the damage if another country halts its exports to us, and if we store the excess we have in peacetime, we can be prepared for that if it comes to it," I explained.

"I see," Liscia said. "So even if it puts us in the red, there's still meaning in nationalizing it."

Liscia was a quick learner when it came to military and diplomatic matters. She was probably the type whose ability or inability to learn a subject was a faithful reflection of her personal preferences.

Incidentally, while we were talking about this stuff, Aisha announced, "Forget about that, I want to eat!"

She looked ready to cry, like a dog that had been forced to wait for a long time.

Lorelei, the singing café, stood on a sunny street corner. This was the place where Juna worked.

When I had heard the words "singing café," I'd imagined a place with a karaoke machine where the customers could sing freely, but the singing cafés in this country were places to enjoy your afternoon tea while listening to the loreleis sing. In the evenings, they stayed open and turned into jazz bars. Were there places like this back in Japan, too?

"You're going to show your face in there, right?" Liscia asked. "Let's hurry up and go in."

"I'm hungry..." Aisha moaned.

With both of them urging me onward, we went through the door and into Lorelei.

From the moment we entered the café, I could hear Juna singing. When I heard that voice, I went weak in the knees.

Oh, right. I did teach her this song, didn't I? I realized.

That was Juna for you: she had mastered singing the English lyrics that even I wasn't so good at.

"Oh, what a wonderful singing voice. I really must hand it to Madam Juna," Liscia said.

"I don't know what the words mean, but it's a nice tune," Aisha added.

Aisha and Liscia both seemed deeply impressed. Well, of course they were. It was a good song.

I had promised to teach Juna the songs of my world, but once I thought about it, I only knew old songs I'd learned because of Grandpa's influence, and songs that had shown up in anime and tokusatsu, because I was into those. I was hesitant to go teaching her anime songs right off the bat, so I'd chosen this song, which was like an anime song, but not: Neil Sedaka's "Better Days Are Coming."

You might know it better as the song Mami Ayukawa covered as "Z - Toki wo Koete," the opening to the mecha anime *Mobile Suit Zeta Gundam*. Now, this is only my personal opinion, but I thought for ordinary music, Hiroko Yakushimaru would suit Juna's voice well, and for anime music, Hiroko Moriguchi's songs would work. I wanted to hear "Tantei Monogatari" and "Mizu no Hoshi ni Ai wo Komete" with her voice.

The café had a relaxing, retro-modern style to it. Sitting ourselves down at one of the tables, we listened to Juna sing for a while. A few minutes later, Juna finished her song and came over to us.

"Why, Your—" she began.

"Hello, Juna," I said quickly. "You may not remember me, but I am Kazuya, the successor to a crêpe fabric merchant from Echigo!"

To cut Juna off, I started talking a mile a minute. Being the smart, talented woman that she was, Juna recognized what was going on just from that. "Oh, yes, Kazuya. Right. It's been so long. How is your father these days?"

"Why, he's too energetic for his own good. Just recently, Mother found out he was having an affair. Now *that* was trouble."

"I see. Kazuya, do be careful about how you handle women yourself," she said, going along with my story.

I couldn't very well have her bowing and calling me "Your Majesty" in a place like this with so many people watching. After all, I was supposed to be in disguise. Still, I had to be impressed with her ability to instantly ad-lib a response to my random nonsense. I definitely wanted her at the castle.

"I'll pay you five times what they pay you here, so will you come be my personal secretary?" I asked her.

"I appreciate the offer, but I think this job where I can let the customers enjoy my songs is my calling, so I'll have to decline." She let me down lightly.

Yep. Even the way she rejects me has class.

"That's a shame. But, they do say that rather than putting wild flowers on display in your room, the flowers are more beautiful left blossoming in the fields."

"Oh, but if you love and adore them, not just put them on display, flowers will shine even in a vase," she retorted.

"I see. I must endeavor to be worthy of loving and adoring them, then."

"Yes, worthy enough to convince the flowers they want you to take them."

"Ha ha ha ha ha."

"Hee hee hee hee hee."

Juna and I laughed together.

As she watched us, Liscia seemed slightly taken aback. "Somehow, when you two talk, it's like you're each probing the other's intentions."

Or so she thought. You're wrong, Liscia, I said silently. Most likely, this was Fig. 1: A younger brother who wants to act more mature than he is being gently chided by his big sister for it.

I'll bet that's how it was. Even though we were practically the same age.

◇　◇　◇

"*Slurrrrrp...*gelin udon truly is delicious, isn't it?" Aisha said happily.

We had decided to stay at Lorelei and have lunch there.

Polishing off her gelin udon as fast as you would a bowl of wanko soba, Aisha shouted "Seconds, please!" while thrusting the bowl out towards our waiter.

A café isn't the place to be eating like that, you know... I thought.

"Still, gelin udon at a café...?" I wondered.

"Did you not like it?"

Juna looked worried, so I shook my head, saying, "Oh, no. I just thought it was odd to be slurping udon in a classy place like this."

"Ever since that broadcast, there have been a lot of people wanting to try it," she explained. "Besides, we aren't through the food crisis yet, so we're grateful to have these sorts of inexpensive ingredients we can use."

"I'm working on it, but...I'm not doing well enough. I'm sorry," I said.

"No, Your... Kazuya, I think you're doing well."

When Juna gave me that gentle smile, it made me feel all warm and fuzzy inside.

Kick! Kick!

Okay, Liscia, stop kicking my shins under the table, please.

"Don't you think Souma treats Juna differently from how he treats everyone else?" Liscia asked.

"Ahh, *slurp*...I had...*slurp*...noticed that, too," Aisha agreed.

"Hey, I can't help it," I protested. "I get nervous when I'm talking to a beautiful, older girl. Also, Aisha, eat or talk. Pick one."

"*Slurp.*"

What, you're choosing to eat? I could have poked fun at her, but that comedy routine was too overdone, so I just let it go.

"This after he told me I was beautiful, too," Liscia said.

"Liscia, I think you're beautiful in a different way than Juna is, you know?" I said.

"Wh-why were you able to hear me?!" she exclaimed.

Uh, if you don't want to be heard, lower your volume a little, would you?

Part of it was that I was strangely conscious of her because she'd let me use her lap as a pillow.

"Y-you could have pretended not to hear," she stammered.

"Like I could let it go by," I retorted. "I'm a healthy young man, so don't say things that are going to make me so conscious of you so often."

"Oh, my, your faces are all red. You're both so innocent." Juna watched us bickering with a smile.

Next to us, Aisha slurped her udon like she was pouting. "*Slurp*...why does he notice the princess's affections...*slurp*...but mine get ignored...? *Slurp.* Ah, I'll have another bowl, please."

"It may not be my place to say it...but perhaps he doesn't take you seriously because you act like this?" Juna suggested.

"Madam Juna?! What have I done wrong?!" Aisha exclaimed.

"That appetite of yours. When I first saw you in the castle, you looked like a brave and dignified woman who was willing to address the king directly, but recently you're just a disappointment who's eating all the time."

"Wh-whaaaaat?!" Aisha looked at us with eyes that seemed to plead, "Tell me she's lying, Your Majesty, Princess."

Liscia and I smiled, then both raised our arms in front of us in an X.

After all, I agreed with Juna 100%.

"Poncho's clearly been stealing everyone's attention from her," Liscia said.

"Where did that dignified Aisha go, I wonder?" Juna asked.

"Wahhh! It's the forest's fault for not having so many different types of food!" Aisha wailed.

"Besides, what do you think you're doing trying to seduce a guy who's already betrothed...?" I added.

"Huh?" All three stared at me blankly.

Did I say something strange?

"Um...Souma? In this country, polygamy is tolerated, so long as you have the wealth to support multiple wives, you realize it's okay...?" Liscia said.

Juna nodded. "It works the other way around, too. Polyandrous arrangements are possible for powerful women, as well. It's uncommon, though."

"If men were limited to one wife, the house could die out if something went wrong, after all," Aisha agreed.

Liscia, Juna, and Aisha told me this with straight faces.

Are they serious...? Ah, no, I guess they probably are serious.

This world's society still hadn't gotten out of the Dark Ages. They didn't have a stable birth rate, and their hygiene and medical knowledge were underdeveloped. On top of that, they were living in troubled times, so there were probably few people living to the average life expectancy. Furthermore, in a Middle Ages-type society, where the "house" is an important concept, the more potential heirs the better, provided you had the wealth to support them. That was probably the reason why they allowed polygamy. Even I could understand that.

"But Liscia's mother is the only queen I've met," I objected.

If it was a polygamous system, wouldn't Liscia's father, the king, have had more wives? I mean, I was getting hassled by Hakuya to hurry up and produce an heir, too.

"Oh, actually, my mother was the one who held the royal authority," Liscia explained. "She's the daughter of the man who was king before my father, you see."

"Hold on, that king married into the family?!" I burst out.

"Yes. After they married, she left ruling the country to him, though. That's why my father could never have slighted my mother by taking another woman as his queen. I can't say for sure that he doesn't have any bastards, though."

"Huh? Was it okay for me to take the throne when he abdicated it to me?" I wondered.

"There's no issue. Father was the one who stood out, but he couldn't have abdicated without Mother's consent."

In other words, that abdication hadn't been an arbitrary decision by the king, but something he'd had the queen's understanding for as well.

"Besides, I was the only one with the right of succession, and I would have had to take a husband anyway, so it's not that big a difference, really," Liscia added. "It's just a matter of whether I hold the royal authority or my partner does."

"Well, couldn't you have been the ruler then, instead, Liscia?" I asked.

"You'd have needed to seek my approval for every one of your reforms, you know? Wouldn't that be a pain?"

"Well...yes."

Now, Liscia wasn't pigheaded in any way, but if I had needed her approval for every little thing, my reforms would have been going much slower. Besides, if the person with ultimate deciding power and the person driving the reformation were separate people, there would be no guarantee that the members of a counter-reformation faction wouldn't try to get between the two and stir up unneeded trouble.

"Your father made a brave decision by transferring everything to me at once, huh?" I said.

"You're right. I'm sincerely able to see how impressive that was now."

Though, it did mean the burden had been shifted to us.

We both sighed in unison.

"So, if you wanted it, Souma, a polygamous relationship is... possible," Liscia said.

"You'd be okay with that, Liscia?" I asked.

"I wouldn't be happy about it, but if it keeps you on the throne..."

"That's being way too understanding," I murmured.

"I'll tolerate up to eight, myself included."

"That's a lot! I couldn't take responsibility for that many!"

Now, when she told me I could have a harem, it's not like the idea wasn't appealing, but...I dunno, I could only imagine it being a lot of work. I wasn't the type who could bear to disagree strongly with women, and I could tell that the more of them there were, the more constrained I'd feel.

"By the way, why did you choose that number?" I asked.

"I can have you all to myself for one day a week," she said.

The weeks in this world were eight days. Incidentally, there were four weeks in a month, making each of them thirty-two days long. There were twelve months in a year, so this world had a three hundred and eighty-four-day year.

Wait, that's why?! I realized, registering what she had said.

When she said that, Juna and Aisha started whispering about something.

"If there were eight of us, do you think we would only get it once a week?"

"It doesn't have to be that way, I'd think? If you and another wife each invited the other on your days…"

"I see. It's not necessarily just once a week! You're brilliant, Madam Juna."

"But wouldn't you want to have him to yourself?"

"Ooh, there's a conundrum."

No, no, Aisha, Juna, why are you getting so into talking about this?!

Having them at the same time… I can't say I wouldn't be into that, but I'd have to become king for that. I was torn between my realistic personality, which wanted to avoid the hard work involved if I took the throne, and my desire to pursue that masculine ideal.

Just then, as I was starting to feel incredibly awkward.

"No, you can't do that! Absolutely not, Hal!"

"Why won't you understand?!"

At a table far away from ours, a young couple in military outfits were having an argument.

The man was a tall human with distinctive red hair. He looked like he was over 190 centimeters tall. He was broad-shouldered, and even through his uniform, I could tell he had a solid build.

The girl, on the other hand, had blonde hair in a short bob, with two triangular ears up top, and was a little on the petite side.

Is that girl a mystic wolf, I wonder?

"That girl's a mystic fox," Liscia told me, but I couldn't tell the difference. "You can tell by their tails. She has a fox tail, see?"

"They're both canines, so can't we just lump them both together as mystic dogs?" I asked.

"If you say that, you'll get both the mystic wolves and the mystic foxes angry. Kobolds are mystic dogs, so it would be like lumping humans together with apes."

"Tell me about all these things I shouldn't say to certain races later, please."

That's another world for you. You never know when you'll step on a landmine like that, I thought.

As I was thinking that, the mystic fox girl was pleading. "I'm begging you, Hal. You can't go to the Carmine Duchy right now! Army General Duke Georg Carmine is hostile to the new king. There could be a civil war!"

"That's exactly why I'm going. If there's going to be fighting, that's a chance for me to get promoted, isn't it?" The one called Hal, who seemed to be a young man of about eighteen, gave her a dauntless smile.

The mystic fox girl, on the other hand, wore an expression clouded with anxiety. "Hal, the way you think about war is too simple. Your father called you back home because he was worried about you being like that!"

"It's none of my old man's business! He's served under Duke Carmine for years, but now that things don't look so good, he's hiding in the capital, the coward! I don't need to listen to him!"

"Your father understands what's happening. Duke Carmine is rebelling without just cause."

The two kept quarreling.

As she was watching them, Liscia clapped her hands together in recognition. "I thought I recognized him! The man is Officer Halbert Magna."

"Is he someone you know?" I asked.

"He's the eldest son of a distinguished family in the army clique. Since his academy days, his combat abilities have put him well above the rest of his peers. He entered the land forces after graduating, but I guess he's returned home since then."

"He sounds surprisingly well known," I mused. "Well, how about the girl, then?"

"I don't know. I've never seen her in the army."

"That girl is Kaede Foxia," Juna answered on Liscia's behalf.

Huh? Why does she know? I wondered.

"Because she's a regular here," Juna said without my asking. "If I recall, she mentioned she's a mage serving in the Forbidden Army."

"If she's in the Forbidden Army, is she an earth-type mage, then?" I asked.

This world's magic could be divided into six elements: fire, water, earth, wind, light, and dark.

Fire, water, wind, and earth manipulated their respective elements for attack spells, while light was generally healing-type magic. Dark was unique in that it didn't, strictly speaking, manipulate darkness. All the unique spells that didn't fall under the previous five elements were lumped together under the "dark-type" categorization.

In terms of magic type, my Living Poltergeists would have been dark.

Every person in this world was aligned with one of these elements, and they could use magic to some degree. As you would know from Liscia and Aisha's training, people could imbue their weapons or attacks with magic of their element, as well.

Those who could cause greater magical effects than ordinary people were called mages. Mages could manipulate flames, cause whirlwinds, form craters in the ground, and sink battleships with their incredible powers.

When mages joined the military, their type determined where they were sent. Fire users went to the army, wind users to the air force, water users to the navy, and earth and dark users (not that there were many of the latter) went to the Forbidden Army, while light users were distributed equally and played a similar role to combat medics.

Honestly, I was opposed to this inflexible way of distributing them, but the army, navy, and air force were under the control of the Three Dukedoms, so I couldn't mess around with them.

Someday, I want to reform that system.

While I was thinking about all that, Kaede and Halbert kept arguing.

"Duke Carmine would never lose to that inexperienced king!"

"Duke Carmine's been acting strange lately! If we start fighting amongst ourselves, only our neighbors stand to benefit! Amidonia wants to reclaim the lands they lost to Elfrieden two kings ago. And as for the Republic of Turgis, with more than half their territory frozen, they want fertile land and a warm water port. If there's a civil war, they're sure to intervene. Duke Carmine must know that..."

Huh, it sounds like Kaede has a good understanding of the situation in the neighboring countries.

The country to the west of this one on the world map, the Principality of Amidonia, had seen roughly half of their territory stolen from them under the expansionist policies of Liscia's grandfather. That was close to fifty years ago, but they were still eyeing this country for any opportunity to regain their lost land. For this country, it was clearly an enemy state.

To the south of Amidonia, on the southern edge of this continent, was the Republic of Turgis. Like Kaede said, it was a frigid land that was mostly frozen.

When you looked at this world's map, the further south you went, the lower the temperature dropped. I didn't know whether that was because (speaking from a Japanese person's perspective) this continent was in the southern hemisphere, or if their concept of north and south was reversed, or even if it was because of some mysterious magical effect, but the further south you went in Elfrieden, the colder it got, and the further north, the warmer it got.

Because of the kind of country they were, "Go north" was a national policy for the Republic of Turgis.

However, of the countries they bordered, the Gran Chaos Empire was massive, so they could ill afford a conflict with them. The mercenary state of Zem was their ally, meaning they couldn't invade there, either. That narrowed their potential targets for northward expansion to Amidonia or Elfrieden.

In other words, both Amidonia and Turgis were like ravenous wolves, ready to pounce on this country at the soonest opportunity.

"What is Duke Carmine thinking when the neighboring countries have designs on our territory?"

"This is Duke Carmine you're talking about. I'm sure he has a plan."

"Aren't you going to think for yourself, Hal?!"

"The fact of the matter is, many nobles have given up on the king and they've gone to serve under Duke Carmine, haven't they? His failure to keep them here is proof of the king's ineptitude."

"I don't know if the new king is competent or not, but up to this point, I've seen no misrule under him! Besides, most of those nobles gathering under Duke Carmine are those who've lost rights under the new king's finance reforms, or who were investigated for corruption and are discontented over having their assets seized, you realize?! Even if you restored their rights, do you really think that would make this country a better place?!"

When Kaede pressed him on it like that, Halbert's gaze wandered. "I'm sure Duke Carmine is thinking this all through."

"There you go, talking about Duke Carmine again. Don't you have an opinion of your own, Hal?"

"J-just shut up, okay?! What, Kaede, do you think you can see the future?! Well, I can! I can!" Halbert lashed out defiantly, but Kaede answered him firmly.

"I can see what's coming! That man scares me. I'm sure that the new king will..."

"Okay, stop," I cut Kaede off, inserting myself between the two of them.

Both of their eyes went wide at the sudden intrusion.

I ignored Halbert's surprised, "Wh-who do you think you are, buddy?!" with a smile at Kaede, who sat with her mouth agape.

"If you keep running your mouth, I'll use my authority to have you arrested, you know?" I said.

"You're...!" Kaede seemed to have immediately realized who I was.

"Yes, I am, so keep quiet, okay?" I said. "Honestly, I don't know how much you understand, but if you talk so confidently about it in a place like this, it could harm the country."

"I-I'm sorry," she stammered. "But...what are you doing here? You're not here to seize Hal for his rebelliousness, I hope?! It's not like that! Hal's just a little weak in the head, he would never rebel..."

Kaede completely misunderstood what I was doing and started to make excuses. Who knows where the analytic ability she'd displayed earlier went, but she was desperately trying to defend Halbert.

"No, I don't care what one single soldier thinks," I said.

"Th-then why are you here?" she stammered.

"Because I was suddenly given time off," I explained. "I was just checking out Juna's place."

"I-I see." Kaede was clearly relieved.

Halbert, on the other hand, had been glaring at me this whole time. "You punk, who do you think you are, butting into our conversation and then threatening Kaede?"

"U-um, Hal? He wasn't threatening me, you see..."

"Shut up! You be quiet, Kaede!"

"Yipe!"

When Halbert slammed his hands on the table and stood up, it frightened Kaede.

"What good is frightening her yourself going to do?" I asked.

"I said, shut up!" He reached out, trying to grab me by the collar, when...

"Urkh!"

He stopped halfway. In an instant, Halbert was surrounded by the three women who were with me.

Normally, being surrounded by three beauties would be a fantastic situation to be in, but I wasn't jealous of his position in the least. After all, Liscia had drawn the rapier from her side and was pointing the tip of it at Halbert's neck, Aisha (who had left her great sword behind because it was too bulky) was holding his face in a claw hold, and Juna, still smiling, had a fruit knife pressed against his back.

Whoa... their power levels are way too high...

"Wait, even you, Juna?" I asked, surprised.

"Violence is strictly prohibited in this establishment," she said with a grin.

"Uh, sure..."

Having found himself in that situation, even the assertive Halbert was sweating. He couldn't move an inch, so he glared at me in frustration through the gap between Aisha's fingers. "You punk! That was dirty! If you're a man, how can you hide behind a bunch of women?!"

"Complain all you like, but it's kind of their job to protect me," I said. "Actually, if I were to stand on the front line without bodyguards, I think that would be a bigger problem."

When I said that, the girls nodded in agreement.

"If you understand that, I wish you wouldn't stick your neck into trouble like this," Liscia scolded me.

Uh, sure, sorry, I'll be more careful.

Halbert's irritated gaze stabbed into me. "You punk, just who are you?"

"Allow me to respond with that great line from a samurai period drama. 'Halbert, have you forgotten my face?'"

"Huh?"

"Why do you suddenly sound so full of yourself?" Liscia slapped me upside the head.

Aw, come on, I've always wanted to say it.

Then Aisha raised her voice and spoke on my behalf. "On your knees! Who do you take this man for?!"

Yeah, that's another line I wanted to use. Wait, Aisha's saying it?!

"You stand in the presence of the (provisional) Fourteenth King of Elfrieden, His Majesty Souma!" Aisha declared.

It felt like I could hear that show's theme music playing, but I'm sure I was imagining it.

Regardless, I gave the disappointing dark elf a light bonk on the head. "You're too loud. We're supposed to be incognito, remember?"

"Ah! I-I'm sorry, Sire!"

"'Sire'...? Don't tell me you're the king?!" Halbert acted surprised long after he should have figured it out. He was the only one present who didn't know by this point, so he seemed a bit slow-witted. Regardless, we couldn't have a calm discussion with him being menaced with a rapier, a claw hold, and a knife, so I had everyone stand down.

Fixing my gaze on the relieved Halbert, I asked him a question. "Now then, Halbert Magna, you were saying something about attacking me?"

"Th-that's..." Halbert averted his eyes.

Oh, come on, was your determination that weak?

"Should I take that to be the will of the House of Magna as a whole?" I asked.

"Wha—?! My old man's got nothing to do with this!"

"Of course he does," I said. "While I might be able to overlook a soldier who was just following orders, traitorous nobles must be tried under the law. They show a clear intent to rebel, after all. In those cases, the charge will be treason against the state. That's a serious crime, you know. At the very least, those within three degrees of consanguinity will be considered complicit in it."

"Wha...?!" Halbert was at a loss for words. All I was doing was forcing him to face the facts, though.

"No... that's too harsh..." Kaede tried to intervene, but I raised a hand to stop her.

"Now, let me just say, I'm not doing this because I hold a personal grudge against you," I said. "That's what the laws of this country dictate. Honestly, I know with long-lived races, it's not unusual for them to have great-grandchildren and great-great-grandchildren around, but even so, the range of people implicated in the crime is way too large. Personally, for a law like this which even punishes innocent young children, I'd like to reform it right away, but I have so many things to do that I just haven't gotten around to it yet."

He was speechless.

"Halbert Magna," I said formally. "You were born into the House of Magna, a proper noble house. So, if you side with the Three Dukedoms, they rebel, and I win, all your kin within three degrees of consanguinity will be executed. That's what the law says, so there's nothing I can do about it, right?"

It would be the law that judged him, not me. There would be no room for me to use my own discretion.

"Now, let's consider what happens if the Three Dukedoms win," I continued.

"Hey! Y-yeah, that's right! As long as we win, it's all good!"

"In the event that happens, what will happen to her?" I placed a hand on Kaede's shoulder.

Halbert was clearly shaken. "No, you wouldn't dare take Kaede hostage!"

"Oh, I wouldn't do something like that. However, she's a member of the Forbidden Army. If the Three Dukedoms rebel, she'll be sent to the front on our side. In other words, she would be your enemy." I looked closely at Kaede. "By the way, what is your relationship with Halbert?"

"W-we're childhood friends."

"Childhood friends... I see."

From the way they'd been talking and acting, I had seen signs of their affection for each other, but...well, there was no reason to point it out here.

"If you're childhood friends, you must care more for one another than you would just any other person," I said. "And? If you join the Three Dukedoms, what do you plan to do about her?"

"What do you mean, what will I do...? About what?"

"We're imagining that the Three Dukedoms win. In that case, I may have been struck down, and you may even have been the one to take my severed head."

"Hah! I'd be guaranteed a promotion, then!"

"I suppose you would," I said. "So, what of Kaede? A cute girl like her, in the losing army. When they find out, what will the soldiers of the winning side do? As a soldier yourself, I think you can imagine, can't you?"

When I pointed that out, Halbert paled. Most likely, he was imagining "that sort" of scene. After the conclusion of a war, it wasn't uncommon to see the defeated ravaged by the victors. Looting, arson, rape, slaughter... the madness of war was that it allowed these acts of barbarity to happen.

Even so, Halbert raised his voice, as if trying to shake off his doubts. "Duke Carmine's forces are well organized! They would never do something so indecent!"

"I don't know what the situation is within the army, but Duke Carmine has more than just the regular forces in his duchy," I said. "There are also those I stripped of their rights or investigated for corruption. Those nobles who've raised the flag of rebellion against me. They have nothing to lose. If they lose, death for both them and their family line awaits. So, they'll throw away their personal assets, hiring a large number of Zemish mercenaries."

The mercenary state, Zem, lay west of Amidonia and north of Turgis. It was a medium-sized country, founded by the mercenary commander Zem, who had used his wits to destroy the country which had hired him and then build his own nation of mercenaries in its place. They had declared themselves to be "eternally neutral," but their primary industry was dispatching mercenaries to other countries, so what that really meant was, "If requested, we will dispatch mercenaries to any country." Their mercenaries were ridiculously strong, so most countries recognized that it was better to have them as an ally than an enemy, and so they had formed mercenary contracts with them.

"That's absurd! There are Zemish mercenaries under contract with the Forbidden Army, too! If they send mercenaries to the Three Dukedoms, as well, they'll be fighting against their own!"

"Oh, that won't happen," I assured him. "I terminated their employment contract with the Forbidden Army a while ago."

Now seems like a good time, so let me talk about the military system of this country.

This kingdom had a total manpower of around 100,000 troops. They were divided like so:

40,000 in the army, led by Duke Georg Carmine.

10,000 in the navy, led by Duchess Excel Walter.

1,000 in the air force, led by Duke Castor Vargas.

(However, one wyvern knight was said to be equivalent to 100 soldiers from the army.)

Of these, only the air force had a knightly title bestowed on every one of its members (it was composed entirely of units of wyvern knights, i.e. "one wyvern plus one or two knights," so that was obvious), but more than half of the army and navy were made up of career soldiers. They trained day and night in the three duchies, and they received a salary from the three duchies.

You could say that the right to self-rule and the tax exemption on the profits from their lands, along with the many other special rights given to the three duchies, were there to support these troops.

Now, the remaining troops, numbering a little over 40,000, belonged to the Forbidden Army, but they were further divided beyond that.

There were the Royal Guard, who reported directly to the king, and the career soldiers who were attached to the Forbidden Army. Then there were the noble estates (which had fewer rights than the three duchies) and their personal forces on top of that. Also, due to our contract with the mercenary state, Zem, there had been a unit of mercenaries under the command of the Forbidden Army, as well, but I had already terminated their employment.

The reason that the Forbidden Army was smaller than the forces of the three duchies had to do with the concept behind this country.

This country had originally been born through many races working together. As a result, a member of the race with the largest population, a human, became the king, but to protect the rights of the other races, the commanders of the army, navy, and air forces were chosen from the other races.

So, if a tyrant took the throne and began oppressing the other races, the system had been set up so that the armies of the Three Dukedoms, being larger than the Forbidden Army, could remove him. Turning that around, if one of the Three Dukedoms was plotting to usurp the throne, the system was set up in a way that if even one of the armies were to side with the king, the rebellion could be put down.

In a peaceful era, this might have been a good setup. However, now the Demon Lord's Domain had appeared, and these were troubled times with every country looking for openings to take advantage of. With this sort of divided command structure, it was possible that we might not be able to respond quickly enough to a sudden crisis. As a matter of fact, I was trying to move forward with reforms, but the Three Dukedoms were giving me the silent treatment.

"Hold on, what do you mean you released the Zemish mercenaries from their contracts?!" Liscia shouted.

"Oh, yeah, I hadn't told you about that yet, had I?" I smiled wryly at the fact that, rather than Halbert, it was Liscia who voiced her surprise this time. "It means exactly what it sounds like. Mercenaries are useless and just eat up money, you know."

Machiavelli had said, "Mercenaries and mixed armies are not to be trusted." According to him, "Mercenaries are tied to you only by their own profit; if presented with greater profit, they will easily betray you. Yet even when they fight, they protect their employer only for their own benefit, and so their loyalty is not to be expected. There is no reason to hire incapable mercenaries, and yet capable ones will always use their wits to seize their employer's position."

In fantasy novels and RPGs, protagonists with the mercenary job often appear, but the way the mercenary business actually worked was wildly different from the image you may have seen there.

Basically, mercenaries were people who made their money on the battlefield. They held no loyalty to any country or prince, quickly changing sides when the balance of benefits shifted.

In a losing battle, they fled immediately. Even when victorious, they would run wild. Compared to standing armies of the same size, their upkeep might cost less, but they were a negative in the long term.

"We don't have the money to pay useless people like that," I explained.

"Even so, the mercenary contract was also proof of our friendly relations with Zem, you realize?!" Liscia shouted.

"True, things have become tense with them since then, but you yourself said, 'Spend always on defense, never on tribute,' didn't you, Liscia? Unlike the empire, they can't afford to invade us themselves. Paying them tribute to bide our time is pointless with them."

The country *was* getting back at me by dispatching mercenaries to the Three Dukedoms, though.

I looked straight at Halbert. "Those bloodthirsty mercenaries are on the side of the Three Dukedoms. Do you think they'll leave a girl in the defeated army—like Kaede—alone? While Kaede is being tormented by the mercenaries, and they're about to kill her because they're done with her, where will you be, and what will you be doing?"

"That's..." Halbert hesitated.

That indecisive attitude of his got me steaming mad. "Will you be lifting your head aloft in joy?! Singing songs to celebrate your victory?! Meanwhile, your childhood friend may have been made their plaything, then left dead at the side of the road!"

"Urkh."

When I shouted at him, Halbert's legs seemed to give out and he had to put his hands on the table for support. He had no comeback to that, and his mouth was closed tightly. Kaede watched him worriedly.

When I saw them like that, I calmed down a little. "Halbert Magna. The path you were about to choose is a dead end. If I win, you will be executed. If the Three Dukedoms win, Kaede will... well, she may not come out of it all right. If you're going to make the gamble of a lifetime, at least make sure the future you want is on the betting table."

He said nothing.

"Before you do anything rash, always think back," I told him. "Think about what is it that you wanted, what for, and for whom? Look around you and think about it."

"What for? And for whom?" Halbert looked around.

His eyes met with Kaede's, which were looking at him with concern. There were no words between them, but Halbert looked like a man released from whatever had been possessing him.

What happens from here on is for them to decide, I thought.

"Sorry, Juna. We were getting in the way of your business, weren't we?" I asked. "We'll be leaving now."

Just before we left, I went to apologize for making a scene, but Juna shook her head. "No. Sire, your words carved themselves into my heart."

After saying that, Juna seemed to hesitate for a moment. She clearly had something to say but was unsure whether it was okay to say it.

I waited a little while, and finally Juna looked up, her face resolute. "Sire, I have something to talk to you about."

◇　◇　◇

"Hey, Souma, there was something I wanted to ask," Liscia said.

"Hm?"

We were inside the carriage we had called to take us back to the castle when Liscia, who was sitting beside me, asked a question.

Aisha was acting as the driver, so we were alone together in the carriage.

"About what happened earlier," she said. "You were trying to persuade Halbert, right? When you said traitors would be judged by the law, you seemed kind of serious."

"Because he hadn't acted against me yet. If he still does after this, I'm not going to show any mercy."

"In the end, you're still a nice guy, huh?" she said.

"Be kind to your allies, severe with your enemies," I said. "That's the kind of king people want to support. It's not like I'm being severe because I enjoy it. The fewer enemies we have, the better."

"Just like I thought...you're a nice guy." Liscia rested her head on my shoulder.

◇ ◇ ◇

The next day...

When I was in the governmental affairs office getting some paperwork done, Hakuya came in. "The head of the House of Magna, Sir Glaive Magna, has brought his son, Sir Halbert Magna, and Forbidden Army Mage Kaede Foxia, and is requesting an audience with you," he reported to me.

Sounds like there's still another dispute to solve, I thought.

When I arrived in the audience chamber accompanied by Liscia and my bodyguard Aisha, there were already three people there kneeling. In front of the other two with his head lowered was a middle-aged man with salt and pepper hair. In his armor, he truly looked like a warrior who had seen many battles. Behind him were Kaede Foxia and Halbert Magna, whom I had met the day before. That being the case, I deduced that the man in front of them with his head lowered must be Halbert's father, Glaive.

"Raise your heads, all three of you," I said.

"Yes, sir."

When Halbert and Kaede raised their heads, I found myself transfixed by the sight of Halbert's face. I mean, he had the marks to show he'd been punched several times. His cheeks were swollen, and he had two black eyes. Those hadn't been there when I'd seen him yesterday, so it must have happened after we'd parted.

"Halbert, you're looking even more handsome than the last time I saw you," I commented.

"Urgh... yes, sir!" A look of frustration crossed his face for a moment, but he didn't fight back the way he had yesterday.

I wonder what happened to him after we parted.

I spoke to Glaive, whose head was still bowed. "Glaive Magna, raise your head."

"I humbly, humbly, beg you, show mercy for my son's recent misconduct!" That was the lament-filled response that came back. He was pressing his forehead against the floor. It was hard to tell since he had one knee up, but he was doing what we'd probably call a dogeza in Japan.

"By misconduct, do you mean what happened yesterday?" I asked.

"Yes, sir! I heard the details from Madam Kaede. While he may have been off duty, he insulted you, Sire, and what's more, boasted that he would join the rebellious Three Dukedoms, which is utterly outrageous! However, my son is yet immature. He said those things because of his underdeveloped brain. Your anger is entirely justified, Sire, but, please, let the blame fall on me for failing to educate him properly!"

Um...that was a little long-winded, but what he's saying is "I'll take the punishment, so please spare my son's life," I guess? I'm not even angry, though.

"Yesterday's events happened when I was there in secret," I said. "I don't intend to make a big deal out of it. From what I see here, he's already been punished appropriately."

"Sire, you are too kind." Glaive apologized profusely, prostrating himself before me.

Halbert and Kaede hurriedly bowed their heads once more.

Finally, Glaive lifted his face. "Now then, Sire. I realize this is incredibly rude, but I have come to tell you something."

"What?"

"Well...it is something best not heard by many people..."

A secret, huh? I had Liscia, Aisha, Hakuya, Glaive, Halbert, and Kaede remain, then dismissed everyone else, including the guards. Aisha seemed out of place, but so long as she was here, if it turned out he was using the promise of secret information as a guise to assassinate me, I had someone to deal with that.

"I've cleared the room," I said. "So, what is it you needed to tell me?"

"Yes, about that..." Glaive began to talk at a relaxed pace.

When we heard what it was he had to say, Halbert's eyes went wide, Kaede looked down, gripping her fists tightly, Hakuya closed his eyes in silence, while Aisha looked around bewildered by everyone else's reactions.

Liscia, meanwhile, had gone stiff and expressionless, not saying a word. There were tears streaming down her face.

As for me, it was a complicated feeling. Anger, exasperation, resignation, sadness... all those feelings got jumbled together in my chest, and I worked my hardest to keep them there.

I spoke in as calm and even a voice as I could manage, so as not to betray my feelings. "Now that you've told me that, what do you want me to do about it?"

"Nothing. I just wanted you to be aware, Sire."

"It's heavy." I stood up, giving orders to Kaede and Halbert. "Forbidden Army Mage Kaede Foxia. This insight is too valuable, and too dangerous, for me to leave you as a mere mage. I order you to serve under Ludwin of the Royal Guard as a staff officer."

"Huh? Y-yes, sir!" she exclaimed.

"Army Officer Halbert Magna. I order you to transfer to the Forbidden Army."

"Huh?! Me, join the Forbidden Army?!"

"That's right. You will be Kaede's second-in-command and report to her. Her rank effectively makes her Number Two in the Forbidden Army. Because she is still a young woman, there is the risk that her subordinates won't take her seriously. In the event of that happening, you are to make sure they do as she says. Understood?"

"Yes, sir!"

Thus, a new, young officer joined the Forbidden Army.

However, I wasn't feeling emotionally at ease enough to be happy a new ally had joined us. As I forced down my violent emotions, my true feelings seeped out through my gritted teeth just once.

"Honestly, these people..."

HOW A REALIST HERO REBUILT THE KINGDOM

The Sighs of Duchess Excel Walter

L ET'S TALK ABOUT the system of nobility in this country.
Once you set aside royalty and the three dukes, the people can be divided into three groups: the nobles and knights, the commoners, and the slaves. (Refugees, as they are not citizens, do not fall into any of these groups.)

We will go into the institution of slavery on another occasion, but what divides the nobles and knights from the commoners is whether or not they hold land.

Because of that, the class of nobles and knights may also be referred to as lords, and the commoners who live on their lands may be referred to as their subjects. (Slaves are considered chattel, and thus are not included in this group.) Lords have many rights within their lands, and at the same time, they have military obligations and other responsibilities to the country.

The titles and lands of the nobility and knighthood are generally hereditary, but commoners who distinguish themselves may be bestowed title and land by the country, raising them to knighthood (for those whose accomplishments are military) or nobility (for those whose accomplishments are in administration).

Furthermore, marrying into a noble or knightly family (in which case, the person provides their own land) is also possible. These people are referred to as new nobles or new knights.

This isn't a distinction that formally exists, but certain hard-headed people who think of new nobles as "upstarts who were not born to be nobles or knights" refer to them this way. New nobles and new knights may pass their titles hereditarily. (Generally, a house becomes accepted after around three generations.)

Conversely, even nobles and knights can, if their crimes are great enough, be dropped to the rank of commoner or slave. In these cases, their lands and title are seized by the country and, in the worst cases, the entire house may lose their status. This is known as "destruction."

The reason nobles and knights distinguish themselves from new nobles and new knights is that, as noted earlier, they take pride in having maintained the status of their house and having avoided this "destruction" for three generations.

There is no need for the nobility and knighthood to manage their lands personally. Particularly with knights, who must spend most of the year serving in the military, management of their lands is left to the members of their household. Royal Guard Captain Ludwin Arcs was one example.

Furthermore, among the nobility, there are those who leave management of their lands to the members of their house, residing in Parnam where they serve in important posts such as top positions in the bureaucracy or as speakers in the Congress of the People. These people are called capital nobles, with the former prime minister (and current chamberlain) Marx being one example.

However, at present, the number of capital nobles had fallen to nearly half of what it had been the year before. The ones who had gone missing were those whose wrongdoing had been uncovered in Souma's government spending audit. Those under investigation had been dismissed from their posts in the capital and were under house arrest in their own lands.

For those whose crimes were minor, if they repaid the money they embezzled and relinquished the family headship to another member of the family, their house would be allowed to continue, but for those whose crimes were great, all their assets were seized, and their house would be destroyed.

Of course, the sort of people who would engage in such corruption could not be expected to quietly acquiesce to the destruction of their houses. They took their personal forces and assets and attempted to flee.

However, because Souma and Hakuya could easily see their intentions, the borders were sealed, and they could not carry their assets out into other countries.

Unable to remain in their lands or flee to another country, they ultimately headed for the duchy of Duke Carmine. They went to Georg Carmine, who was hostile to the king, and waited for an opportunity to rebel.

The central city of Carmine Duchy was Randel.

While not as great in scale as the royal capital Parnam, it was still sizeable compared to other cities, with a large enough population to become a city-state on its own.

General of the Army Georg Carmine's castle was here, and a castle town had grown up around it. However, past generals had been indifferent to the city's management and so, unlike Parnam which could change greatly with the direction the king chose to take it, the town had a nostalgic feel to it, probably the same now as it had been 100 years ago.

On a street corner in that city of Randel, a single carriage was parked. Inside the carriage was a beauty in her mid-twenties. Any man who saw her would almost certainly have let out a sigh of admiration.

Even wrapped as it was in a kimono similar in style to the ones worn in Japan, her voluptuous figure was still apparent. However, the reptilian tail which stuck out from the buttocks of her kimono and the tiny antlers that sprouted out from beneath her blue hair made it clear that she wasn't just an ordinary human.

From inside her carriage, she listened to the hustle and bustle of the town around her. There must have been a tavern nearby, because she heard a group of drunkards grumbling quite clearly.

"Seriously, that new king... just who does he think we are? Hic!"

"Indeed. It is we who have supported this kingdom for so many long years."

"But the king goes and ignores us, pushing forward policies on his own!"

"Why did King Albert leave the country to that whelp...?"

"His retainers are no better! They're a bunch of inexperienced novices, too! What's with that gloomy black-robed jerk?! What's with that human pig?!"

"Heh heh heh, I'm sure he only values those who are good at flattering him."

"The young *are* prone to such things! He throws out experienced people like us, only listening to people who'll flatter him. A king like that won't last long."

"That's right! Let's take this country back with our own hands!"

"Yeah! For the kingdom we love!"

"For the kingdom we love!"

For the kingdom, is it...? My, how they do like to run their mouths. The woman in the carriage sighed. *Even that sigh was alluring.*

You people are the ones who betrayed the country with your illegal acts. When it came time for you to face the law, you fled, so it certainly takes some gall for you to say the king threw you out. And the king only values those who flatter him? Were you not watching when he gathered personnel? That king would use even those who were dissatisfied with him so long as they were worth it. He uses Sir Hakuya and Sir Poncho because they are capable. The reason he doesn't use you is because you are not.

Since they didn't even understand that much, she couldn't bring herself to bother ridiculing them.

It's been a few months since the crown was transferred to His Majesty, Souma, yet he hasn't made any major policy blunders or lost the support of the people. To the contrary, he's shown extraordinary ability in the way he's steadily resolving the food crisis we feared. No matter how much they respected King Albert for his sagacity, it's nonsense to ask, "Why did he choose that whelp?"

The woman rested her elbows on the windowsill, her chin in her hands.

To think the nobility has fallen so far from the proud and high-minded people who founded the country. Their ancestors must be turning in their graves.

Though she appeared to be in her mid-twenties, this woman recalled the dawning age of this kingdom more than 500 years ago. She thought back to her comrades, smiling sadly.

As a descendent of sea serpents, it would be more than another 500 years before she would be taken to their side.

"It's times like this when belonging to a long-lived race is the hardest. I've gotten used to bidding farewell to the short-lived, but then I'm forced to see unpleasant things like this. I envy *you people* who have been able to die without a care for what would come after."

With those words, Navy Admiral Excel Walter, one of the three dukes, gave a self-deprecating laugh.

"Sea Princess!"

When a voice addressed her from outside the carriage, Excel sat up straight. "Yes?"

"Ma'am, a report has arrived from Canaria," the voice said.

"Show it to me," she commanded.

"Yes, ma'am. It is here." The speaker pushed the documents through a gap in the carriage door.

Excel took the documents, opening them and perusing their contents. As she read them, her face finally broke into a smile.

I see... so that's how you've judged him. Yet you still wish to be at his side, you say. Hmm... that's all well and good, but I do think the loving praise dripping from your writing is going to give me heartburn. Really, now, I must envy your youth.

Excel froze the documents with a sigh, then let them go. The documents fell, shattering into pieces when they struck the carriage floor.

Allow me to correct myself. When you live so long, there are times when you'll find new light in the most unexpected of ways. This feeling is something you people who have died can never taste, isn't it?

Serves you right.

Excel wore the smile of a young girl, not showing so much as a hint of her true age.

HOW A REALIST HERO

REBUILT THE KINGDOM

CHAPTER 5

The Legendary Old Man

MANY PEOPLE were lined up in the audience chamber of Parnam Castle, where both the hero summoning and talent award ceremony had been held. These were the bureaucrats of the finance ministry.

Each wore an exhausted expression on his face.

Their cheeks were sunken, and they had bags under their eyes. Some wore dry smiles, while others looked to be on the verge of collapsing. Despite that, each one of them had a twinkle in their eye.

Theirs were the eyes of warriors who had survived a bloody battle.

Since I had become king and launched my reforms to save an economy on the brink of collapse, they had served as my hands and feet, working hard, like horses drawing a carriage. Anyone who had been working to enrich themselves had been dismissed, leaving only the serious ones behind. These were people who worked hard, reluctant to take time off even to sleep.

One of them might spend an entire day comparing the

numbers between sets of documents, while another might spend most of the day on horseback, going around to ensure funds were being used correctly. They had been spending their days returning home only to sleep. Many of them didn't even return home, they just slept in the castle's nap room, returning to work as soon as they woke.

Some had families.

Some had children.

Some were recently married.

However, they cast aside the time they would have spent with their families, continuing to work.

The face of a wife dissatisfied that her husband put work before her, the face of a child lonely because his father wouldn't play with him, the face of a newlywed wife sincerely concerned for her husband... the bureaucrats averted their eyes from these faces, telling themselves it was just for now, and worked diligently.

Earnestly trying to save this country from collapse.

Earnestly trying to protect those in this country whom they loved.

I looked down at them while sitting on the throne. I probably didn't look much better than they did at this point. While I could rest unused parts of my consciousness in shifts, I was handling five times my regular workload and working 'round the clock. While my body might have been fine, I could feel my spirit being ground down.

"That's a fine look you've all got on your faces, now." I rose, speaking to them in a quiet voice. Then I went down to them, placing my hand on one thin man's shoulder. "Your eyes are hollow and lifeless. You've got the face of a ghoul."

They all said nothing.

"I know how it's been," I said. "These days of forgoing sleep, fighting with the numbers day in and day out, ignoring the pleas of your families that you stop coming to the castle. You people are my greatest treasure! Take pride in that! With every moment you've spent putting your souls to the grindstone, you've been saving the people of this country!"

"Ohhhhhhhhhhhhhhhh!"

Pale and emaciated, anyone could see these men were the indoors-y type, yet now they roared like barbarians. They thrust their fists into the air, chanting, "Souma! Souma!" I waited a moment for their fervor to settle, then continued.

"Thanks to all of you, we've managed to secure the funds we need at present. Now, Project Venetinova can begin in earnest. When this project comes to fruition, this country's food crisis will be completely resolved. It will be because of all of you fulfilling your duties, setting this struggling economy straight and finding the funds to make it happen! In place of the people, I thank you!"

"King Souma!"

"King Souma!"

"You have toiled hard in the shadows for this country! Unlike heroes, your names won't be left in the history books. However, you have saved far more lives than any hero could save on the battlefield! I, Souma Kazuya, will remember that fact for all my life! You are the nameless heroes of this country!"

"Glory to our king!"

"Glory to King Souma and Elfrieden!"

"You've really outdone yourselves," I continued. "Thus, I bestow upon you this gift. I grant you a five-day vacation, starting tomorrow! Return to your families, rest your bodies, and restore your spirits!"

"Ohhhhhhhhhhhhhhhhhhhh!"

That's the largest cheer yet today, I thought. *I can understand how you feel. You're all starved for rest. I'm sorry for running this place like a sweatshop.*

"Truthfully, I want to pay you a bonus, but if I were to dip into the funds you've worked so hard to find to do so, it would defeat the purpose. I'm really sorry."

They were silent.

"In place of that, after conferring with the prime minister, I've decided to give you each one expensive bottle from the castle's wine cellar! Have a celebratory drink or sell it as you please!"

"Ohhhhhhhhhhhhhhhh! Your Majesty! King Souma!"

As I looked at the cheering bureaucrats, I nodded, full of emotion myself.

However, Liscia, who was standing beside me watching, was clearly put off by this scene.

"Souma, you're exhausted," she said.

"I won't deny it," I answered.

As soon as we returned to the governmental affairs office, Liscia spoke to me, seemingly concerned.

Yeah, I shouldn't have been that hyper. Looking back at it, I was acting a little loopy.

"It's because I was up until almost dawn working. The lack of sleep was giving me a high," I responded while lying down in the bed set up in the corner of the governmental affairs office, as I usually did.

"I won't insist it be lavish, but please get your own room," Hakuya had once said sourly to me. "If the ruler of the nation sleeps in the governmental affairs office, he's not setting the proper example for his subjects."

But I couldn't give up the convenience of being able to work as soon as I woke up, so things had stayed as they were. I figured I would probably be sleeping in here until things settled down a little in the country.

Liscia went to sit down at the end of the bed. In that moment her small, shapely buttocks suddenly appeared in front of my eyes, so I turned and looked the other way despite myself. Liscia always wore that tight-fitting officer's uniform, so I could easily make out the lines of her hips.

"But, Souma, you're able to rest your consciousness in shifts, right?" she asked.

"Huh? Uh...yeah, sorta. But we were almost at the point where we could afford the budget for a large-scale project, so I ended up working my full consciousness for that last push."

When I said that, Liscia sighed a little. "I know you're working hard, but don't make me worry. Because you're irreplaceable, all right?"

"Ha ha, if it comes to it, you can just summon another hero, can't you?" I asked.

"You dummy! If you say another word about that, I'll slap you!"

I turned my face to look at Liscia. There was real anger in her eyes.

"Even if we summoned another hero, that person wouldn't be you," she snapped. "You're the one I want, Souma."

"R-right..." I faltered.

"Never forget. You're the one I want to be king, Souma. I'll accept no substitutes. If my father were to demand the crown back, I'd fight him at your side."

When she made that incredible declaration with a straight face, all I could do was nod my head.

Somehow, it felt like I'd seen a portion of her motherly courage there. Liscia was going to make an amazing bride someday. That I was planned to be the groom, however, was something I still didn't feel right about.

Liscia seemed satisfied with my response for now. "So? You were talking about a budget, but what do you need all that money for?"

"Oh, for a start, I was thinking I'd build a city."

"A city?" she asked.

I had Liscia fetch a map of the country from my work desk. Looked at as a whole, the territory of the country looked like a < shape, and I pointed to the center of it.

"We'll build a coastal city here. Also, we'll be moving forward with road construction at the same time. If we have a transportation network from a coastal city to all the other cities, we can control both marine and land transportation. That should allow us to make distribution much smoother. Honestly, it's a wonder to me how such prime real estate has remained untouched up until now."

Incidentally, northeast of that spot was Lagoon City, a coastal city ruled by one of the three dukes, Navy Admiral Excel Walter. Currently, Lagoon City was the largest trade port in this country, but at the same time it was also a naval base with docks for battleships. With a trading port where goods from around the world gathered and a naval base with its need for confidentiality linked to each other, there were mismatched priorities. In a crisis, that could lead to trade being stopped.

For that reason, too, it was urgent that we build a new city with a trading port.

"This coastal city will be the beating heart of this country, and the roads that stretch out from it will be its veins," I explained. "If distribution is smooth, when there is a shortage of some goods in the south, they can be shipped in from where they're plentiful in the north. Do you know what that means?"

"Um... you buy goods where the prices have been lowered by abundance, then resell them in places where the price has risen due to demand...or something like that?" she asked.

"No, no, I'm not a merchant. The king can't be the one doing that."

"You can't?" She seemed surprised.

"What good would it do to take money from my people when I'm trying to make them prosperous?" I asked.

Well, if we'd been speaking purely about foreign trade, she'd have been right, but for domestic trade, we needed to think not as individuals, but as a country.

"Certainly, at first, there will be merchants who do that and make money hand over fist. However, eventually, the supply shortage will be resolved. Once supply and demand are in balance, the high prices should gradually come back down. We can plan for price homogenization across the country. Basically..."

"...people will be able to buy the things that were too expensive for them before?" she finished.

I gave Liscia's answer a satisfied nod. "Currently, the largest rising demand in most of this country is foodstuffs. To stabilize prices on those, we urgently need to secure distribution routes. Besides, more than half of this country's border is with the sea. We should be able to harvest a lot of maritime products. If those can be hauled overland, we can solve the food crisis in no time."

"Even now, we're able to bring dried and pickled goods inland, you know?" she said.

"Well, can you live on dried and pickled fish forever?" I asked. "Me, I'd get tired of it."

"Well, yes, I suppose I would, too."

Dried horse mackerel is tasty, but I definitely wouldn't have wanted to eat it every day. The salt in it is there to fight bacteria and decay, so you can't change the flavor, even if you do get tired of it. Fish spoils fast to begin with, and even dried, it will turn in a matter of days. That was why the speed at which we could ship fish and shellfish inland was so important.

"That's what the transportation network is for, huh?" she mused.

"Exactly. Now, then..." I gave a big yawn and closed my eyes. "Let me sleep for a bit. When I wake up, we'll go to the planned site for the new city together. Ludwin and his men are probably already there getting started. I need to go see them..."

"Okay." She nodded. "Sleep tight, Souma."

"Yeah, good ni—huh?!"

There was a soft, warm sensation on my right cheek. I opened my eyes in shock, but Liscia was already gone.

Oh...a goodnight kiss... th-that's what it was, right? They're not that uncommon in other countries, right? Yeah, it's fine, it's totally normal. Nothing special about it. Liscia did it casually, I'll bet. There shouldn't be any deeper meaning to it. Probably. I'm sure.

In the end, I never did manage to get to sleep.

◇　◇　◇

Do you remember how before, when I talked about how the technology of this country was all messed up, I mentioned that there were steel battleships, only they were drawn by massive sea dragons? When Liscia and I arrived at the planned site for the new city, we were greeted by one of those steel battleships.

Battleship *Albert.*

Bearing the name of the former king, it was the sole battleship in the possession of the Forbidden Army, and the flagship of the Royal Navy.

Its shape was like the *Mikasa,* which was the flagship of the Combined Fleet at the time of the Battle of Tsushima. There were two main batteries, one each at the fore and aft, for a total of four guns. It was also equipped with auxiliary guns along the sides, although the main batteries and auxiliary guns were all loaded onto the vessel, not fixed artillery. Also, because it wasn't loaded with an internal combustion engine, the lack of a smokestack was another difference between the two.

Its power source was a sea dragon. (These looked like plesiosaurs, but with short, thick necks and goat-like horns.) With a giant sea dragon pulling it, this battleship could run through the water. For an ordinary ship, one dragon was enough, but this ship was a two-dragon model.

Now seems like a good time, so let me explain about some of the imbalances in this country's technology.

You might find it strange that a country which hadn't even reached the industrial revolution had these sorts of near-modern warships. However, thanks to this world's magic and mysterious creatures, they were able to do things they otherwise couldn't.

Even if something is made of iron, if it's been built with the proper calculations for buoyancy, it can be made to float. In other words, the outer frame of a battleship can be built even with Middle Ages technology. The reason they hadn't been built until after the industrial revolution was because the engines that would be needed to move them didn't exist. In an era where your only means of propelling a boat are catching the wind with sails or rowing with oars, an iron ship wouldn't be able to do anything but float there.

However, in this world, there were powerful sea dragons that were strong enough to tow an iron ship. By training them to pull the ships, ocean navigation became possible. That was why iron ships were built.

It was the same for the large cannons aboard the battleship. This world already had gunpowder. Now, that in and of itself wasn't strange. Even on Earth, there are traces of gunpowder having been used which predate the appearance of black powder, one of China's three great inventions. In the second century, during the time of *Romance of the Three Kingdoms,* the general defending Chencang used an explosive weapon (something like a firecracker) to pulverize the invading army led by Zhuge Liang's weapons.

However, in this world, there were no arquebuses.

Because they had magic for their long-range attacks, they had never developed firearms. Earth mages could fire off stones like a machine gun, fire mages could drop attacks that were like napalm bombs, wind mages could launch a vacuum slash from incredible range, while water mages could, at shorter range, penetrate obstacles with water pressure.

Furthermore, there existed what were called "attachable spells." By attaching spells with various effects to an object, that object could be made stronger or able to cut better. Because of this, weapons with higher mass, which could have more spells embedded in them, tended to be more powerful.

Thus, an arrow was stronger than a bullet, a spear stronger than an arrow. To explain further, with a bullet's small mass, even if you embedded an attack spell in it, it couldn't pierce a suit of plated armor with a defensive spell embedded in it. It could be said that this was why they'd never developed guns.

However, while they didn't have rifles, they did have cannons.

This was because the use of other elements was limited over the water, so they'd been developed as a means of making long-range attacks.

This world's magic was said to come from mixing special waves emitted by people with a substance called magicium in the atmosphere to produce a variety of phenomena. Magicium had an elemental alignment (with the exception of darkness), and the composition of the magicium in the atmosphere was greatly influenced by the terrain. Over the water there was mostly water magicium, meaning magic from the other elements was weakened there, and so on for other areas.

Because of this, if they were to use magic in naval battles, all elements but water would be weakened, and they would end up in a situation where water elemental magic didn't have a long enough range. However, it could still be used to control the currents for steering, so water mages were assigned to the navy.

Which was precisely why cannons had been developed to attack ships. Ultimately, technology only develops where there's a demand for it.

End of digression. Now let's get back to the Battleship *Albert*. When I saw the *Albert,* here is what I thought:

What am I supposed to do with one ship? It's only when they're defended by destroyers and cruisers that a battleship or carrier can exhibit their true power. What I have here is no more than a scarecrow.

"Well, you know, it was assumed it would be operating alongside the navy." Liscia's words only made it sadder. Clearly, this thing was a white elephant.

"In that case, if we leave the flagship to the navy, don't you think that would save us some of the upkeep costs?" I asked.

"B-but...we were able to use it to transport materials, weren't we?" she asked.

"Well, yeah, I guess..."

We had used this needlessly big battleship to transport materials for the coastal city. Once we had removed the armaments from inside it, that had freed up a good amount of carrying capacity. With the transportation network not in place yet at this stage, it had allowed us to ship the materials here many times faster than we could have sending them by land.

"But, in that case, it would have been even more effective if we'd built it as a transport ship to begin with," I said.

"Ugh! Don't be so negative about everything!" she protested.

"I'm fighting with the budget, so when I see something gobbling up funds, I can't help myself."

Then Aisha came along, bringing Ludwin with her.

"Your Majesty, I've called Sir Ludwin for you," she said.

"Your Majesty, Your Highness, I welcome you to the planned site of the new city." The handsome captain of the Royal Guard, Ludwin Arcs, saluted with a smile. At the castle he always wore silver armor, but here he was dressed more casually. With the white shirt and leather vest he wore, he looked like a handsome sailor who might show up in a pirate movie.

I was using the Forbidden Army to work on constructing the city. Of course, I was hiring several craftsmen from the civil engineering and construction guild, too, but with the scale of the project, they couldn't handle everything.

That's why I was using the Forbidden Army, thinking I would wrap this up quickly with human-wave tactics. After I'd gone to the trouble of teaching the soldiers combat engineering skills, it would have been a waste not to use them. I had two-tenths of the Forbidden Army's standing forces here, with the remaining eight-tenths building the transport network that would connect all the cities.

"So, how is progress on the construction?" I asked.

"We've already finished roping off the site. Work is going steadily... or it *was*..." Ludwin said hesitantly, a bitter smile on his face.

"I keep telling you, you need to stop construction!" one person shouted.

"Listen, old man. We're building this city on the king's orders, get it?" another answered.

I heard voices arguing inside the tent that served as the construction office.

"I'm telling you this for the king's sake! You mustn't build a city here!"

"You just don't get it, do you, old man? It's not like we're trying to evict you or anything."

"You're the ones who don't get it!"

No, it wasn't an argument—it was more like this old man was one-sidedly yelling at them.

I spoke to Ludwin. "So, basically, an old man who lives in the area is vehemently opposed to us building the new city?"

"Yes. A local fisherman. Mr. Urup."

"I did tell you not to aggressively buy up land or anything like that, didn't I?" I asked.

"Of course. We're looking for residents to apply anyway, so the prior residents can stay right where they are. We won't charge them for the land, either. When we work on the landscaping, we plan to rebuild their houses at no cost."

"Hmm... those sound like good conditions to me," I said.

As far as I could see, there were nothing but deserted-looking fishing villages around here. It had to be hard just to eke out a living in a place as rural as this. If a city were built, with the influx of people, many of the inconveniences of living here would go away. Not only were they not being chased out of a place that would offer them a better future, they were even having their houses rebuilt for free, so what was there to be opposed to?

"Why is that old man opposed to it?" I asked.

"Well..."

"I'm telling you, you'll incur the wrath of the sea god!" I heard shouting from inside the tent again.

The sea god?

"You see, he says this is the sea god's domain and building houses will anger him, or something like that."

"What, you even have sea gods in this world?" I asked.

Liscia and the others all shook their heads vigorously.

"I've never heard of one before," Liscia said.

"I, too, am unaware of one," Aisha agreed.

"It's probably just an old man's nonsense," Ludwin added.

It seemed nobody had heard of one.

A sea god, huh? I wondered.

"I've never heard of this sea god in my life," a voice said from inside. "Would you please not interrupt construction with your strange religion?"

"It's no religion! The sea god is real! If you violate the sanctity of his holy land, eventually you will anger him and be destroyed! In fact, the sea god goes on a rampage once every hundred years or so!" the man shouted.

Hm?

"When I was a boy, the sea god went on a rampage once. At the time, all of the people who had built homes in the sea god's holy land were swallowed up by him!" he added.

Could he be talking about what I think he is...?

I entered the tent. Inside were a young Forbidden Army soldier and a tanned old man wearing a towel twisted into a headband.

"I'm sorry, sir. Could you tell me in detail about what you're talking about?" I asked politely.

"Who are you?" he demanded. "I'm busy talking to this fellow..."

"Wh-why, Your Majesty!" the soldier stuttered.

"His Majesty?!" When he saw the soldier stand and salute me, the old man let out a bizarre cry.

"Hey there," I said. "I'm the (provisional) King of Elfrieden, Souma Kazuya."

I went to shake his hand.

"The name's Urup," the old man responded with a tense look on his face.

Once we had finished greeting each other, I immediately dove to the heart of the matter. "Now then, Urup. Back to what you were talking about before."

"Hm?! R-right! Your Majesty, please, reconsider building this city!"

"Old man, are you really going to trouble His Majesty himself with your nonsense?" the soldier demanded.

"No, I want to hear him out." I gestured for the soldier who was trying to stop him to stand down. "Can you tell me more about it?"

"B-but of course." And so, Urup explained the local legend to me.

Apparently, this land had originally belonged to the sea god, but he had lost it after being defeated by the land god in battle. However, the sea god still believed this land was his, and when people built houses on it, he would destroy the people who lived in them.

This was why there was a rule in the nearby fishing village that no one should build houses here.

Once they had heard Urup's story, Liscia said, "It's too vague. I don't really get it."

"Listening to him was a waste of time," Aisha added.

Both of them seemed exasperated, but I felt differently.

Partway through his tale, I'd had Ludwin bring a map, asking just how far the sea god's holy land stretched. Then, once I had narrowed down the range of "the sea god's holy land" enough, I looked at the map and told Ludwin, "We need to make major changes to the city plan."

"Hold on, Souma, why are you saying that all of a sudden?!" Liscia demanded.

"Do you believe what this old man is saying, Sire?!" Aisha cried.

"If we make changes now, there will be a major delay in construction," Ludwin protested.

I could understand how they felt. I didn't want to do something so bothersome, either. However, when I considered the peace of the new city, it had to be done.

"Souma, you can't mean to tell me you really believe in this sea god?" Aisha asked.

"No, there's probably no sea god," I told her.

"Then..."

"Liscia, legends are people's memories." I pointed to my temple. "Legends are something we hand down. So, why do we hand them down, you might wonder? Because our forefathers decided it was important to do so. Worthless stories won't be handed down. If this one has been handed down, there's a lesson to be found in the legend, or wisdom for everyday life in it."

"And you're saying this 'curse of the sea god' is like that?" she asked.

"Yeah. In this legend, the lesson is *don't build houses in a specific area*. If people ignore that lesson and build houses there, they're sure to be destroyed." I looked straight at Urup and added, "By a tsunami, right?"

Urup's eyes went wide, and he suddenly began to tremble.

"Y-yes! By a tsunami! Everyone in the houses there, they were washed away, houses and all!"

"Was there a big earthquake before the tsunami came, perhaps?" I asked.

"H-how did you know?!" Urup cried, as if he had just remembered that now himself. Perhaps the sight of people being washed away, houses and all, was so shocking that he had unconsciously been suppressing the memory.

"In other words, the sea god's true identity is a tidal wave triggered by an undersea earthquake," I said.

Even on Earth, it was only recently that the mechanism behind earthquakes had been discovered.

We'd had to wait until the 20th century, when the interior structure of the Earth had been discovered. Until that point, even if we'd experienced an earthquake as a phenomenon, we had said it was because of reasons like "volcanic activity" or "underground water turning into steam and causing a hollow cavity to form."

I used my hands to demonstrate one plate subsiding under another, like you often see on news programs' earthquake coverage, but all I got was a bunch of blank stares.

"Ummm... sorry. I don't really get it," Liscia said.

"Plates? Vibration? Are you talking about magic, Sire?" Aisha asked.

"I'm lost, too," Ludwin added. "When it comes to things that advanced, I don't know if they teach it even at the Royal Academy."

Not one of them understood. It was ahead of their time, so I couldn't blame them.

"Okay, forget the mechanism behind how it works, then," I said. "The important thing is, when there's an earthquake underwater, sometimes it causes a tsunami. In other words, Urup's 'wrath of the sea god' doesn't occur because people build houses there; it's a periodic thing."

"My word... it will happen even if we don't build houses there?" Urup's eyes were wide.

I traced the contours of the coastlines on the map and showed them. "I could also mention, this country's coast is in a < shape, and this spot is in the corner of it. Places like this will be damaged more heavily than other coastal areas in a tsunami. The reason for that is something you wouldn't understand even if I tried to explain it to you, so just accept that that's how it works."

If I'd built a miniature model of the coast and poured water in so they could see the waves converging, they might have been able to understand. That'd take effort, though, so it could wait.

"Still, if this place is so dangerous, won't the new city be at risk?" Liscia pointed out.

I groaned. "Hrm... some spots might be better than this, but all coastal regions are about the same, and I can say for sure that this is the closest port to the center of the country. From what I'm hearing, there's a long period of time between them, and they only happen once in a hundred years, so if we design the city assuming it will be hit by a tsunami, it should be okay."

With that, Ludwin and I looked at the map, hammering out the details of our plan.

"First, we should pile up dirt and raise the ground level," I said.

"Right now? If we do it by hand, it will take quite a while," he answered.

"Have earth mages in the Forbidden Army prioritize working on it. It will have an impact on the building time, but there's no other choice."

"Understood." He nodded. "Now that I think of it, I've heard that Duchess Walter's coastal city has these things called seawalls. Should we make those here as well?"

"Seawalls, huh? It'll hurt the view..." I gave it some consideration. "If possible, I want this trade port to be usable as a tourist destination, as well. Besides, the walls wouldn't be able to stand up to an unprecedentedly large tsunami, anyway."

"We shouldn't build them, then?" he asked.

"Let's see... actually, I'd rather build a city that doesn't rely on seawalls. It seems like the civil engineering and construction guild has an expert on flood control, so let's summon him and get his opinion."

"Understood," he said. "Now, as to the specifics of the city plan..."

"Thanks to old man Urup, we know roughly the area that the tsunami can reach," I said. "We'll avoid it when we place the residential, commercial, and industrial districts. Of course, that goes for important facilities like consulates, as well."

"You're not going to develop the area that the tsunami reaches?" he asked.

"The fishing harbor and wharf can't go anywhere else. As for the rest, we'll develop it as a seaside park."

"I see. You'll develop on the assumption that it's going to get washed away."

"Yeah," I said. "Oh, one other thing, old man Urup."

"Hm? What is it?"

"I'm going to make you a state-registered storyteller, so see to it that the Legend of the Sea God gets handed down, please. I'm going to make it a public service job which requires certification, so work hard to train the next generation to tell the story before you die."

"M-me, a public servant?!" he exclaimed.

"Yeah. In addition to the 'don't build houses where the tsunami can reach' lesson from earlier, work in 'if you feel an earthquake, assume there will be a tsunami,' and 'because a tsunami is coming, evacuate to high ground,' as well. You can blame the sea god's wrath, just make sure the tale is one that's easy to hand down."

"Understood! I shall spend the rest of my life on it!" he cried.

"Good. By the way, about the castle wall that will surround the city..."

The three men talked enthusiastically about the plan for the city. Liscia and Aisha watched them with wry smiles.

"His Majesty looks like he's enjoying himself," Aisha commented.

"He *is* enjoying himself," Liscia nodded. "Compared to hunting for funds, at least."

"I wonder why it is, but I think I've finally seen the youthful side of His Majesty."

"Youthful... huh. The reason Souma doesn't seem youthful is almost certainly because..."

"Hm? What is it, Princess?" Aisha asked.

"No. It's nothing. Hey, Aisha."

"What is it?"

"Aisha, do you...like Souma?" she asked hesitantly.

"Yes! I have great respect and affection for him!"

"I see. Well, then. Let's work to support Souma so he can keep smiling."

"Yes! But of course!" Aisha cried.

At the time, I didn't realize at all that a conversation like this had taken place.

◇　◇　◇

Thirty years later, an earthquake and unprecedentedly large tsunami struck the area.

The land was inundated by turbid waters and many boats were washed out to sea, but surprisingly few lives were lost. Because everyone in the area had grown up hearing the Legend of the Sea God from the storytellers, they were able to begin evacuating as soon as they felt the earthquake.

After the disaster, a statue titled "The King and the Old Man" was built in the seaside park.

It was a statue to commemorate the old man who, at the time

of the new city's construction, had risked his life to make a direct appeal to the king and tell him how to prepare for the tsunami, and the wise king who had listened to his plans. If the two of them could have heard, they'd have laughed wryly, saying, "That's over embellishing it."

Particularly for old man Urup, who had once been the storyteller, but now appeared in stories of his descendants as the Legendary Old Man, what sort of expression did he have on his face while he watched over them from the next world?

HOW A REALIST HERO REBUILT THE KINGDOM

CHAPTER 6
Relief

I'M HALBERT MAGNA, age nineteen.

I'm the eldest son of the Magna family, well known within the Elfrieden Kingdom's land forces. I myself used to belong to them, but after some stuff happened, I was forced to transfer to the Forbidden Army.

To add insult to injury, my commanding officer was my childhood friend, the earth mage Kaede Foxia, who liked to end her sentences with "you know." To think, now I had to take orders from her... I wished it were all just a joke.

On top of that, what was I doing now? Right now, rather than a sword, I was swinging an entrenching tool (a round-edged shovel which can also be used in close quarters combat) instead.

Marching orders had come for the Forbidden Army, and when I arrived on the site, I was tasked with piling up dirt, hollowing out the middle, pouring in a gooey liquid (?), reinforcing the sides with gravel, then planting saplings on either side. After that, I would set up the street lamps filled with the lightmoss which is common in the capital, the kind which absorbs light during the day and is phosphorescent at night, repeating these same tasks over and over.

To sum it up simply, I was doing roadwork.

Summer had ended, but the sun was still hot, and I was digging up dirt and making piles with it over and over.

"Why...does the Forbidden Army...have to do...roadwork?"

"You there. Stop prattling and get to work, on the double."

Wiping the sweat from my brow, I looked over to see Kaede standing on top of a simple scaffold, smacking the railing with her megaphone as she gave orders. She must have been feeling the heat badly herself. Her trademark perky fox ears had drooped down like dog ears.

"Hey, Kaede, is this really...?" I began.

"You can't do that!" she protested. "Hal, you're my subordinate, you know. You must address me properly as the site foreman."

"Foreman, is this really a job for the Forbidden Army?"

"This is the sort of work that the Forbidden Army does now, you know," she answered.

"Surely we could leave this stuff to construction workers."

"There just aren't enough of them, you know? This is part of a plan for a kingdom-wide road network, you know? We've hired unemployed people from the capital as well, I hear, but we're still so short of hands, I'd even ask a warcat to help."

Even so, would you normally have the military do this sort of work? I thought.

"Besides, we can't just have construction workers come here alone, you know," she said. "The further you go from a settlement, the more powerful the wild creatures get, after all. And if we hired adventurers to protect them, it would cost a fortune."

"So, in the end, we're just cheap labor, is that it?" I asked.

"If you understand that, then get to work, on the double," she said.

"You're an earth mage. Can't you do this faster with magic?"

"I can't afford to expend my magic here, you know," she said. "Hal, are you going to dig tunnels through the mountains in my place?"

I said nothing.

I went back to my work of digging up dirt and piling it up.

It's better than being forced to dig a tunnel without magic, at least, I thought. *What kind of old-fashioned hard labor sentence is this...?*

◇ ◇ ◇

Noon came. We went back to the camp and were given a two-hour break.

Inside the tent we ate, chatted, or used the simple beds (they were no more than stretchers that had grown a little fur) to take an afternoon nap. Apparently, the king strongly encouraged naps after eating. It was something about how it improved work efficiency.

So, work in the Forbidden Army literally came with "three meals and a nap," but once people found out what kind of work was involved, there was no way they would be jealous of us.

Anyway, I wasn't going to make it through the afternoon if I didn't eat, so I wolfed down the lunchbox I had been supplied.

Today's lunchbox was meat and vegetables between bread. Delicious.

The meat was lightly spiced, which felt like it helped relieve my exhaustion. It was apparently a dish called "shogayaki" which that king had come up with. It was a menu he was experimenting with now that the production of the seasonings the king was having the mystic wolves make for him—"miso," "soy sauce," and "mirin"—had gotten on track.

In the Forbidden Army, we were often served the king's experimental menus like this. The meals were one of the few things that made me happy that I had been forced to transfer to the Forbidden Army. The meals we'd gotten in the land forces had prioritized quantity over quality. The kind of thing you'd picture from the words "a man's meal." Honestly, eating here even once had been enough to convince me I didn't want to go back.

"That king... if nothing else, I've got to recognize his gift for cooking," I admitted.

"They really are delicious, you know," Kaede agreed. "The dishes our king comes up with."

At some point, Kaede had sat down next to me, and she was eating the same menu.

"Also, it's incredible that we can eat fresh veggies every day, you know," she continued. "They come in from the closest village to here that's hooked up to the castle by road. The reason roads are great is that they make it easy to maintain supply lines, you know."

"The roads we're building are being useful right away, huh?" I asked.

"With this transportation capacity, you can almost call the food crisis solved already, you know. We can bring food from the areas with a surplus to the areas where there are shortages. We'll be able to transport foods that we couldn't before because they didn't keep long enough."

"Is he doing this because he knows all that stuff?" I asked. "That king, I mean."

"He's an incredible man, you know. His foresight is almost frightening."

Well, I thought Kaede was amazing for being able to understand all of that, too. She could be a bit silly in some ways, but Kaede had some pretty high base specs. She could use magic, and she was sharp, too. That was probably why she had been chosen by the king himself.

As her childhood friend, it did frustrate me a little, though.

I need to do my best, too.

"Well, now that you've eaten, will you be taking a nap, Hal?" she asked me.

"Well... I am tired. Guess I will."

"In that case, you can rest your head in my lap, you know," she said.

"Bwuh!" I spewed my tea.

Everyone was suddenly looking our way. More than half of those glances were from men who clearly wanted to kill me.

Now, even though I'm biased as her childhood friend, Kaede is cute. It's nothing to write home about, but her figure's not bad, and those fox ears and tail really work in her favor. It wasn't surprising that she was treated like an idol in the Forbidden Army.

The king had told me to serve under her so the men wouldn't look down on Kaede, but, honestly, I think that with one request from her, these guys would gladly have gone to their deaths. That was why their murderous rage was directed at me, for being so close to her.

I coughed desperately. "What are you saying?!"

"People were talking about how the princess did it for the king in the park in the capital a little while back, you know," she said.

"I'm amazed they could do that in a place where so many people could see..."

Well, they're engaged and all, so maybe it's not that odd, I added to myself. *It's far better than not getting along at all.*

"People are saying we'll have a royal heir by next year. Though, partly because the king is from another world, the betting pools for the heir's name haven't been able to narrow down a list of candidates."

"You're talking an awful lot about something that's none of your business," a voice said.

Kaede yelped.

When I turned to look in the direction of the sudden voice, I saw King Souma, sighing and slumping his shoulders, and Princess Liscia, her face a deep shade of red, standing at the entrance of the tent.

"Hey, you two. How've you been?" King Souma asked, addressing us casually.

"I'm full of energy, you know," Kaede managed. "Your Majesty, I see that you and the princess are the same as ever."

"Yeah, we haven't changed much, have we, Liscia?" King Souma asked.

"You're right. It makes me wish you'd show a little more awareness of your position as king."

King Souma and the princess sat down at our table, as though it were perfectly natural for them to do so and started having a friendly chat with Kaede.

Huh? Wait? What's going on?

King Souma and the princess were sitting across from me and Kaede while the dark elf who'd been with them at the café stood waiting by the entrance. Since I felt better just knowing that blue-haired woman wasn't around, that was probably evidence I'd been traumatized by the experience I'd had last time.

Then King Souma turned the conversation to me. "Halbert, have you gotten used to things in the Forbidden Army, as well?"

"Yes, sir! I have no issues!"

"So formal..." he muttered. "Where did the spirit you had before go?"

"I apologize for my behavior that time!" I said immediately. "I was terribly rude to you, Your Majesty..."

"King's orders: don't be so uptight and formal. Also, no more of that 'Your Majesty' stuff. Souma's fine."

"No, but..."

"*Hal,* did you not hear me? That was an order."

"I...I understand...Souma."

"That's good. I was just thinking I'd like a guy my age who I can chat casually with," King Souma—Souma—said, seeming satisfied.

What the hell, man? Seriously? I thought. *Well, if he's requesting it himself, fine. I don't feel much respect for his authority, anyway.*

"So, why are you here, Souma?" I asked.

"For an inspection, that's all. I want to see how the roadwork is progressing."

"You don't need to tell us to take our jobs seriously. We already do," I said.

"So it seems. I took the road coming here."

"You'd better be grateful," I said. "We're breaking our backs to build it for you."

"And I reward you with good food and wages, don't I? You're receiving plenty of compensation."

I got used to talking casually with him in no time. Souma'd never felt like a king to begin with, anyway.

When he saw we were finished eating, Souma rose from his seat. "Now then, you two, why don't you join me for the road inspection? I'd like to explain road construction to Liscia."

"What, isn't Kaede good enough for that on her own?" I asked. "She's the one in charge here."

"I want to show her the actual work of making the road, you see," he explained. "Besides, it's at times like these when you should do what your superiors want and take the chance to build connections. It'll come in handy later, you know?"

"How is it going to help me?" I demanded.

"Well, we're studying how to make instant gelin udon right now," he said. "Just add water and anytime, anywhere, even out in the field, you'll be able to enjoy gelin udon. I might be able to arrange for some of the samples to make their way to your unit..."

"Right this way, Sire. I'll show you around." I rose to my feet and saluted Souma.

Instant gelin udon. Now we were talking. I wasn't going to let this chance to add some variety to our already-limited selection of field rations slip away.

The princess and Kaede seemed amused by my sudden change in attitude, but I didn't let that bother me. Food was my number one priority, after all.

The five of us—me, Kaede, Souma, the princess, and the dark elf guard—arrived at a section of road that was currently being paved. There, Souma asked me to demonstrate the work procedures for everyone.

First, I piled up dirt to create the road's sides.

"Once he's piled up the dirt on both sides, we pour that gooey stuff over there in the middle," Souma said, explaining road construction to the princess.

"What is that gooey stuff?" she asked.

"Roman concrete. It's a mixture of volcanic ash and lime. It will harden as time passes. It also has a unique viscosity, so it doesn't crack easily. If you want to see how tough it is, look at that over there. I think you'll understand."

After saying that, Souma pointed to a giant lizard that was larger than many buildings. The giant lizard was towing several wheeled container cars behind it. The container cars were packed full of construction materials and provisions for the soldiers.

The giant lizard was a rhinosaurus, also known as the great horned lizard. This super-sized lizard was distinctive for the two great tusks which grew from atop its nose. (If Souma had been describing it, he might have described it as "Take a rhino, add a Komodo dragon, divide by two, then multiply the size by ten.") They were omnivorous and gentle, easily becoming attached to people, so they were used in big cities to haul large volumes of cargo like this. When they were enraged, they had an unstoppable charge, so I had heard of them being used to assault castles, as well.

"It's so tough that even if that rhinosaurus rammed it at full speed, it won't crack," Souma explained.

"That *is* incredible," the princess said. "It's that hard?"

"No, actually, it's flexible where it needs to be, so it distributes the force that's put into it. In the world I came from, there were buildings made with this concrete over 2,000 years ago that are still standing."

2,000 years? Four times longer than this country's existed? I thought. *Wow, that's amazing.*

"Moving on, the street lamps he's setting up on either side of the road are the same as the ones in the capital. There are a lot of wild creatures, so I doubt people will move by night often, but with these, they won't get lost if they do. As for the roadside trees he's planting, they're 'warding trees' from the God-Protected Forest."

"'Warding trees'?" the princess asked.

"Aisha, you explain."

"Yes, sir! These warding trees constantly emit waves that monsters and wild animals dislike. They probably do it to keep giant boars from eating them. In the God-Protected Forest, we plant these warding trees densely around our villages to prevent incursions by monsters and animals."

"I see," the princess mused. "They're like a simple barrier, huh?"

When he heard the princess's response, King Souma gave a satisfied nod. "Now that's what I call local know-how. Anyway, if we planted them densely over a wide range like a road, there's no telling what that'd do to the ecosystem. So rather than fully block them off, we'll leave a reasonable number of gaps so that we're just discouraging them from approaching."

"Why? Wouldn't it be better to stop them entirely?" the princess asked.

"Okay then, Liscia. If the ashen wolves and red bears, which change their hunting grounds seasonally, can't migrate because of the road, and they stay where they are instead, run out of prey, and then start attacking livestock and houses, what will you do? Or, what if giant apes and giant boars, which will end up staying in one place the same way, come down to the villages to tear up the fields and, in so doing, spread leeches that previously only existed in the mountains to the village. What if that happened?"

"I get that we absolutely shouldn't do it, but why are your examples so specific?!" she asked.

"Because coping with dangerous animals is a problem that all local self-governing bodies must face," Souma said, an exhausted look on his face.

What's a "local self-governing body"? I wondered.

Unlike me, Kaede seemed to understand, and she was thoroughly impressed.

"Wowwie... you've thought it through that far. I should have expected no less from our king, you know," she said.

"Hmm. Well, all I did was bring along a bunch of knowledge from the world I was in before," Souma said.

Kaede's eyes sparkled, and Souma blushed a little as she stared at him.

As she watched those two, the princess seemed a little miffed.

"Um, Princess?" the dark elf asked.

"What?" the princess demanded.

"That's one scary look you've got on your face."

"I-is it? Well, you're not one to talk, are you?"

"Huh?"

Then, at that moment...

"No!"

There was a sudden cry. Wondering what it was, I turned to look in its direction and saw the dark elf looking at a letter, her face distorted with emotion. There was a white bird perched on her quivering shoulder.

Was that a messenger kui?

Using a kui's homing instinct and ability to pick up on waves emitted by its master at a long distance, it was possible to communicate between an individual and a fixed location. Except for the Jewel Voice Broadcast, which almost felt like cheating, this was

the fastest method of communication. So, did that mean someone had contacted her?

"What is it, Aisha?" Souma asked.

The dark elf spoke through quivering lips. "I've just received
word from the God-Protected Forest that there's been a major
landslide!"

◇ ◇ ◇

"I've received a message from my father, the chief of the dark
elf village," Aisha said. "'Last night, a sudden landslide swallowed
up around half the village,' it said. There had been a lot of rain in
the God-Protected Forest lately. There are...many people missing... ohh..." Aisha's voice caught.

Her homeland and family had just been hit by a terrible disaster. It had to have been quite a shock to her.

I'm concerned, but I don't have time to comfort her, I thought.
In this situation, as the king, what moves should I be making?

While I was silently thinking that, Hal said, "Hey, you could
at least comfort her..." but Kaede was already pulling him away by
the ear before I could say anything back in response.

"The king is thinking right now," she lectured. "You mustn't
interrupt him, you know."

I watched her drag Hal off. What a good childhood friend
she was.

Okay, I've sorted out my thoughts. I raised my face, acting
immediately.

"This unit will go to aid the dark elf village!" I declared.

Hal held his ear and blinked at me repeatedly. "This unit? There are only around fifty of us."

"Disaster relief is a battle against time," I told him. "We don't have time to turn back to the capital. Fortunately, the God-Protected Forest is closer to here than to the capital. First, I'll dispatch this unit as an advance team!"

I gave each of them their orders.

"Liscia, return to the capital and request they dispatch a relief unit. Also, talk to Hakuya and have him send food, clothing, tents, and other relief supplies to the dark elf village."

"I understand, but...don't you have a 'consciousness' working back in the capital? If you do, wouldn't it be faster to contact him through that?" Liscia asked.

"I can't. Living Poltergeists only has an effective range of 100 meters or so. Dolls can ignore that range limitation, but they can't do paperwork, so I didn't leave one behind."

If I'd known this was going to happen, I would have left at least one doll behind. If I had, I might have at least been able to communicate that something had happened.

Too late for regrets now, I guess, I thought.

"So, there you have it," I said. "Someone needs to go make the request in person."

"I get it," she said. "Leave it to me."

"When you go, bring the bodyguards we brought here with you! It'd be no joke if something were to happen to you on the way there."

"I think I'll be fine, but...understood. You take care of yourself, too." Liscia immediately ran off.

If I stopped to think about it, it was amazing that I was making the princess of a nation play messenger girl, but Liscia probably didn't mind. We were of the same mind on these things.

"Aisha, how far is it from here to the God-Protected Forest?" I asked.

"Half a day on a fast horse," she said. "At a normal march, it'll take two days no matter how we hurry."

"Two days... when did the disaster strike?" I asked.

"It was during the witching hour, from what I gather."

"It's already been nearly half a day, then? The soonest we can arrive is two and a half days after the disaster. Having only half a day before we reach the seventy-two-hour mark is going to be rough."

Hal looked confused. "What's that? What do you mean by 'the seventy-two-hour mark'?"

"In natural disasters like this, that's the line after which the death rate for those in need of rescue shoots up. It's three full days after the disaster strikes. It's called the 'seventy-two-hour wall.'"

"Sorry. Could you say that in a way that's easier to understand?" he asked.

"It means that a lot of lives can be saved in those seventy-two hours."

"I get it now. Wait, in that case, we can't dawdle here! Shouldn't we be getting our butts to the God-Protected Forest, pronto?! It's gonna take a full two days, isn't it?" he demanded.

"I know that," I said. "Do we have a carriage?"

"The original plan only called for us to use carriages when we came here and when we left. If we need to get enough carriages for fifty people, that's going to take time."

"Damn!" I said. "Is there no other way to move around...?"

I noticed something. Hal and the others looked to see what I was looking at, then gulped.

I was looking at the beasts pulling the container cars. If you take a rhino, add a Komodo dragon, divide by two, then multiply the size by ten, you would have these giant lizards, the rhinosauruses. They were big, but they could run continuously at high speeds comparable to a steam locomotive.

"Hey, Hal, Kaede," I said.

"What?" Hal asked cautiously.

"What is it?" Kaede asked.

"It'll probably make us all nauseous, so will you be okay?" I asked.

"I'm quite resistant to motion sickness, you know," Kaede said.

"I'll deal with it," Hal muttered.

"You will? I'll tough it out, too, then."

I immediately gave the order to fifty members of the Forbidden Army.

"Unload all the freight from the container cars! Fortunately, the road runs near the God-Protected Forest, but once we get into the woods, we'll be traveling on foot! The lighter our load, the better! Leave the materials where you unload them! Even if they're lost, you won't be blamed for it! I'll give a written apology to Hakuya and get off with a little scolding! Also, bring all the food with us! We can't do something lame like show up to offer aid, then have to sponge off the locals for food!"

"Yes, sir!"

Following my orders, the Forbidden Army soldiers speedily unloaded the container cars.

As you might expect from people who'd been doing nothing but construction work, they moved fast. The way they efficiently worked together to carry off the materials made them look like skilled movers. They really did feel reliable.

"No, we're soldiers, remember?" Hal complained.

"Stop prattling and get to work, Hal," Kaede said.

Kaede was using her magic to easily move materials that would normally have taken a few big strong men working together to lift.

Earth magic was, in the end, the magic of gravity manipulation. It didn't create earth or stone from nothing; it manipulated what already existed. That was probably why she could do tricks like this. It was a huge contribution.

Right now, I was probably the least useful person here. Since I had below-average strength, even if I joined in with the soldiers, I would probably just be in the way.

As I stood there watching them work for lack of anything better to do, Aisha came up to me. "Your Majesty..."

She looked weak, as if she might break down at any moment.

Ever since I'd recruited her, Aisha had been at my side as a bodyguard, so I felt like I had seen a lot of her expressions. Her determined face when she made a direct appeal to me, her imposing warrior face, her childlike face when she was eating something, the face like an abandoned dog that she made when she had to wait for that food... I had seen many expressions from her, but this one was new.

To see a girl who was so much more powerful than me looking so weak pained my heart. Aisha was always protecting me as my bodyguard, but now it was time for me to protect her. I placed my hand atop her head, which was roughly the same height as mine.

"S-Sire?" she asked.

"Leave this to me." I pulled her in, resting her forehead on my shoulder. "I have no power, and I'm far weaker than you, Aisha, but I'm in a position to make a lot of people move. So, leave this to me. If there are lives that can be saved, I'll save all that I can."

"Sire... Siiiiiiiire!" Burying her face in my shoulder, Aisha began to cry.

I gently patted her head.

Until we were ready to go, I comforted the crying Aisha.

The God-Protected Forest was a forested area to the south of the country.

The name apparently came from the legend that a giant god-beast that took the form of a goat-antelope protected this forest.

That said, there had been no claimed sightings of it in recent years, and now the only proof of its existence was that its divine protection kept locusts from attacking the forest, kept droughts from drying it up, kept cold waves from freezing it, and kept the trees green at all times. This god-beast that only showed it existed through its divine protection...did it *really* exist?

The dark elves were the ones to claim their forest was under the god-beast's protection.

The forest had to be approximately as big as the Sea of Trees around Mt. Fuji. They called it a forest, but it was actually the autonomous domain of the dark elves, and that xenophobic race had never let the other races enter their forest. Even Aisha had come to appeal to me for a crackdown on trespassers.

This time, there were close to fifty (hundreds once you considered the units to follow) humans coming to provide relief, and we would be entering the forest, but this was by request of the chief's daughter, Aisha, so it would be treated as a special case, apparently. The dark elves lived in the forest, defended their independence, and hated outsiders.

As a matter of fact, despite the catastrophic landslide they had suffered, they apparently hadn't sent a request for aid to the capital. If Aisha hadn't been contacted, we might never have known the disaster had happened at all. It was admirable of them to try to solve their problems on their own, but it was stupid for them to let the number of deaths shoot up because of it.

"They've become hardheaded because they don't even try to look at the outside world," Aisha spoke sadly as we walked through the God-Protected Forest. "Because I contacted you, Sire, and you listened to my opinions, there were signs of that beginning to change, but..."

Her voice became indignant.

"This isn't an era where we can live in the forest alone. With the threat of the Demon Lord's Domain, we never know when they'll begin to move south! If we shut ourselves away in our forest, do they believe the god-beast will really save us when the time comes?! The god-beast is the protector of the forest, it's not the protector of the dark elf race!"

"Y-yeah..." I said, taken aback.

"That's why we dark elves should study and learn about the wider world!" Aisha was impassioned. It felt like the first time she'd looked so respectable in a while.

"Besides, if I stay in the forest, how would I eat Your Majesty's delicious foods?!" she added.

I take that back. Aisha was still Aisha.

Well, it's better that she's like this than to have her be tense and anxious, I thought.

Soon after we arrived in the dark elf village, we were met by a handsome man who looked to be in his twenties.

"Oh, Your Majesty!" he cried. "How good of you to come."

His handsome face bore a certain resemblance to Aisha's. Could he be her big brother?

He was tall, probably at least one hundred ninety centimeters. I could tell from the accessories he wore on his head and arms that he was of a high rank, but the fine-looking robe he wore was covered in dirt. He looked a little tired, as well.

As she stood before that young elf, Aisha thumped her hand on her chest once. "Father, I have brought His Majesty here with me."

"Well done," he said. "Your friendship with His Majesty must have come about through the guidance of our god-beast."

"Father?!" I exclaimed.

My surprise brought a smile to the young elf's exhausted face.

"My king, it is a pleasure to meet you. I am the chief of the dark elves and Aisha's father, Wodan Udgard. Thank you for taking such good care of my daughter."

"Oh, sure. Um... you're awfully young."

"Pure-blooded elves stop aging once their bodies mature to a certain point," he explained. "We live three times longer than humans, too, so while I may look young, I've still lived eighty years."

I see, I thought. *That's about the same as the elves and dark elves you see in stories, huh? Those say that elves are long-lived, stay youthful for a long time, and that they're all beautiful. Though, my chamberlain, the half-elf Marx, was an old dude, wasn't he? Do half-elves age differently, I wonder?*

Setting that aside, I whispered to Aisha, "He seems welcoming. I thought dark elves were supposed to be xenophobic?"

"My father is the head of the cultural liberalization faction, so he's understanding of cultural exchange with the outside. Father was also the only one who approved of me going to make an appeal to you."

"I see. The reason you don't worry about the rules is because of his influence, huh?" I said. I shook hands with Wodan. "I am the acting king, Souma Kazuya. I am here by the request of Aisha to provide relief."

"It's good of you to come," he said. "Also, you're the king, so please, you don't need to be so formal with me."

"Righty-o. Is this better?"

"Yes. Still, I never expected the king himself to come here."

"I happened to be doing an inspection at the time," I explained. "I've brought the fifty members of the Forbidden Army who were at hand as an advance party. A few days from now, a second group with relief supplies should arrive."

"I'm grateful. The truth is, I'd love to have the whole village come to welcome you, but given the circumstances, I hope you'll understand."

"I know," I said. "It really is an awful situation."

The dark elf village was in the center of a thick circle of warding trees. There were villages like this dotted around the forest, and the dark elves lived in them. If you were to look at the God-Protected Forest as a country, this village would be the capital, and there was an order of magnitude more dark elves living here than anywhere else.

The eastern third or so of that village had been carved away by the landslide. It looked like a slightly elevated slope on the eastern side had collapsed. Perhaps due to the long spell of rain, there was a large amount of water flowing over the exposed surface. The ground might have loosened a fair bit. Our one salvation was that it was sunny now. If it had been raining, we would have had to worry about another collapse while we worked.

"What are the damages like?" I asked.

"We've recorded nearly one hundred casualties already. There are still more than forty missing, as well."

That's a lot, I thought. *It's going to be a battle against time to see how many we can rescue.*

"Let's begin the relief operation immediately," I said. "However, there's a risk of secondary disasters, so it would be a good idea to have the women evacuate. Also, have some people keep an eye on the mountain, please. If the mountain moves in the slightest, or there are any weird noises, have them report it. If it were to collapse again while we're carrying out relief operations, that would be a serious issue."

"I will do that at once," he agreed. "Is there anything else you would like to ask of me?"

"Please compile a list of the missing. We'll erase them from it as we manage to ascertain their safety."

"Understood."

Once I worked things out with Wodan, I gave orders to Aisha and the Forbidden Army.

"Aisha."

"Yes, sir!"

"Have the women evacuate to a place that doesn't look like it will collapse. Consult with Wodan to decide where is best. You will escort them and ensure they're delivered there safely."

"Yes, sir! Understood!"

"Good," I said. "Starting now, the Forbidden Army will begin operations to search for those whose safety is unconfirmed. You guys have a lot of skill at digging, I'm sure. Listen closely, and if you hear voices calling for help in the dirt, carefully rescue them!"

"Yes, sir!"

"However, be absolutely sure that you don't do anything you can't handle. If it looks like there may be another collapse, retreat even if you're in the middle of saving someone. The rescuers cannot be allowed to take even a single loss. Understood?"

"Yes, sir!"

Nodding at the Forbidden Army soldiers' response, I shouted an order. "We will now commence relief operations!"

◇ ◇ ◇

The relief effort was an all-out battle.

Everyone came together, doing everything they could. They called the names of the missing, listened closely, and if there was even the slightest response, they would carefully move the dirt and sand aside.

It didn't matter who was a soldier and who was a man from the village. They worked together, moving the earth and cutting apart fallen trees, then pulling out the people trapped underneath. Kaede used her magic to move huge rocks, while the women from the village were feeding the displaced and tending to the wounded.

As for me, I had teamed up with Hal, and we were carrying out search operations.

"Hal, under that thick tree! Someone's still breathing!" I called.

"Huh?! I don't hear any voice," he said.

"Well, they're there! Just dig!"

Hal had a doubtful look on his face, but when he dug where I told him to, he found a little girl's hand. "Seriously...? Just you wait, we'll have you safe soon!"

Hal moved the earth aside, pulling the dark elf girl out.

She already had brown skin, so it was hard to tell, but her complexion was looking bad. After being trapped in the moist earth for all this time, that was to be expected.

It was a good thing that the summer heat was still lingering. Were it a little later in autumn, she might have died from the cold while she'd been buried.

When I came back with a blanket, Hal was holding the girl and patting her on the back. "You did well. You're going to be okay now."

"Wah...wahhhhhhhhhh!"

"It's okay! You're okay now!" Hal desperately tried to calm the wailing girl.

If you ask me, men are useless at times like these. Hal and I were both at a loss for what to do, just repeating "It's okay," over and over.

I wrapped the girl in a blanket, waiting for her to calm down before calling over a nearby Forbidden Army soldier. "Take this girl to a safe place."

"Yes, sir! As you command!" the soldier said.

Once we had seen the girl off, Hal said to me, "I'm amazed you knew she was there. I couldn't hear her voice at all."

"Even while we're talking, I'm searching," I said.

"Do you know some sort of searching spell?" he asked.

"Not quite. This is what I'm using." When I stretched my palm out to Hal, a little thing burrowed out of the ground and jumped up onto it.

Hal looked at it, blinking. "Is that...a mouse?"

"A wooden one, yeah."

It was a mouse carved out of wood, about ten centimeters long. I had been manipulating it with my Living Poltergeists ability to search for survivors under the rubble. My ability was able to operate at long distances if I used dolls, but it seemed they only needed to be shaped like a living creature, not necessarily a humanoid one. Even as I was showing this one off to Hal, there were another four wooden mice moving around almost like real mice and looking for those in need of rescue.

"It's a wonder that you were carrying around something like that," he said.

"I found them in a shop while I was on my date with Liscia," I said. "I thought I might use them for something, so I put them in the rolling bag with my other self-defense items."

By the way, that bag had also held two small-sized Little Musashibo dolls which I now had on patrol in the area. Even in places where the landslide had damaged the roads, those light-weight little guys could jump around easily enough.

"Your ability is more amazing than I'd ever have thought," he said.

"Yeah. I feel like this is the first time outside of administrative tasks that I've gotten some use out of... urkh!" I hunched and started vomiting.

"Whoa, what's this, out of nowhere?!" Hal called out to me, sounding concerned. "H-hey, Souma."

"Blech..." I managed, then coughed violently.

"A-are you all right? Why'd you suddenly start puking?"

"S-sorry. While it was searching, one of my wooden mice...it suddenly found a really badly damaged body..."

"Damaged...?"

"The eyeballs were—"

"No, stop! I don't want to hear it!" Hal looked away and plugged his ears.

I looked at the dirt in front of us.

When the news covers disaster areas, they focus on the tragedies of the affected and the hopes of the survivors. However, now that I was experiencing it firsthand, it was a hell greater than I had imagined. This reality was too harsh for a general audience. It would break their hearts.

Still, I didn't have time to be thinking about that.

"Hal! I've found two people in need of rescue, in the shadow of a rock fifty meters ahead of us and to the left."

"On it!"

For now, I just had to kill my emotions.

We diligently continued with our relief efforts. We managed to dig a great many dark elves from the earth and rubble.

All of them were injured in one way or another, and many had serious injuries that couldn't be taken lightly even once they had been rescued. Often, by the time we managed to dig them out, they had already died.

At first, the ratio of living to dead among the rescued was half and half, but now it was leaning more heavily towards the dead. When I considered that, of the close to one hundred casualties

Wodan had mentioned when we had first arrived at the village, only two-tenths had been dead, it was clear that things were getting worse as time passed.

The searchers were showing signs of heavy exhaustion, as well. They had been resting in shifts, but it had now been three days since the disaster occurred.

It was hard on the dark elves, of course, but also on the soldiers who had come a long way and then spent a full day searching. They had already dug out a fair number of those in need of rescue (some alive, some not).

I thought it would be wise to check in with Wodan to confirm how many people were still missing. If we could narrow down the number of victims, we could focus our manpower on searching the areas where we thought they would be.

As I was thinking that, I heard a desperate cry.

"O god-beast! Why have you let this happen?!"

When I looked, I saw a young (?) dark elf man who resembled Wodan wailing as he struck his fists and head against the ground.

Aisha had returned from evacuating the women and children, so I asked her about him. "Aisha, who is that?"

"That's...my uncle, Robthor Udgard, He's my father's younger brother."

"From the way he's crying and wailing, I guess that means..."

"Yes," she confirmed. "His wife and child—in other words, my aunt and her daughter—have yet to be found."

"That must be...difficult. Are you okay, Aisha?"

"Well, you see, if my father is the head of the liberals, my uncle is head of the conservatives. I didn't have much contact with them. His daughter was still young and cute, though, so it pains me to see this happen to her."

"I see..."

We were well past the seventy-two-hour deadline. If she hadn't been found yet, that meant...

Robthor looked in our direction. When he saw us, he walked over towards us, stumbling as he did.

"King... oh, King... why?"

Robthor grabbed me by the lapels, causing Aisha to yell at him, but I motioned for her to stand down. Rather than gripping them tightly and trying to lift me up, he was just grasping at them, as if clinging to me. If I simply brushed him away, he would probably collapse.

"O, King. I have done all I can to protect this forest. So why has it taken my family from me...?"

I was at a loss for words. I looked over to Aisha.

"My uncle opposed the periodic thinning," she said. "He said it was unthinkable that dark elves, as protectors of the forest, should cut down trees needlessly. The place which collapsed was one where we couldn't do periodic thinning because of my uncle's objections," she explained.

That's... I don't know what to say...

"O, King! Tell me why! Why would the forest I protected destroy my family? If I had cut down trees like Wodan and his lot, would my family have been spared?!"

"There's...no way to know that," I said.

"No!" he howled.

"True, if you carry out periodic thinning, take care of the undergrowth, and increase the land's ability to hold water, it's possible to create conditions that reduce the likelihood of a landslide. However, it only makes it less likely. In a case like this, where heavy rain over a long period was the cause, it could have happened anywhere."

"You're saying we just had bad luck, then..." he murmured.

"In terms of where the landslide happened, yes. However, periodic thinning means there's always work going on in the forest. The workers may hear strange noises, see the forest seeming to shift, and notice other warning signs that a landslide is about to occur. If they notice, there are things that can be done. People could have been evacuated."

This has also been said to be an advantage of using mountains for terraced rice-fields.

You would think cutting down the trees to make room for rice paddies would make landslides more likely, but it reduces the odds of landslides which result in human casualties. Because people must go into the fields all the time, they quickly notice the warning signs, and that makes it easy to respond. The strongest countermeasure against landslides is to watch the forest at all times. The elves didn't have debris flow detection systems like modern-day Japan, so that made having people on watch even more important.

"I've protected the forest all this time... was I wrong to do that?" he moaned.

"Your belief that you were protecting the forest was wrong," I said. "Nature's not so fragile that it needs people to protect it."

Aisha had told me before that the trees in the God-Protected Forest were long-lived. That was why they hadn't noticed that it had turned into a bean-sprout forest and the ground had been weakened. Even though they had simply been lucky that nothing had happened until now, they'd convinced themselves they were protecting the forest.

"If it's egotistical for man to destroy the forest, so, too, is it egotistical to try to protect it," I said. "Nature is meant to go through cycles of death and rebirth, yet we're trying to keep it in a state that's convenient for us. All people can do is manage things through periodic thinning, keeping the forest in a state where we can coexist with it, trying our best not to wake it from its slumber."

He seemed speechless.

At that moment, one of my wooden mice discovered something.

"There! I found a parent and child!" I cried.

"Wh-where?!" he stammered.

"Hold on. They're in a collapsed house ahead and to the left of us, two meters from the mountain ridge!"

We rushed to the spot, moving the sand and dirt aside. When we did, we found a little girl and a woman I assumed was her mother in a gap between the collapsed lumber. The mother was holding her girl tightly, trying to protect her. When Robthor saw them, he let out a breathless sigh. Clearly, they were his wife and daughter.

When we pulled them out, the woman had already perished.

Just as I was thinking all hope was lost, Aisha raised her voice. "Sire! The child is still breathing!"

"Get her to the relief team immediately!" I shouted. "Don't let her die!"

"Understood!"

After wrapping the child in a blanket and seeing her and Aisha off, I looked to Robthor, who was crying beside his wife's body. I thought maybe I should let him be, but this man still had things he needed to protect. I couldn't have him stopping here on me.

Placing a hand on his shoulder, I said quietly, "She protected your daughter to the very end."

"Yes..."

"Pull yourself together! It's your turn to do it now!"

He seemed startled. "Yes... yes...!"

Speaking through sobs, Robthor nodded again and again.

Sometime after that, the second relief team that Liscia had gone back to call for arrived. With the search for all missing persons completed, the advance team was relieved of their duties.

For the reconstruction work, the more numerous and better-equipped second team would take over.

After offering one last silent prayer for the fallen, the advance team returned to the capital. The mud-covered and exhausted members of the advance team were packed into the container cars like frozen tuna about to be shipped out. Right about now, Hal was probably laying his head in Kaede's lap and taking a good rest.

I was in a similar state myself, riding in the carriage with Liscia, who had come to pick me up.

We had left Aisha behind in the village. With her homeland in that awful shape, there was no way she would have been able to focus on her duties. For the time being, I had told her to wait in the God-Protected Forest.

As I leaned against the window, dozing off...

"I wasn't able to do anything this time," Liscia said sadly.

"You went to call a relief party, didn't you?" I asked. "Everyone worked their very hardest. Actually, if there's anyone who was unable to do anything, it was me."

"Hardly. I hear you were a great help out there," Liscia tried to reassure me, but I shook my head.

"I'm the king. In times of crisis, giving commands in the field isn't the king's duty. A king's duty is to prepare for a crisis *before it happens*. I...didn't do enough of that."

"That's not—"

"I think the Forbidden Army worked well as a relief unit. Still, there were more places where I came up short. Means of communication, long-distance shipping, accumulation of aid supplies in each area, medical teams attached to the relief party, psychiatrists to treat patients with PTSD. I came up short on all those things. Because I was so focused on the food crisis and the issue of the three dukes, I was lax in my preparations."

I looked at my reflection in the window, covered in mud and wearing an expression of exhaustion.

Liscia was looking at me with concern, but I pretended not to notice.

Epilogue

IN THE CENTER of the Carmine Duchy, the city of Randel, in the meeting room in Randel Castle—the residing castle of Duke Georg Carmine—the three dukes who controlled the land, sea, and air forces of this country had gathered.

At the head of the table was the lord of this castle, Georg Carmine. This lion-faced beastman had a burly, muscular build that was apparent even through his military uniform. He had the appearance of a warrior who had weathered many battles. Beastmen did not live longer than humans, but even at the age of fifty, he showed no signs of decline. His very presence was enough to make the atmosphere tense.

Seated to Georg's right was the Admiral of the Navy, Excel Walter. Wearing a kimono that was similar in style to the ones worn in Japan, she was a beautiful sea serpent with antlers poking through her blue hair. Sea serpents were a race that could live for over a thousand years, and she herself had already reached an age of more than five hundred, yet she still looked to be in no more than her mid-twenties. However, contrary to her appearance, her command showed all the experience that came with her age.

Sitting across from her was the General of the Air Force, Castor Vargas. He looked like a gallant young man, but the two oni-like horns which grew through his red hair, the membranous wings which grew from his back, and his lizard-like tail marked him as a half-dragon, a dragonewt. He was close to one hundred years old, but as a member of a race that lived to five hundred years, he was still treated as a youngster. He, too, looked like he was in a foul mood.

Looking at the other two, Excel sighed. "I was under the impression we were meeting here to avoid a needless conflict."

"What, Duchess Excel, are you afraid of that whelp?" Castor took an aggressive tone with Excel. "Has the once-feared sea serpent Duchess Excel grown old?"

"Oh, me? And who was it who tried to seduce this old granny fifty years ago, hmm?" Excel asked.

"Urkh."

"Also, when you address me, it's not 'Duchess Excel;' it should be 'Mother,' shouldn't it?"

"Right."

With that playful rebuttal, she deflated Castor.

In truth, Excel had been Castor's first love. Perhaps because he had been unable to forget her even after his attempts failed magnificently, when he had later met Accela, her daughter who was closer to him in age, he had fallen in love with her at first sight and they had married. In short, Castor was Excel's son-in-law. She was not someone he was able to argue with and win.

"Castor, do you still mean to oppose the king?" she asked.

"Of course! I don't care if he's a hero, or whatever else they want to call him, that fake king usurped the throne, forced Princess Liscia into a betrothal, and unjustly seized power in this country! How could I serve a guy like that?!"

"The only ones who tell it like that are the nobles being investigated for corruption," she corrected him. "King Albert abdicated of his own will in favor of the man he felt would be a better successor. The king's relationship with Princess Liscia is close, too."

"I don't know about that! He may just be making it look that way! If he wanted to rebuild this country, he could have done it as a vassal! Was there some problem with the former king's reign?" he snapped.

Excel wisely said nothing.

There were no problems with it, but there were no good points to it, either, and that was a problem, thought Excel, but to say so would be too disrespectful to the former king, so she refrained.

Excel had found the speed with which Albert had abdicated dubious, but all signs since then had pointed to it being a wise decision. Excel didn't remember Albert as a ruler who could make such a decision, but perhaps it merely meant he had grown as a person.

"Besides, we three dukes have protected this country for many long years. I can't stand the way he's belittling us!" the man snapped. "The letter he sent me as soon as the throne was abdicated to him was 'Serve me, or not, make your choice,' you know?"

"It was, 'If you will cooperate with my reforms, I will provide food aid and build roads for you'...right?" she asked.

The three duchies had a lower population than the crown demesne, and because they had armies to supply, they had reserves, so they had not felt the food crisis as deeply. However, when the food crisis hit, the three duchies opened their reserves and began rationing, so all the merchants who'd dealt in foodstuffs had gone bankrupt due to lack of demand. Next, because of the rise in unemployment, shops had gone out of business because their wares wouldn't sell. Then, in a chain reaction, the craftspeople who had supplied them had gone under as well.

On that point, Souma had weathered the crisis by providing subsidies only to the poor, not distributing more than necessary, encouraging people to eat foods there had been no custom of eating before, and increasing the country's transport capacity by building roads. In doing this, he managed to minimize the degree to which the economy shrank. Furthermore, of the three duchies, only the Walter Duchy had independent maritime trade routes and had been able to just barely stop the negative feedback loop by selling off their excess merchandise to other countries.

But that's something I was able to do because my duchy has a port city, Excel thought. *Neither the Carmine Duchy nor the Vargas Duchy have inland trade routes. With his large army, along with the fleeing nobles and their personal retinues to care for, the Carmine Duchy must be suffering from serious economic problems. If that's the case, why is Georg so adamant about opposing the king?*

As she was thinking that, Castor roared, "'I'll feed you like a pet, so obey me,' is basically what that means! He's looking down on us!"

"If it's for the benefit of your people...what else is there to be done?" Excel asked.

"I don't like it! Does he think he can tame us with a little bait?!"

"I doubt the king needs a pet with pride and little else," Excel said.

Castor slammed both his hands down on the table. "What is with you today?! It's like you're defending the king! I know you don't like him, either. That's why you ignored the king's requests for assistance!"

"Kindly don't act as if we're the same," she said tartly. "What the sea serpent race must prioritize above all else is the peace and safety of our beloved Lagoon City. If he will just guarantee me that, I'm prepared to obey him."

The sea serpent race, with Excel at their lead, had a unique system of values.

Sea serpents always thought of the needs of their city, Lagoon City, first and foremost. Their ancestors had once lived on an island in the Nine-Headed Dragon Archipelago, but after losing in a power struggle within those islands, they had been driven out to sea, becoming wandering pirates.

Then, at the end of their long years of wandering, their ancestors had finally built a base of operations at what was now Lagoon City. The sea serpents protected themselves on this land which they had finally gained for themselves with love and with pride.

The sole reason they had participated in the founding war of this multiracial state, the Elfrieden Kingdom, had been to protect Lagoon City.

"If it will benefit Lagoon City, I'll wag my tail for anyone, and if they threaten Lagoon City, I will eliminate them, no matter how great they are in number. That is the pride of the sea serpents," Excel explained.

"Hmph, wagging your tail is something to take pride in?" he snorted.

"Yes. I fight to protect the things I must. I'm not an infant who throws a tantrum just because he doesn't like someone. If it can be resolved by talking, there's no better outcome than that. It would be absurd to start fighting amongst ourselves now, when our neighbors are eyeing us for an opportunity to strike."

"The Principality of Amidonia, huh?" he muttered.

He was referring to the country which bordered Elfrieden to the west.

When they had found themselves on the receiving end of the expansionist policies of the king prior to Albert, the Principality of Amidonia had lost close to half its land. Now, they were watching closely for any chance to regain their lost territory. Amidonia seemed eager to intervene in the dispute between King Souma and the three dukes, having already sent them a letter saying, "If you intend to depose the false king, we are prepared to dispatch troops to aid you."

"Honestly, what a stubborn bunch," he snorted. "Their intentions are so transparent."

"I'm sure they've sent a letter to the king, too," Excel said. "I doubt the king will take them up on it, but they may dispatch 'reinforcements' anyway. You see what I mean? About how foolish it is for us to quarrel now."

"Hmph. Fine, then why don't you just go to the king's side already."

"There are a number of things I want to see and judge for myself, and then I plan to do just that. Things about the king, and about you."

Excel turned a silent glance towards Georg Carmine. After some light pleasantries when she had first been brought into the room, he had closed his eyes and said nothing. Was he listening to Excel and Castor make their cases, or was he thinking about something himself? She didn't think he was sleeping, but Excel was beginning to become irritated with his demeanor.

"Georg, what are you thinking?" she snapped.

"What do you mean, what?"

"Oh, my. So, you were awake after all," she said. "Of course I'm asking why you, the one who is most patriotic and loyal to this country of all of us, would take hostile actions against the new king."

"Duke Carmine, you don't like that fake king either, right?" Castor demanded.

"I wasn't asking you, Castor," Excel said. "Answer me, Georg. Setting aside his legitimacy, his reign has been a stable one. Why would you go out of your way to cause turmoil like this?"

With Excel pressing him for answers, Georg opened his

mouth gravely. "I judged him incapable of ruling this country. That is all."

"And why is that? What is it about his abilities, with which he will soon overcome the food crisis and economic difficulties that were pushing this country to the brink, that dissatisfies you?"

"In order to accomplish that, that king cast aside many things without hesitation." Georg opened his eyes. That alone was enough to make the atmosphere in the room tense.

Excel and Castor both gulped. He was the youngest person present, yet in appearance and mentality, he was the most mature of all of them. This was the imposing presence of the greatest warrior in the country.

"I've heard that that king was summoned from another world," he said. "Because of that, he has no attachment to things and can discard them without hesitation. If he deems them inefficient, then be it history, traditions, soldiers, or vassals, he'll throw them away. Am I wrong, Duchess Excel?"

"That's..." Excel found herself at a loss for words. It was true. She could see King Souma's reign had that side to it.

"Vassals who've served this country for many long years were abandoned by that king," he continued.

"Yes. That was because they were corrupt."

"Will you still say that, even if they turn on him as a result? I believe you yourself just spoke of the folly of endangering the country at this time. That king is the one who sowed the seeds for it."

"You say that, but you're the one who's sheltering those nobles," she said.

"Those with a grudge against the king will be useful pawns in defeating him," he responded. "Of course, I have no intention of reinstating those people once the war is over."

Excel shuddered at the way the corners of Georg's mouth rose as he spoke those words. *Does this man mean to work the corrupt nobles to death in a war?!*

He would strike down the king, work the corrupt nobles to death, and even if he couldn't dispose of all of them that way, he would find some excuse after the war to execute them. These were people for which any number of reasons could be found.

Then, with the current king's faction and the corrupt nobles having vanished from the capital, only an empty lot on which Georg might build whatever he wished would remain. He could reinstate King Albert as his puppet, if he so wished. Or he could rise to become king himself.

Excel stood up. "Have you been driven mad with ambition for the throne?!"

"H-hey now, calm down," Castor intervened, trying to smooth things over. "This is Duke Carmine you're talking about. I'm sure he's not planning to usurp the throne, right?"

Georg shook his head. "Of course not. Once King Souma is removed, I will have King Albert take the throne once more, and we will support him."

"I'm not convinced." Excel lowered her posture. She was feigning calmness, but she was actually quite flustered.

The situation is worse than I anticipated. This is the worst possible scenario... perhaps I need to act on the assumption that Georg already has undisclosed ties with Amidonia. Ugh, if Castor was any judge of character, we might have worked together to reign in Duke Carmine. Excel cursed her son-in-law for his short-sightedness.

Her daughter had married into his house and had since borne her two grandchildren. She was worried what might happen if she let Duke Carmine win, but if Excel were the only one to join the loyalist faction and King Souma were then to win, as the wife and children of the traitor Castor, what would become of Accela and her children? Under this country's laws, when a serious offense was committed, relatives of up to three degrees of consanguinity were guilty of the same crime. If she cut ties with the House of Castor, the House of Walter would avoid that chain of responsibility, but if she did that, Accela and the children would...

"Castor," she said.

"What?"

"Cut your ties with Accela, Carl, and Carla."

"Are you trying to say we're going to lose to that whelp?!" he shouted.

"It's in case the worst should happen. If you intend to face the king, at least be prepared for the possibility."

Excel glanced over at Georg, but his eyes were closed, as if to say he had no intention of intervening. Even though she was discussing what would happen if he lost... was this a show of confidence, perhaps?

On the other hand, Castor, who had been asked to cut ties with his wife and children, had a troubled look on his face. "Accela and Carl, maybe...but Carla, I can't."

"Why not?!" Excel demanded.

"Because she'll never listen to me."

At that moment, the doors to the conference room slammed open.

A beautiful young girl entered. Her flaming red hair and shining golden eyes were quite distinctive. She was sixteen or seventeen years old. She wore heavy armor in a metallic red color, and from her back and rear protruded the wings and tail of a dragon.

"Carla..." whispered Excel.

This was Castor's daughter, Carla.

She had gotten her facial features from Excel and was a fair young beauty, but when it came to her temperament, Castor's blood seemed to have won out. Instead of doing anything feminine, she had joined the air force unit led by Castor, training day in and day out.

Because of her beautiful face, many sons of the nobility and gentry had sought her attentions, but she had said in no uncertain terms that "I will never take a man weaker than me as my husband."

In fact, she was the second strongest in the air force after Castor, and so she had handily trounced every one of her suitors. As a father, Castor was relieved, but as a parent, his feelings were more complicated, and he worried she might wait too long and never be able to get married.

Seeing Carla appear here, Excel had a bad feeling about what was going to happen.

As she had expected, Carla said, "Grandmother! If Father has decided to fight, then I shall fight, too!"

Excel shouted back, a vein pulsing on her forehead, "No, you must not! Do you mean to become a traitor at your age?!"

"I cannot forgive him for unseating King Albert and trying to force himself on my friend, Princess Liscia!" she declared. "I will punish him for his insolence personally!"

"You've misunderstood!" Excel shouted. "King Souma is..."

"It's no use, Mother. Once she gets like this, Carla won't budge an inch." Castor shrugged his shoulders in resignation.

"You people. Honestly..."

Even as Excel held her head in consternation, Georg remained silent.

◇　◇　◇

On the eastern side of the territory of the Principality of Amidonia, which was longer on the map than it was wide, the city of Van was the capital.

Some had felt it was too close to the Elfrieden Kingdom to be a capital, but its selection had likely been a manifestation of their unbroken determination to regain the stolen eastern territory.

In the governmental affairs office in the castle in the center of Van, a middle-aged man with a handlebar mustache was reviewing documents.

His cloaked figure looked somewhat plump, but this was only because he had broad shoulders. He was not actually obese. In fact, under his cloak, he was extremely muscular.

This man was Prince Gaius VIII of Amidonia.

"Oh ho..." he said.

"What is it, Father?" A young man in his twenties who stood waiting at his side queried. He had a handsome face, but his eyes had a cold glint which chilled those who looked at them. He was the crown prince and heir apparent of the Principality of Amidonia, Julius Amidonia.

Gaius handed the document he had been reading to Julius. "It's from Georg Carmine. It seems he's ready to 'stand up.'"

"I see," Julius said. "At long last. I've heard of the swift, severe attacks he would make in his younger years, never giving us time to catch our breaths. For a personage of such ability, he was awfully slow to act now."

"He's grown old, I'm sure," his father said. "Were his mind still keen, he never would have taken us up on our offer."

"True."

After Julius returned the document to him, Gaius rose from his seat. "We will move when the new king declares war. Send reinforcements to the kingdom."

"Oh...? And to which side?"

"Which? To the king's side, we say, 'We are with the three dukes,' to the three dukes' side, we say, 'We are with the new king.'"

"I see," Julius said. "We have no reason to obey either side that way."

"Heh heh heh. Precisely."

Gaius and Julius looked to one another and shared a dark smile.

Beside them, a pair of cold eyes was watching.

Good heavens... sometimes I just ain't sure what I oughta do about my old man and my idiot brother.

The cold eyes belonged to a young girl.

She was sixteen or seventeen years old. She had an attractive face like Julius, but not his air of cruelty. If anything, her eyes were small and beady, and with her round face, she had the stuffed animal-like adorableness of a raccoon dog. Her hair was tied in two braids at the nape of her neck.

This girl who looked good in those braid-style twintails was the first princess of this country, Roroa Amidonia. However, contrary to appearances, her inner voice was sharp-tongued (and spoke in mercantile dialect).

This country ain't long for this world as is. Are these idiots tryin' to shorten what little time it has left? she thought.

Amidonia was a mountainous country. It had plentiful metal resources, but on the other hand, it had little arable land, so it was always faced with food shortages. The food crisis in neighboring Elfrieden was bad, but nothing compared to what this country faced. Even a slightly poor harvest would mean people starving to death.

I do understand why the old man's tryin' to get even a little more fertile land for us, I do, but he's pourin' every last cent that I worked so hard to scrimp and save for him into military fundin'. Roroa ground her back teeth together in frustration.

While Roroa was a princess, she also had uncanny financial sense, and she supported this country's financial policies from the shadows. After getting the economy moving through foreign trade, she limited exports of resources and encouraged the export of finished products to protect and develop their industries. The reason this country on the brink hadn't seen its economy collapse was in large part thanks to Roroa's monetary sense.

However, Gaius had been unable to fully make use of Roroa's money-raising ability.

If they'd been usin' the funds I'd earned to develop industry, they mighta been able to bring in even more funds, but these warmongerin' economic nitwits go and spend it all on the military. What makes it even worse is that they sincerely believe "If we strengthen the military, we can steal whatever we need." Are they morons? You spend money to make money, it's that cycle that's important. If you're just dumpin' money into somethin', that's called wasteful spendin'! But even if I were to scream that at them, they probably wouldn't listen to me...

"You agree, too, right, Roroa?" her brother said.

"Yes, Brother." When the conversation suddenly turned to her, Roroa replied with a big fake smile. Though, in truth, she hadn't been listening to a word they said.

The end may finally be here for this country. Oh, how I envy the Elfrieden Kingdom. With their large population, they must have a lot of tax revenue they can move around, and best of all, their king's the sort who'd be able to understand what I'm talkin' about. Honestly, I'm so jealous of our neighbor's wallet... wait. Their wallet?

At that moment, Roroa realized something.

If I'm jealous of my neighbor's wallet. Why don't I just combine it with my own? As legally as possible... Maybe I can do that? Yeah, maybe I can. In that case, I can contact the old man in charge of guarding Nelva...

Roroa began formulating a plan of her own. High risk, high return.

They say that as Roroa embarked on the greatest intrigue of her life, her smile resembled her father's and brother's just a little.

◇　◇　◇

At the capital of the Elfrieden Kingdom, Parnam:

I was in the governmental affairs office in Parnam Castle, listening to the final report on the food crisis.

"As you see in the materials provided, we can expect good results from the fall harvest. Furthermore, the transportation network you laid out has accelerated the people's movements, and now goods have spread across the land without overabundances or shortages anywhere. Of course, this applies to foodstuffs, as well. From these facts, I believe we can treat the food crisis as, by and large, solved for now."

"That's good to hear," I said. "It makes all the hard work worth it."

It had been a long road, but now I could finally take a breath and relax. As the person who'd been grappling with this problem all this time, it was an especially emotional moment for me. However...

"Yes. With this, we can now safely move on to *the next stage*," Hakuya said, with no regard whatsoever for my emotional moment.

The next stage, huh?

"We...really have to do it, don't we?" I asked.

"Does it weigh on you?" he asked.

"Well, yeah. I understand the necessity of it, though..."

Yes. This was necessary.

The political theorist Machiavelli had said this in *The Prince:*

"If a prince should stain his hands with cruelties, even in peaceful times, he will have difficulty holding the state. However, for some tyrants, even after infinite cruelties, they live long and secure in their countries, defending themselves from external enemies and never being conspired against by their own citizens. I believe that this follows from cruelties being properly or badly used.

"Those which may be called properly used are those applied in one blow at a time when it is necessary for one's security. If a prince does not persist in them afterward, ruling in a way that advantages the people as best as he is able, he may even be remembered as a great ruler. However, one who fails to strike out the root of trouble from the beginning, dragging things out and inflicting repeated cruelties, uses them badly."

This passage was one reason that Machiavelli's *The Prince* had been, for a long time, criticized by the humanists of the Christian church. However, the cruelties he had spoken of there did not refer to massacres of ordinary people. He was talking about using trickery to permanently dispose of political opponents.

If you can stabilize your hold on power with one act of cruelty, then govern well afterward, it is a happy thing for the people. On the other hand, if you spend all your time worrying about what your political opponents think and don't advance any worthwhile policies, not striking out the root of trouble in one blow, purging traitors again and again, you will lose the trust of the people.

The prince who Machiavelli had held up as his ideal, Cesare Borgia, had massacred the influential nobles who had welcomed him during a feast, securing absolute power for himself.

Oda Nobunaga had used his severity well, taking the Oda Family from rural daimyos to becoming great daimyos in a single leap. However, in the end, because Nobunaga had persisted with his severities, he had shortened his own life, ultimately dying to a betrayal by one of his vassals.

In other words, cruelty was like a prince's treasured sword that could cut through anything, but if he grew addicted to using it, it was also like a cursed sword that would eventually destroy him.

"As I've said before," I said, "I've deemed your plan a cruelty."

"Yes," he agreed. "You also said, 'If we are to do it, let it be in one stroke.'"

"You can do it that way, I assume?" I asked.

"The preparations have already been made."

"Very well, then."

I could say it was for this country, but I wasn't that attached to the place.

I didn't have a just cause, or a great one. But when I questioned why I was doing it, suddenly Liscia and the others' faces came to mind. Those who lived, smiling, in this country: Liscia, Aisha, Juna, and Tomoe.

I thought of the bonds I had lost in the old world. I thought of the bonds I had formed in this new one.

I already thought of those girls as my family.

"Kazuya, build a family. And, once you have, protect them, come whatever may."

...I know, Grandpa. I'll protect my family to the end, no matter what comes our way.

To do that, just this once, I will become a cruel king.

"We will now begin the *subjugation*."

HOW A REALIST HERO

REBUILT THE KINGDOM

The Story of a Certain Group of Adventurers

ADVENTURERS.

As the people who challenged and cleared out dungeons and the many mysteries that lay within, theirs was a profession filled with romanticized adventure. However, at the same time, they were also jacks and jills of all trades, taking quests issued by the guild (protecting merchants, slaying dangerous beasts, and more) in exchange for rewards. Now, here is something about these adventurers. Among the newest urban legends spreading in Parnam, the capital of Elfrieden, there is one known as "The Adventurer Who Wears a Kigurumi."

It was said that this adventurer wore a kigurumi, a sort of full-body costume, that was 1.7 meters tall. His weapon was a naginata, slung over his back. He had a roly-poly body but was able to move quickly and was apparently very talented. He formed no party, taking on dangerous beast subjugation quests solo, but occasionally, if there was a party seeking temporary members, he would join them for a dungeon crawl.

Incidentally, his name was registered with the guild as "Little Musashibo."

◇　◇　◇

"Uh... so, you're the adventurer who's temporarily joining our party?" a male warrior asked doubtfully.

A roly-poly kigurumi was standing in front of the quest board in the guild. It stood before a party of four adventurers (party composition: one male warrior, one male priest, one female thief, and one female mage).

In the kigurumi's hands was a naginata, on his back a wicker basket. His face was covered with white silk (in fact, it was sewn on), and the acorn eyes and bushy eyebrows that peered out from it were adorable.

Who was that? Was he a snowman? Was he a round-bottomed doll? No, he was Little Musashibo!

"..." (Little Musashibo waved his arms around wildly, meaning, "That's right.")

"Oh, could it be that you're the kigurumi adventurer people have been talking about lately...?" Dece asked. He was a male swordsman with an attractive face that wouldn't have been out of place in a boy band.

"..." (Little Musashibo nodded.)

"A-are you now...?" Dece's expression became a little strained.

Considering Little Musashibo's silly appearance, that reaction was only to be expected. The rest of his comrades were bewildered, too.

"Oh, come on, I know we're short a person on the front line, but does that really mean we need to bring in a guy like this?" demanded a beautiful young girl whose defiant eyes left a strong impression. Her voice was full of venom. This girl with a slightly punk sense of fashion was the female thief, Juno. The adventurers called thieves were, of course, not actual robbers. They were a support role in the party who detected enemies and disabled traps in dungeons and could handle melee combat as well.

The kindly-looking male priest, Febral, rebuked her. "W-well, his outfit may be ridiculous, but everything I've heard indicates he's a reliable adventurer. I don't think there should be an issue. We aren't delving into a dungeon today, and the difficulty for this is supposed to be beginner level, anyway."

His role as priest was also just what people called a healer. It didn't indicate any sort of religious belief.

"Oh, sure, what's the harmmm? He's kinda cute, anywayyy!" This light and airy beauty, the female mage Julia, started to playfully lean against Little Musashibo, enjoying his softness. Little Musashibo acted a little annoyed by this.

With a dry laugh at the scene, Dece extended his hand to Little Musashibo. "Anyway, it'll be a pleasure to work with you today."

"..." (Little Musashibo shook his hand.)

"...Are you not able to talk?"

"..." (Little Musashibo nodded.)

Dece said nothing for a moment. Then he burst out, "Oh, come on, is this really going to be all right?"

There was no one who could address these doubts.

With Little Musashibo joining them, the party headed for an underground passage in the capital.

Apparently, these tunnels had been originally created to let the royal family escape in the event of an enemy attack reaching the capital. Because of that, to confound intruders, the passages had been built as a complex maze with three levels.

On this occasion, the adventurers had received a quest calling for the "exploration of the underground passages and investigation of creatures living therein (and if possible, their removal)."

Because this country had been free of war and chaos since the time of the former king, King Albert, the importance of these tunnels had diminished, and they were no longer being properly maintained. As a result, giant rats and other such massive creatures had soon made their home in them. With the situation inside the tunnels at this point, it wouldn't have been out of place to call them a dungeon.

Now, here was the thing about those underground tunnels. Apparently the recently-enthroned king wanted to repurpose them and had posted this quest with the guild for that reason. Until the underground passages were safe and secure, any number of people were welcome to challenge it. The reward paid would be dependent on the creatures hunted. It was a low-risk, low-reward quest suited to beginners.

The adventuring party, now with the addition of Little Musashibo, was progressing through those underground tunnels. In the cold, wet air, an irritated Juno poked Little Musashibo's head.

"Hey, don't let this guy stand in front! He's blocking my line of sight."

"Having a front-liner stay in the back would be pointless," Dece snapped. "Deal with it."

With Dece telling her off, Juno clicked her tongue in displeasure. That was when it happened.

A giant snake suddenly appeared before the adventurers. The snake was ten meters long and thick enough to wrap one's arms around. It raised its head, hissing menacingly at the adventurers. Immediately, Dece and Musashibo moved up.

"We'll handle the front line! Everyone else, support us from the rear!"

"..." (Little Musashibo gave a thumbs-up.)

In the next moment, the giant snake struck. It went for Dece. From there on, the snake ignored Little Musashibo for some reason, only trying to attack Dece.

"Wait, why's it only going for me?!" Dece cried.

"?!" (Little Musashibo was confused.)

Because snakes search for their prey by detecting their body heat, it could not detect anything from Little Musashibo, which was just a kigurumi.

Dece took a tail slap from the giant snake and, while he did manage to block it with his shield, he was thrown off balance. Taking advantage of the opening, the snake slithered between the two of them, attacking the three people in back. The first to be targeted was Juno, who had been acting as support in the middle guard.

"Whoa, why's it ignoring that kigurumi and coming at me?! I—I can't stand snaaaaakes!"

It seemed that the sudden snake attack had made Juno's legs give out. With her falling on her rump and unable to move, the snake opened its mouth wide and came at Juno. At that moment, just when she was sure she was going to die...

Slash!

Just as the snake was about to sink its fangs into Juno, Little Musashibo used his naginata to cut it clean in two from behind. With a cut in the middle severing its head from its tail, both halves of the snake continued to thrash about for a while before eventually falling silent.

Little Musashibo swung his naginata to clean the blood from it.

Having regained her senses, Juno shyly said to Little Musashibo, "Th-thanks..."

"..." (Little Musashibo gave her a thumbs-up and then patted Juno on the head.)

When she saw Little Musashibo not boasting, but showing concern for her instead, Juno brought a hand to her chest. She must have been terribly frightened, she thought, because her heart was racing for some strange reason.

H-he's a weirdo...but he's not a bad guy, it seems.

Having reevaluated her opinion of the man (?), Juno chased after the rest of the party.

The party continued their exploration. When they entered the second level, the attacks by giant creatures only became more intense. Now they weren't only facing single enemies; some attacked in packs.

"..." (Little Musashibo cut down a swarm of giant bats with a whirlwind attack.)

"Oh, you're pretty good."

"..." (Little Musashibo gave Dece a thumbs-up.)

"Hm? Hey, pal..."

"..." (Little Musashibo tilted his head to the side, as if to say, "What?")

"There're a number of little bats hanging off your back, you know..." Dece said.

"?!" (Little Musashibo flailed around.)

"Yeesh... here, I'll get them for you," said Dece.

Little Musashibo had no sense of pain, and therefore hadn't noticed he was getting bitten.

A few minutes later...

Splish, splash.

"..." (Little Musashibo had fallen into a hole full of water and was thrashing around.)

Splish, splash.

"..." ("Hurry, help me," he appealed to the party members.)

The sight made Julia and Febral feel warm and fuzzy inside.

"He looks like he's playing around," said Julia.

"He does," Febral agreed.

"Hey, let's hurry and help him!" Juno said. "Come on, you too. Grab a hold already."

Juno reached out, pulling Little Musashibo up. Having been

rescued, Little Musashibo bowed to Juno again and again.

"..." ("Thank you so much! I will never forget your kindness!" he was saying.)

"Y-you don't need to thank me," Juno stammered. "I owed you for before. It's only natural for comrades to help one another."

"..." ("You're willing to recognize me as a comrade?!" He was overcome with emotion.)

"Wh-who cares! Come on, let's go already."

"..." ("Ah, wait for me!" He chased after Juno.)

Little Musashibo's slow, easy footsteps faded into the distance. The remaining members of the party were dumbfounded.

"Juno... was she just talking with that kigurumi?" Dece asked.

"That was what it looked like to me," Febral nodded. "The kigurumi didn't say anything, though."

Julia giggled. "If she was, it may have been the power of love..."

"Love?!" The two men's simultaneous response echoed through the dark tunnel.

A few hours later, the adventurers finally reached the third level.

Perhaps it had been built to be spacious, because the ceilings looked to be twenty meters high, and the paths were wide. This third level was the lowest in these underground passages. Though there had been some little mishaps along the way, their progress down here had been nothing if not smooth.

"This is no challenge," Juno said. "I can see why they said it was beginner level."

"..." (Little Musashibo cocked his head to the side as if to say, "Really?")

"We're used to the monsters in dungeons, see," Juno explained. "No matter how ferocious they are, we're not going to lose to some animals."

"..." (He looked at her as if to say, "You say that, but you were awfully scared of that snake...")

"Th-that one doesn't count! Everyone has things they're afraid of!" Juno burst out.

"..." (He shrugged his shoulders as if saying, "Sure, sure, I get it.")

"Hey, if you've got something to say, say it!" she fumed. "If I got serious..."

The rest of the party looked on dumbfounded as the two argued back and forth in the underground tunnel. (Though Juno was the only one talking.)

"Seriously, how is that conversation working?" Dece asked.

"I am inclined to start believing Julia's suggestion of 'love,'" Febral said.

Then it happened.

"Huh?! Everyone, be on your guard!" Juno shouted.

The relaxed atmosphere was blown away, and everyone got into battle positions. The way they could do this like flipping a switch was part of what made adventurers so impressive.

Dece asked, "Juno, how many are there?"

"One," she answered. "But it's unbelievably huge."

Thieves had sharp senses and could use the slightest sound or vibration to judge the precise number and size of opponents in another location.

"How big're we talking here?" Dece asked.

"That giant snake was nothing in comparison," she replied.

"This is just an underground passage, right?" Julia asked. "Why is there something so big here?"

Febral was the one to answer. "I've heard that, in underground spaces like this, creatures can grow to sizes that would be unthinkable under normal circumstances. Once they reach a certain size, they have no natural predators and, because temperatures stay about the same here year-round, they just keep growing bigger rather than dying."

"So, you're saying there's one up ahead that got big like that?" Dece asked.

The moment those words left Dece's mouth, the air shook. It didn't take a thief's skills to know that the massive whatever-it-was was almost upon them.

"It's coming!" Juno shouted.

The creature appeared. Its massive body nearly reached the ceiling, which was already high for an underground tunnel. It had slimy skin, and, unlike its mouth which looked like it could open big and wide, its eyes were so small they didn't realize they were eyes at first.

"A salamander!" the four shouted in unison.

Only one person (?), Little Musashibo, said, "..." ("A ridiculously huge salamander?!"), having a different reaction from the rest.

Dece couldn't believe his eyes. "Oh, come on. Normally salamanders are maybe two meters long, at most, you know?"

"..." ("This world's salamanders are usually the size of Komodo dragons?!") Little Musashibo was surprised, but nobody was able to notice.

"This one looks like it's clearly more than ten meters long," Dece said.

"So, they can grow to become this large..." Febral sounded impressed. "However, it is an issue that it's a salamander. Their mucus is highly acidic. It would be dangerous to attack with melee weapons, and it's resistant to heat. On the other hand, if we can freeze it, this could be an easy fight..."

"We don't have anyone who can use ice magic," Dece said. "If flames worked, Julia could've handled it with her magic, but... how about you, Mr. Kigurumi?"

"..." ("Nuh-uh." He shook his head.)

"Well, there's nothing else for it, then. Let's run," said Dece, the party leader, calling for a retreat. "Our quest was to explore and investigate. There's no need to overextend ourselves. If we just report that we found that thing, the castle ought to be able to send out a subjugation team later."

"I get what you're saying, but can we get away so easily?" Febral asked.

As Febral pointed out, the salamander had the adventurers firmly in its sights.

Dece ground his back teeth, bringing up his shield and moving forward. "We'll have to get away. Febral and Julia are fastest, so they go first. Juno doesn't have a lot of gear, so she can go next. Mr. Kigurumi, can I count on you to bring up the rear with me?"

"…" ("Okie-dokie!" He gave a thumbs-up.)

"Okay…split!"

They all moved when Dece gave the order.

Febral and Julia ran back along the path they had come from, while Dece and Little Musashibo stayed behind, keeping the salamander in check. Juno put her legs to good use, running around nimbly and confusing the salamander. The salamander tried to go after the two who had fled, but with Dece and Little Musashibo blocking it and Juno's movements leaving it bewildered, it couldn't make much progress forward.

Eventually, it must have gotten impatient, because the salamander let out a cry and swung its long tail. When it did, the mucus that had been attached to its tail flew everywhere.

"Oh, shoot! Everyone, look out!" Dece shouted.

"Eek!" Julia screamed.

The highly acidic mucus rained down and struck the adventurers. It stuck to Dece's shield, Juno's breastplate, the back of Febral's vestments, and Julia's long skirt, hissing and releasing an unpleasant smell as it dissolved the cloth and metal.

"Salamander mucus will melt flesh, too! Strip off any equipment it got on!" Febral shouted as he pulled off his top.

When they heard that, Dece dropped his shield and Julia stripped off her skirt, continuing to run with her underwear showing.

"Hold on, it got my breastplate!" Juno shouted.

"Well, hurry up and take it off! If you don't, forget your breasts, you'll be showing your bare ribs instead!" Dece shouted.

"Urgh..."

With Dece shouting at her, Juno stripped off her breastplate and shirt, going topless. She did her best to cover herself with her right arm while holding her short sword ready in her left, but she was turning bright red from embarrassment.

"Juno, just go already! Mr. Kigurumi, are you all right?"

Once Dece confirmed that Juno had started running, he looked over at Little Musashibo to find its face was covered in mucus.

"H-hey! What're you doing?! Take off that kigurumi already!"

"..."

Despite Dece's worries, Little Musashibo shook his head back and forth. On a closer look, while he did have mucus on him, there was no sign of any melting.

"Hold on, is your kigurumi acid-resistant?" Dece asked.

"..." (Little Musashibo gave him a thumbs-up.)

For Little Musashibo's "skin," his well-paid creator had used his wages liberally, having nothing else to spend them on, and so it was made of special, high-quality, bladeproof, bulletproof, cold-resistant, heat-resistant, acid-resistant fibers.

For a moment, Dece was struck dumb. "Ha ha ha...! Okay, in another ten seconds, we'll run, too. Get ready...three, two, *one!*"

On the count of one, both of them turned on their heels and ran off. The salamander gave chase. However, perhaps due to the size of its massive body, it wasn't very fast.

Just as they were thinking *We may be able to escape!* the salamander swung its tail once more. Because it did so while running this time, the mucus splattered all over in random directions.

"Ugh!" Juno howled.

"Juno!" Dece shouted.

The mucus didn't hit Dece or Musashi, but unfortunately it did graze Juno's leg. Juno crouched down, holding her leg tight. It looked like she couldn't move through the extreme pain. At this rate, it was going to catch up to them. That was when...

"...!" (Little Musashibo ran forward.)

"Uwah!" Juno yelped.

...Little Musashibo lifted her up in his arms, throwing her into the wicker basket on his back. Then, with Juno still in the basket, Little Musashibo ran off with slow, easy steps. Juno poked her head out of the basket, looking at Little Musashibo's face in profile as he ran.

"Uh, um...thanks."

"..." (Little Musashibo gave her a thumbs-up.)

Then, just in the nick of time, Dece and Little Musashibo ran through a narrow hole.

Having made the difficult escape from the salamander and returned to the surface, the adventurers made their report to the guild. While they hadn't succeeded in slaying the salamander, their sighting report was deemed valid, and they were paid a hefty sum for it. It sounded like a subjugation force would be dispatched to deal with that salamander soon. Regardless, the quest was now complete.

With their reward in hand, the party set out to divide the

spoils among themselves. However, for whatever reason, Little Musashibo made no attempt to take any for himself. Dece was at a loss for what to do.

"That's not fair. We owe you for saving Juno! Please, take your reward," Dece pleaded.

"..." (Little Musashibo silently shook his head.)

"Are you really, *really* sure you don't want any?"

"..." (Little Musashibo nodded. Then he waved, "Goodbye.")

Little Musashibo walked away from the party with slow, easy footsteps. Julia and Juno, who had already changed into fresh clothes, watched that man (?) go with bewildered looks on their faces.

"I wonder, what was that person (?) really?" Julia asked.

"Don't ask me," Juno said. "Was that thing even a person?"

"I'll bet there was a little fairy insiiiide..." Julia teased.

"I doubt it," Juno said. "But, if there was... I'm sure..."

I'm sure it was a good fairy, thought Juno.

Little Musashibo departed, leaving behind only a mystery. Was the mage right, and was he a fairy?

And thus, another urban legend was born in the capital.

◇　◇　◇

Within the large communal bath inside Parnam Castle was the torso of a large-sized Little Musashibo soaking in a tub, Souma who was washing the acid and mud off it, and Liscia who was watching him with a cold look in her eyes.

"Is it just my imagination or is it even bigger than when I saw it last time?" she demanded.

"That was a prototype," he explained. "I used it as a model when I sent out the job request to craftsmen in the castle town."

"Ah! Don't tell me the 'Kigurumi Adventurer' they're talking about all over town is..."

"Yeah, it's probably this guy... wait, Liscia? Why the scary look?"

"First the mannequin, now this! Are you trying to convince people that Parnam is the demon capital?!" she shouted.

"Ow, that hurts...! Wait, whoa!"

When Liscia threw a bucket at him, Souma ended up diving, clothes still on, into a cold-water bath. While in the water, Souma thought back on everything Little Musashibo had experienced today.

I never would have imagined there was a giant creature like that under the capital. I'm glad we were able to find it before damage reports started to come in, but I put Juno and her friends in danger.

He had optimistically assumed that even novice adventurers ought to be able to handle the wild animals living in there, so he had messed up and set the difficulty level too low. It had nearly meant adventurers dying needlessly on a quest that he himself had set. The reason he hadn't taken the reward at the end was that he felt it was the least he could do after the trouble he'd caused Juno and the others.

Though the biggest reason was that it would be wrong to accept the reward for a quest he set himself.

Regardless, I really do have to reflect on what happened today. Although...

"Uh, um... thanks," Juno had said.

When he recalled Juno's face when she shyly said that as Little Musashibo carried her, the corners of Souma's mouth naturally rose a little.

The adventure itself was fun. I hope I'll get the chance to do it again.

That was what Souma thought as he sat there soaking in the dirty water.

The Little Tanuki Princess of Amidonia

THE CAPITAL of the Principality of Amidonia, Van.

As might be expected from a nation of warriors, the city was surrounded by high walls and the buildings were ashen gray, free of excessive stylistic flourish. Perhaps because their ruler's focus leaned so strongly towards the military, the layout of the city was a convoluted mess full of alleyways.

Right now, a young girl was running through those alleyways. She was sixteen years old, perhaps, with a petite, slender physique. Her face had regular features, and she tied her hair back in twin braids.

This was the daughter of the current Sovereign Prince Gaius VIII, Roroa Amidonia.

She had an air about her that was different from her stern and austere father Gaius or her coldly calculating brother Julius. The way she was curious about anything and everything made her as adorable as a little animal.

When she went out into the city, people were always quick to call out to her.

"Oh my, it's little Roroa. Hello there," said a woman preparing to open up shop.

"Hello, Ma'am. Turnin' a nice profit?"

"Not at all. The economy's poor everywhere."

"I see. Sorry 'bout that. My stupid old man's not so good at governin'."

"You must be the only one in this country who could say that," the woman said with a strained smile. As was not uncommon in militaristic states, any criticism of those in power would quickly get a person arrested here. The only reason Roroa could get away with talking the way she did was because she was the first princess of this country.

However, Roroa replied with a smile that didn't feel at all like it came from a princess.

"Just you wait. I'll do somethin' about it."

"Hahaha, I'll look forward to that."

"Sure!"

With a wave to the woman, Roroa ran off again.

◇ ◇ ◇

On the shopping street in Van, there was a store that dealt in men's apparel. The little sign out front read "The Silver Deer" in a stylish font. Roroa opened the door to the Silver Deer with great force, calling loudly to the owner.

"Seeeebastiaaaan~♪ Leeeet's plaaaay~♪"

"...Lady Roroa."

When she did, a middle-aged man with graying hair who was dressed like a bartender came out. He seemed like the sort of stylish and deep-thinking man whom the aroma of black tea would suit well, but he was holding his head, as if suddenly afflicted with a headache.

"Don't shout people's names so loudly. What do you mean, 'let's play'?"

"Geez, you're no fun, Sebas."

"It's Sebastian, and I'm working right now..."

"Hmm? I didn't get the feelin' you had any customers."

Roroa looked around the store, but she didn't see any customers. The store had a nice atmosphere to it, and many of the items on display were tasteful, so it was strange to see business so dead.

"Well, the men of Van never were much for fashion," Sebastian said with a wry laugh.

The Silver Deer had branch stores all around Amidonia, but despite the store in Van being the head office, its sales were terrible. Given the austere ruggedness that was the national character, men in Amidonia didn't concern themselves with what they wore, and this trend was especially pronounced in Van.

"Normally, it'd be women who'd go for stylish stuff like this, though."

"The day I start to stock stylish clothes for women is the day this store goes under."

In the patriarchal society of Amidonia, women were looked on with disdain if they were seen walking outside in needlessly showy attire. That was why Amidonian women only wore clothing in subdued colors, so even if this store were to stock stylish clothing for women, it wouldn't sell at all.

This was another thing Roroa was dissatisfied about.

"Honestly, it's stupid. The market is defined by customer demand. Expandin' the market's what leads to economic development, but our society's placin' limitations on customer demand."

While Roroa was a princess, she also had a rare sense for economics. Together with people like Colbert, the Minister of Finance, she had been moving around the country's financial capital to make a profit and enrich the country. However, her father Gaius spent most of that profit almost entirely on expanding the military.

"Really, if I want to rebuild this country, maybe I'll have to level everythin' first. That would take the fixed ideas people have got into their heads and blow them all away."

"Honestly, could you not say such dangerous-sounding things in my establishment?" Sebastian said with a sigh of dismay. "So, Lady Roroa, how may I be of service today?"

"Hm? Oh, right. I wanted to ask you about somethin'."

As Roroa said this, she edged up to Sebastian like a needy kitten. With these sorts of gestures, she really was like a small animal.

"Listen, are you connected to merchants outside the country, Sebastian?"

"Well, yes, to a degree."

"So, basically, that means you've got information 'bout a bunch of other countries, then. Well, in that case, there's somethin' I was hopin' ya could tell me about the Kingdom of Elfrieden."

"About the Kingdom of Elfrieden?"

The Kingdom of Elfrieden was one of the countries that neighbored the Principality of Amidonia. What was more, around fifty years ago Amidonia had lost nearly half its territory in a war with the Kingdom. Because of that, among other things, they were regarded as a bitter enemy.

"So, what is it you want to ask?"

"Oh, I overheard my old man sayin' there was a sudden change of kings there, you know."

"Ahh. You must be talking about how King Albert ceded his throne to Souma Kazuya."

"Yeah, that was it! I wanted to ask you about Souma!" When she finished speaking, Roroa crossed her arms and tilted her head to the side. "I know a bit myself. He's that hero they summoned from another world, yeah? I don't get how he ended up becomin' king, but what I really don't get is, even though he's a hero, we ain't hearin' any stories about him doin' anythin' heroic. Aren't heroes supposed to, you know, blow away monsters and easily clear dungeons, and stuff like that?"

The way Roroa spoke using little gestures for all of this put a smile on Sebastian's face.

"True enough, I haven't heard any stories like that about the king in question."

"I know, right? My old man thinks some inexperienced young pup's been put on the throne, and he's right and ready to take advantage, but...somethin' bugs me about it. I've heard their last king was a mediocre leader and too nice for his own good, but would he really hand over his throne so easily if this guy was just some kid?"

"I suppose not."

Roroa was clever. She had a greater ability to see through to the heart of matters than either her father or brother. If she could have taken the throne, the principality would surely have developed greatly. However, she lacked the cruelty she would need to harm her father and brother and take the throne for herself. While Sebastian thought it regrettable that she would never sit on the throne, he also looked favorably on her for not having a personality which would allow her to do that.

That was why Sebastian gave Roroa the information he had.

"I've heard that this Souma is building roads to fight a food crisis, or something like that."

"Huh? Buildin' roads to fight a food crisis?"

For a moment, Roroa was caught by surprise, but soon she let out a hearty laugh. That laugh, however, wasn't one for mocking a misguided policy.

"Ahahaha! I see, he wants to build a transportation network to boost their transport capacity and get through the crisis that way. Well now, he's young, but he's still comin' up with better policies than my old man."

Roroa had accurately seen through to the core of Souma's policy. By increasing the fluidity of distribution, he meant to adjust for surpluses and shortages of supply. Roroa wiped her eyes and caught her breath.

"Yep! This new king Souma's got my attention. Sebastian,

would you mind usin' your network to get me as much info on Souma as you can?"

Seeing how full of energy Roroa had become, Sebastian shrugged his shoulders.

"I don't mind, but...what's in it for me?"

"Think of it as an investment in the future. I'm pretty sure we're gonna make a killin' on this."

As she spoke those words, Roroa wore a daring smile.

HOW A REALIST HERO REBUILT THE KINGDOM

Aisha: Day of Departure

IT HAPPENED in the vast wooded region in the south of the Elfrieden Kingdom, also known as the God-Protected Forest.

This forest, said to be protected by a god-beast, was also the domain of the dark elves.

The dark elves possessed great martial prowess, taking pride in their role as woodland protectors. They thought of themselves as a people who lived and died with the forest. They did not socialize with other races, and, while they were a part of the kingdom, that was only because they had determined that should the kingdom fall, the God-Protected Forest would be in danger.

However, the situation in the forest had changed recently. Ordinarily, entry into the God-Protected Forest was forbidden to all but those of the dark elf race, but now the members of other races in the kingdom had begun to trespass. The cause of this was the food crisis which had arisen after the appearance of the Demon Lord's Domain. Other races in the vicinity, struggling to find anything to eat, had begun to enter the forest in search of its natural bounty.

However, the forest's bounty was not without limits. The dark elves could understand that the food crisis was making life difficult for these people, but they needed the forest's bounty to sustain themselves. As a result, there were clashes on the outskirts of the forest between dark elves guarding against intrusion and members of other races intent on entering the forest.

If things were left to follow their own course, there was the risk that this could develop into a larger armed conflict. Something had to be done.

Having resolved to do just that, one young woman was about to depart from the forest.

◇　◇　◇

"Goodbye, Father. I will return soon," said a girl with light brown skin who looked to be eighteen or nineteen, slinging a great sword over her back.

This was Aisha Udgard, the only daughter of Wodan Udgard, chief of the dark elf village.

"I swear that I will emerge victorious in the martial arts tournament and stand before the king," Aisha added, thumping her chest once with pride.

Recently, it seemed the throne had passed from one king to the next. What was more, they had heard that the new king was now casting a wide net in search of talented people. As part of that process, he would be holding the Best in the Kingdom Martial Arts Tournament, where fighters would compete to demonstrate their gift of martial ability. If she won this tournament, she would be able to attend an award ceremony held by the king himself. In other words, she could meet the king in person. If she had that chance, she could make an appeal to him about the plight of the forest.

The clashes are already beginning to escalate beyond what we can handle ourselves. I must have the new king take steps to prevent intrusions!

That was Aisha's plan.

"Must you go?" As he watched her leave, Wodan seemed concerned. "A direct appeal to the king will be seen as an affront. This young man, Souma, he's just recently taken the throne. There's no telling what decision he will hand down. There's no need for one so young as you to go, is there?"

Seeing her father's concern, Aisha silently shook her head. "Father, you know how capable I am in battle. I am the strongest in our village. It should be possible for me to win the tournament and meet with the king. There, I will appeal to him directly about the plight of our forest."

"Hmph! A human king will never listen to our requests," a contemptuous voice said. This was Wodan's younger brother and Aisha's uncle, Robthor, who had also come to see her off. Robthor had always been a conservative, but lately, every time there had been a clash, he had taken the warriors with him and headed to the site. This had led him to develop a mistrust of other races.

"Uncle, first we must meet with him and talk," Aisha said. "Fortunately, I have heard the new king is a wise one."

"You are too optimistic," her uncle retorted. "You may find that he is cunning instead."

"All the same, I must first see for myself what kind of man he is."

"Hmph! Do as you will."

With those words, Robthor walked off in a huff. With a bitter smile at his younger brother's behavior, Wodan placed a hand on Aisha's shoulder.

"Regardless, I just ask you come home to me safely. No matter what the result, I will not fault you for it. So long as you return safely, that is all I ask."

"Yes! Absolutely!" Aisha nodded firmly, and Wodan nodded back.

"That said," he continued, taking on a look of concern, "you've never left the forest before, have you? That's what worries me."

"What is there to fear? Even among the men of this village, none can match my strength."

"Not all of the dangers in the outside world come from those hostile to you." Wodan tried to put it in terms Aisha would understand. "Aisha, you are an excellent warrior. However, you are something of a glutton."

"A-am I, really...?"

"If someone on the outside were to treat you to delicious food, might you not carelessly follow them wherever they took you?"

"I-I will not forget my task!" Aisha protested, but Wodan didn't seem too inclined to believe her.

"Then what of when your task is complete? What if the one offering you food is a man? If a man tames you with food, will you so wish to be with him that you no longer desire to return to the forest?"

Now his complaints had just turned into those of a father worried that his daughter might hang around with bad men, so Aisha responded indignantly, "I will never take a man weaker than myself as my husband! And I will not be tamed with food!"

"Really, now..."

"It's true! I swear, I will not give in to the temptation of food!"

"O-okay..."

Somehow...this seems like a lost cause, Wodan seemed to be thinking.

"Have a little more faith in me!" Aisha said indignantly. "Now, I must be going!"

And so, Aisha departed from the God-Protected Forest.

Later, Wodan received a messenger kui (something like a messenger pigeon) from Aisha. In the letter, it said that she had won the tournament and had been able to make her appeal to the king as planned. It said that the king had given a favorable response and that she had not been faulted for appealing to him directly. Furthermore, it said that he had offered valuable insight into how to manage the forest.

It said all of these things, but they only accounted for about two-tenths of what she had written. Of the remaining eight-tenths, two-tenths extolled how marvelous the new king was, five-tenths related how delicious all the foods she had eaten while staying with His Majesty were, and her report on recent happenings made up less than one-tenth of the letter.

While Wodan was relieved his daughter had completed her task successfully, he knew that what he feared had come to pass and let out a deep sigh as her father.

"Well, she seems cheerful. I suppose that is good enough," Wodan muttered, looking towards the capital.

◇ ◇ ◇

Around that time, Aisha's voice rang out cheerfully from the Parnam Castle cafeteria: "Your Majesty, seconds please!"

Tomoe's People-Watching Diary

MY NAME is Tomoe Inui.

I'm a ten-year-old mystic wolf. When the Demon Lord's Domain showed up, I was chased out of my home in the north and came to the Elfrieden Kingdom as a refugee. My mom and little brother came with me, too.

That's who I was, but a little while ago, I was adopted by the old king and queen of this country.

They did it because I could talk to animals and monsters, and that caught the eye of the new king, Big Brother Souma. He told me it was a very important ability. They adopted me, but my real mom and my little brother Rou were allowed to live in the castle, too, so I could always see them.

That meant I had two moms now. Mom and the old queen both took good care of me, so I was very happy.

Today, I would like to talk about the people in my life.

First, I'll start with Big Sister Liscia.

She is the old king and queen's daughter, and she has an arranged marriage with Big Brother Souma. I am her little sister by adoption, too. She is brave, and strong, and pretty, and cool. She is a great big sister.

"Souma, are you really going to import something like that?"

"Yes. I absolutely need to have it, and I can't get it in this country, after all."

"Okay, I understand. But...what are you even going to use volcanic ash for?"

"Well, just you wait and see."

That's what Big Sister Liscia is like, but...

"Thanks for all your help, Liscia."

"Wha...? It's no big deal...I mean, you're doing it for the country..."

She still can't come out and be honest about her feelings for Big Brother Souma.

"Why, Madam Tomoe. Have you come to eat lunch?" Aisha called out to me in front of the Parnam Castle cafeteria.

Ms. Aisha Udgard is a dark elf, and she is always protecting Big Brother Souma. She is really strong. I've heard that even if a whole bunch of men ganged up on her, they still couldn't beat Aisha. She is pretty, too, and tall, and "busty." I admire her figure. Will I be like that someday?

That's what Aisha is like, but...

"Hey, Aisha. Poncho is developing a new sauce for dishes made from flour. There are some samples left over. Do you want to eat them?" Big Brother Souma poked his head out of the cafeteria and called for her.

"I'll follow you for the rest of my life, Your Majesty!" Aisha ran right to him.

It's so weird. Aisha is a dark elf, but when Big Brother Souma and his food are in front of her, she shakes her bottom back and forth. It makes it look like she has a tail.

There is another person I admire. Her name is Juna.

She is a good singer with pretty, blue hair. She has grace and feels like a mature woman, and I admire her, but in a different way than Big Sister Liscia and Aisha.

She looks like she is always taking a step back from where everyone else is and looking at the big picture. She supports everyone from the shadows. She is very mature. I admire her more and more all the time.

That's what Juna is like, but...

"..."

"Um...Juna?"

"Oh, what is it, Tomoe?"

"...No, it's nothing."

"Hm?"

...there are times Juna looks a little lonely when she watches Big Brother Souma with Big Sister Liscia or Aisha. But when Big Brother Souma turns to look at her, she always puts on a gentle smile to hide it.

I think if she feels lonely, she should say so, but Juna never lets Big Brother Souma see her like that. I don't understand adults.

There is a certain room I always go to visit.

It belongs to this country's prime minister, Mr. Hakuya Kwongmin.

When I knocked and went in, Hakuya was staring at a pile of

papers. Big Brother Souma seemed busy, but Hakuya was always just as busy. Even though he is always so busy, Hakuya makes time for me.

When Hakuya noticed me come in, he said, "Oh, Little Sister. Is it that time already?" He said it with a little smile.

I gave a short bow. "Thank you for your time again today, teacher."

"Okay," he said. "Well then, let us start by reviewing this country's history today."

"Okay!"

Ever since I came to this castle, Hakuya has been teaching me reading, writing, math, and even this country's history. Hakuya knows a lot, and he is a good teacher. I'm not being forced to study; I had asked him to teach me.

Even if it was because of my ability, I am grateful that Big Brother Souma and Big Sister Liscia adopted me as their honorary little sister, so I want to be a smart little sister that they can be proud of.

When I told Hakuya that, he said, "I'm sure His Majesty and Lady Liscia want you to have fun like a child your age..." with a strained smile.

Still, I want to be able to help my big brother and sister as soon as possible. I want to make it so we can all walk together in this country. That's why I'm going to study hard!

Knock, knock.

"Your Majesty, may I have a moment?"

"Hm?"

"I have brought your little sister."

"Zzz..."

"Ah, she fell asleep again, huh?"

"Yes. She works hard at her reading, writing and math, but this always happens when we get to history... do you suppose my history lectures are boring?"

"Don't let it get you down. She's ten, so you can't really blame her. I'll take her over to her mother later. Lie her down in the bed over there for me."

"Yes, Sire."

"Honestly...there's no need for her to try to grow up so fast."

"She's at the age where she wants to act mature. You must have had a time in your life like that, too, didn't you?"

"You're right. But for now..."

Good night, Tomoe.

HOW A REALIST HERO REBUILT THE KINGDOM

Juna: Better Days Are Coming

THE ROYAL CAPITAL of the Elfrieden Kingdom, Parnam.

The singing café Lorelei stood on one corner of the shopping street in this castle town.

This business, with its headquarters in Duchess Excel Walter's Lagoon City, was a popular one which allowed its customers to enjoy tea and snacks by day and alcohol in a stylish atmosphere by night as they listened to the beautiful singing voices of the songstresses who worked there.

There was one songstress whose popularity was top class even by their standards; a blue-haired diva said to be descended from loreleis, Juna Doma.

Her beautiful face ensnared all who gazed upon it, her every gesture carried a quiet elegance, and her singing voice was strong and beautiful.

In the event held just the other day to seek those who were gifted, she had won in the categories for "Beauty" and "Talent," and even during her audience with the king, it was said that her voice had stolen his heart.

That top songstress, Juna, was singing at Lorelei again today.

The song was "Better Days Are Coming."

It was one of the songs Souma had taught her.

Closing her eyes, she sung with power. In her mind, envisioning that young king.

He's truly...a mysterious gentleman...

As Juna sang, she thought back to her memories with King Souma.

◇ ◇ ◇

"Well then, it's a pleasure to be working with you, Your Majesty."

"Oh, yes... it's a pleasure..."

In a room in the castle, Souma and Juna were seated facing one another.

Aside from these two, the only ones in the room were two maids standing by at the doors. On Souma's side there was only a chair, but on Juna's there was a desk with paper and writing implements. Compared to the bold Juna, Souma seemed a bit nervous and fidgety.

"You know, I just can't seem to get used to doing this."

Perhaps it was Juna's mature aura, but despite being roughly the same age, as well as the fact that he was the king, Souma tended to speak formally around Juna.

That was too gracious for Juna, but even if she asked him not to, it seemed unlikely he would change the way he spoke.

"Well, I really do need you to get used to it. Besides, you were the one to suggest we do this, you know?"

"That was...well, yes. But still, singing in front of someone else is a bit hard for me..."

"It's only embarrassing at first. That will change to pleasure once you get used to it."

"You're making it sound kind of indecent, you know?! Anyway, here goes."

After saying that, Souma hesitantly began to sing.

Souma sang a song from the world he had come from. Juna wrote the melody down as sheet music. This had all begun with Souma's wish to share the songs of his world with the people of this one.

At first, Juna had listened to the music files in his smartphone directly. However, because the batteries had died after a little while, they had switched to this format. First Souma would sing, Juna would write down the sheet music, then she would sing it back to him to check that it matched.

Then, when the song was complete, Juna would give it lyrics in this country's language, doing her best not to change the meaning. Because Souma's musical sense wasn't good enough to capture the harmony or the intricacies of the melody, the result always ended up sounding like a cover version, but even so, a good number of Earth's songs had come to this world through this process.

Of course, since they were all songs Souma knew, the selection was blatantly biased toward his own tastes, meaning there was inevitably more songs from anime, video games, and tokusatsu.

Right now, Souma was singing the opening theme to a certain game.

"Does it go like this...?"

After she finished writing down her sheet music, Juna hummed the melody.

The song was "Reset" by Ayaka Hirahara.

At that moment, "Ah!" Souma's eyes opened wide, and the tears began to stream down his face. When she saw that, the normally calm and composed Juna stopped singing and rushed over to Souma's side.

"I-is something the matter?! Have I done something wrong?!"

"No...that's not it...that's not it at all..."

Having said that, Souma covered his eyes with one hand and faced upwards.

"I loved this song and the melody too; it has a nostalgic feel to it. So, when I heard you sing it, I just couldn't help myself. It brought back memories..."

Juna understood. She had heard that this young king had been summoned here from another world.

In other words, he had been forcibly torn away from his homeland.

Juna's song must have brought on a bout of homesickness.

"Sire..."

Juna placed her hand atop his. She thought she might be reprimanded for her impertinence, but the maids standing by the door turned a blind eye to her.

Juna spoke to Souma in the gentlest voice she could manage.

"Sire...please, do not strain yourself."

"Juna?"

"There are more people who care for you than you realize. The princess, Madam Aisha, as well...and myself. I wish to do all I can to support you."

Having moved his hand away from his eyes, Juna looked straight at him and gave him a smile.

"It's okay to cry if that will let you smile again afterward. If you can't let the princess indulge you because she's younger, please allow me to do it instead. Women from port cities are broad-minded. Allow me to swallow up your little tears with a compassion as vast as the sea."

"That almost sounds like a confession of love," Souma said, giving a wry smile through his tears.

"Hee hee, who knows if it is?"

"Are you teasing me?"

"No, there was no falsehood in my words just now."

Having said that, Juna pressed Souma's head to her bosom.

"If the princess brings out your strengths, then I will hide your weaknesses."

◇ ◇ ◇

As she sang, Juna thought back to that day, to the tears Souma had shed.

When I said I wanted to support him...the words came so easily. I'm sure...it was because I was speaking from my heart...

When the song entered the chorus, she saw the door to the café open.

Three people came in. A young human man, a girl, and a dark elf. Perhaps because they were in disguise, all of them were wearing uniforms from the Officers' Academy.

When she saw the young man, an unintended smile came to Juna's face.

It's okay, Your Majesty. No matter how painful things are, as it says in this song, "better days are coming." We won't let you ride the "ship of sadness." (In the original song this had been a "train," but because those did not exist in this world, Juna had translated it as "ship.")

Having made up her mind, Juna put all her strength into singing.

What They Wanted to Be

Liscia: Souma, was there something you wanted to become?

Souma: What's this, all of a sudden?

Liscia: Well, we forced you to become the king for our own sakes, right? That's why I thought I'd at least ask. Well?

Souma: Hmm...a public servant. Basically, I was aiming for a bureaucratic job. Though, if you ask if I actually wanted to become one, maybe not so much. I just wanted the stable employment... Ah! But when I was little, I wanted to become a nursery school teacher. You know, like what Tomoe's mother does at the castle.

Liscia: Wow, I didn't expect that. Do you like kids?

Souma: It just makes me smile seeing the things little kids will do and say, you know? Though teachers look after other people's children, so I'm sure it would have been a hard job. What did you want to be when you were little, Liscia? Did you want to be a soldier instead of a princess?

Liscia: Me? When I was little, I wanted to be...a bride.

Souma: R-right...

Souma & Liscia: *W-well, this got strangely embarrassing...*

HOW A REALIST HERO REBUILT THE KINGDOM

Liscia: Picking an Outfit

"**A**UGH! What should I wear?!"

In a room in the castle in Parnam, capital of the Elfrieden Kingdom, Liscia was going over the contents of her dresser while muttering to herself.

This was Liscia's bedroom. Because of her long years in officers' school and military service, along with her own strong-willed and too-serious personality, it didn't look anything like what you would expect from the room of a seventeen-year-old girl.

Technically, she had once been this country's princess, and so she did have gorgeous dresses. Because she tended to take good care of her possessions, the dolls her parents had given her long ago were safely stored in her dresser, but it was very true to Liscia's personality that she didn't leave such things out in the open.

Yet Liscia, with her level-headed personality, was now scattering her clothes all over the room. The cause of this lay in the words from the man who was the (provisional) current king of this country, as well as Liscia's betrothed—Souma.

"We've got a day off. How about we go on a date in the castle town?"

Ever since Souma had been given the throne by her father, Albert, he had been grinding his bones to dust, working his very hardest. She knew that was why Prime Minister Hakuya had to force him to take a day off. Even from what she had seen herself, Liscia knew Souma was working too hard.

Still, suddenly being asked on a date had left Liscia in a state of confusion and disarray.

Liscia had never had any serious romantic prospects before. In her years at the Officers' Academy, there had been many sons of the nobility who had cozied up to her because of her status, but their ulterior motives had been plain to see, and so none of them had ever measured up to the straight-laced Liscia's expectations. Before she knew it, she had become more popular with the girls than the boys, and her status as an unattainable romantic conquest had earned her the nickname "The Golden Ice Palace."

Honestly, Liscia thought that reputation was overblown. She wasn't pushing the boys away. There were just no worthwhile boys. As proof of that, now that she had been asked out on a date by a boy she was starting to develop feelings for, she was losing her head over it.

"Hey, Serina, Tomoe, which outfit do you think would look good on me?"

Liscia held up two outfits for the two of them to examine. Tomoe was a mystic wolf girl who had recently become her adopted sister, and Serina, her personal maid, was like a big sister to Liscia. The two of them had been watching Liscia, and Serina found the scene half-heartwarming and half-exasperating to see.

"Um... everything looks good on you, Big Sister," Tomoe ventured. "And I think...no matter which you wear, Big Brother Souma will say you look good in it."

Tomoe had offered some harmless and inoffensive words of encouragement. Serina, on the other hand...

"If you are clinging to a ten-year-old girl for support, that is truly pitiful."

Her words were blunt.

"Urkh..." Liscia muttered. "Fine, you choose for me, Serina."

"What are you saying? You choosing the clothes for yourself is what gives them meaning. Your feelings for the man in your heart, and how you wish to be seen by him, will make themselves evident in the clothing you select."

"Th-the man in my heart... Souma's not like that, not yet..."

"If you dawdle too long, your position as his first queen will be snatched away by another wife he takes later," Serina said briskly. "I know. Perhaps I should present myself before His Majesty? Dressed up in an outfit that I selected myself?"

"Y-you can't!" Liscia exclaimed.

"Hee hee, I was joking. Look how flustered you are. It's simply adorable."

"Geez!"

Serina was a capable maid, but she had a bad habit of bullying cute girls. In other words, she was a total sadist. But rather than inflict physical pain, she preferred to toy with them psychologically and embarrass them with her words. These days, the one who received the most of her "affection" was Liscia.

"H-how does this outfit look?" Liscia asked, holding up a brightly colored women's military uniform. It was something that wouldn't have looked out of place in a theatrical production about the French Revolution.

Serina buried her face in her palm. "Why...why is it a military uniform?"

"B-because Souma said...I look good in them, maybe?"

The embarrassed way Liscia said that was full of maidenly charm, and a feast for Serina's eyes, but...

"A military uniform simply will not do," Serina said with a sigh. "It is true that you look good in them, but that's no outfit to be wearing on a romantic tryst. Besides which, on a special day like this, rather than let him see you the way you usually are, do you not think it would be better to show him a different side of yourself?"

"A different...side of myself..." Liscia murmured.

"Tomoe. How does the princess look from your perspective?"

"She's brave and cool," Tomoe said, her eyes sparkling.

Serina nodded in agreement. "Yes. That is how other people see you, Princess. Now, if the cool, brave princess were to show a side of herself that was different from usual, do you not think that might seize His Majesty Souma's heart?"

"A side of myself that's different from usual..." Liscia murmured.

"For instance, I know... why not go with something more sensuous?" With those words, Serina pulled out a red cocktail dress.

It had an open back and quite the risqué neckline as well.

While she owned dresses like these for social events, Liscia couldn't imagine that they suited her, and she had never once worn them. "Y-you want me to wear this?!"

"Normally, you have yourself wrapped up so tightly," Serina said. "That does make it fun to get you undressed later, but why not try keeping his eyes glued to you by showing off some of that sexiness you normally wouldn't?"

"I'm sensing an indecent aura from every word you say! And, hold on, I'm worrying about what to wear on a date here! I couldn't wear a thing like this around town!"

"Well, true enough, they would mistake you for a lady of the night, I'm sure," Serina nodded.

"You recommended it knowing that?!"

"In that case... what do you think of this one?"

Ignoring Liscia's protests, Serina pulled out another outfit. It was a pink one-piece dress with lots of white frills.

"Th-that's..."

That one-piece had been something her mother had practically forced her to accept as a present about half a year ago. Probably, she had been worried for the masculine Liscia, and "Become a girl who will look good in this" had been the message she had wanted to give her out of motherly concern. However, because it wasn't to Liscia's taste, she had buried it in the back of the closet without so much as trying it on.

"It's cutesy, I suppose you could call it," Serina said. "This could help develop a whole new side to yourself, Princess."

"I don't want to let it do that! All those frills are absolutely dreadful!"

"I think you would look adorable in it, like a doll..."

"No! Never!"

After that, they pulled out many outfits, arguing back and forth over them. At last, Tomoe, who was hesitantly watching from the sidelines, raised a hand to speak.

"Um..."

"Ah, what is it, Tomoe?" Liscia asked.

"Um... you two are both very famous. If you're going to the castle town, don't you need to wear clothes that won't stand out too much?"

Liscia was silent.

Now that she mentioned it, she was right. Hakuya had been saying something about showing off how close they were to the people, but if the future king and queen were just walking around in broad daylight, it would cause a stir. In other words, she shouldn't have been picking out a suitable outfit for a date, she should have been picking out clothes that wouldn't make it obvious who she was. Liscia's legs gave out, and she collapsed to a floor that was littered with clothing.

As she looked on, Serina, who had realized this the entire time, wore a beaming smile.